# CRITICAL ACCLAIM FOR LEIGH RUSSELL

'A million readers can't be wrong! Loyal fans of Geraldine Steel will be thrilled with this latest compelling story from Leigh Russell. New readers will discover a terrific crime series to get their teeth into. Clear some time in your day, sit back and enjoy a bloody good read' – **Howard Linskey**

'Taut and compelling' – **Peter James**

'Leigh Russell is one to watch' – **Lee Child**

'Leigh Russell has become one of the most impressively dependable purveyors of the English police procedural' – **Marcel Berlins,** *Times*

'A brilliant talent in the thriller field' – **Jeffery Deaver**

'*Death Rope* is another cracking addition to the series which has just left me wanting to read more' – *Jen Med's Book Reviews*

'The story keeps you guessing until the end. I would highly recommend this series' – *A Crime Reader's Blog*

'A great plot that keeps you guessing right until the very end, some subtle subplots, brilliant characters both old and new and as ever a completely gripping read' – *Life of Crime*

'Russell at her very best and Steel crying out to be turned into a TV series' – **The Mole,** *Our Book Reviews Online*

'This is an absorbing and compelling serial killer read that explores the mind and motive of a killer, and how the police work to track down that killer' – **Jo Worgan, *Brew & Books Review***

'An absolute delight' – ***The Literary Shed***

'I simply couldn't put it down' – **Shell Baker, *Chelle's Book Reviews***

'Highly engaging' – **Jacob Collins, *Hooked From Page One***

'If you love a good action-packed crime novel, full of complex characters and unexpected twists this is one for you' – **Rachel Emms, *Chillers, Killers and Thrillers***

'I chased the pages in love with the narrative and style... You have all you need within *Class Murder* for the perfect crime story' – **Francesca Wright, *Cesca Lizzie Reads***

'All the things a mystery should be, intriguing, enthralling, tense and utterly absorbing' – ***Best Crime Books***

'A series that can rival other major crime writers out there...' – ***Best Books to Read***

'Sharp, intelligent and well plotted' – ***Crime Fiction Lover***

'Another corker of a book from Leigh Russell... Russell's talent for writing top-quality crime fiction just keeps on growing...' – ***Euro Crime***

'A definite must read for crime thriller fans everywhere' – ***Newbooks Magazine***

'For lovers of crime fiction this is a brilliant, not-to-be missed, novel' – *Fiction Is Stranger Than Fact*

'An innovative and refreshing take on the psychological thriller' – *Books Plus Food*

'Russell's strength as a writer is her ability to portray believable characters' – *Crime Squad*

'A well-written, well-plotted crime novel with fantastic pace and lots of intrigue' – *Bookersatz*

'An encounter that will take readers into the darkest recesses of the human psyche' – *Crime Time*

'Well written and chock full of surprises, this hard-hitting, edge-of-the-seat instalment is yet another treat… Geraldine Steel looks set to become a household name. Highly recommended' – *Euro Crime*

'Good, old-fashioned, heart-hammering police thriller… a no-frills delivery of pure excitement' –*SAGA Magazine*

'*Cut Short* is not a comfortable read, but it is a compelling and important one. Highly recommended' – *Mystery Women*

'A gritty and totally addictive novel' – *New York Journal of Books*

## Also by Leigh Russell

### Geraldine Steel Mysteries
*Cut Short*
*Road Closed*
*Dead End*
*Death Bed*
*Stop Dead*
*Fatal Act*
*Killer Plan*
*Murder Ring*
*Deadly Alibi*
*Class Murder*
*Death Rope*
*Rogue Killer*
*Deathly Affair*
*Deadly Revenge*

### Ian Peterson Murder Investigations
*Cold Sacrifice*
*Race to Death*
*Blood Axe*

### Lucy Hall Mysteries
*Journey to Death*
*Girl in Danger*
*The Wrong Suspect*

# LEIGH RUSSELL

# EVIL IMPULSE

A GERALDINE STEEL MYSTERY

**NO EXIT PRESS**

First published in 2021 by No Exit Press,
an imprint of Oldcastle Books Ltd,
Harpenden, UK

noexit.co.uk
@noexitpress

ISBN
978-0-85730-422-3 (print)
978-0-85730-423-0 (epub)

2 4 6 8 10 9 7 5 3 1

Typeset in 11.25 on 13.75pt Times New Roman
by Avocet Typeset, Bideford, Devon, EX39 2BP

Printed in Great Britain by Clays Ltd, Elcograf S.p.A.

For more information about Crime Fiction go to crimetime.co.uk

*To Michael, Jo, Phillipa, Phil, Rian, and Kezia*
*With my love*

# EVIL
# IMPULSE

## Glossary of acronyms

DCI  – Detective Chief Inspector (senior officer on case)
DI   – Detective Inspector
DS   – Detective Sergeant
SOCO – scene of crime officer (collects forensic evidence at scene)
PM   – Post Mortem or Autopsy (examination of dead body to establish cause of death)
CCTV – Closed Circuit Television (security cameras)
VIIDO – Visual Images, Identification and Detections Office
MIT  – Murder Investigation Team

# Prologue

Their expressions differed each time, some pleading, others defiant, but the terror was always present. More exciting than their writhing bodies, their naked fear was addictive. No other thrill could ever be as satisfying as gazing into victims' eyes when the realisation hit them that they were going to die, no revenge as fitting as the power to end a life in righteous execution. The death penalty was delivered in secret, but that was fine too. The knowledge that justice had been served was its own reward. Other people might not understand, but there was a higher power whose approval was assured.

Death had not been the original intention, but it was difficult to ensure their silence without it. Removing the first victim's tongue had seemed like a clever idea which had proved horribly messy. In the end, it had been impossible to spare the woman's life. In no time at all she had choked to death, but not before she had lost a lot of blood. The memory was still sickening, even after such a long time.

Moving the corpse would have been pointless once she was dead because it was obvious she had been killed on her own blood-soaked bed. So she had remained there, a bloody heap of flesh, until eventually someone must have stumbled on her body. But by then, it was all over.

After that, there had been no more blood. Apart from the mess, it was too unpredictable. Every physical touch left a trace, leading to the risk of identification by some overzealous forensic team. Suffocation required no direct contact with the victim, alive or dead. And there was no blood. Given that death was unavoidable if the victim was to remain silent, suffocation had to be the most sensible option. With a suitable method established, it was simply a matter of selecting the next victim.

Unsuspecting women proved surprisingly easy to come by.

# 1

SINCE HER RETIREMENT TO York, Mandy had taken to walking along the towpath as soon as she woke up in the morning. It was important to keep to a routine so, regardless of the weather, she went out every day before breakfast. The walk was a pleasant one, and she enjoyed observing the changes of the seasons. The trees were beginning to turn golden and brown, and the sky was overcast more often than not. Glancing down at the river bank that morning, her attention was caught by a blue creature moving gently up and down on the water. Looking more closely, she realised that what she was looking at was not an unusually brightly coloured fish, nor even a strange bird, but an item of clothing caught in the fronds of a river weed. As she stared at it, she was shocked to see what looked like a hand protruding from one end of a blue sleeve. She closed her eyes, and let out an involuntary cry on opening them again, because she had not been mistaken. Concealed within a sodden sleeve was a human arm, perhaps still attached to a corpse hidden below the water.

Mandy looked around frantically for someone to help her but she was alone on the towpath. With trembling fingers, she pulled out her phone and called the emergency services to report what she had spotted in the river.

'Yes, a dead body… yes, I'm sure it's dead,' she faltered, after giving her name and location as precisely as she could. 'That is, I can only see one hand, but that's definitely dead. That's all I can see of it, a hand. Everything else is out of sight under the water... no, I haven't touched anything... yes, I'm sure it's dead.' She did not need to look at the hand again to describe it in detail. 'The skin's kind of green and grey.'

It seemed to take a long time for the police to arrive. Meanwhile, a couple of other people had walked past along the towpath. Mandy made no attempt to detain them. She could not bear to draw attention to her horrible discovery, which might entail her having to find it and look at it again. In addition, she had a vague notion that the site ought not to be disturbed before the police had a chance to examine it for clues. There could be a significant footprint in the earth that would lead investigating detectives to the killer, assuming there had been a murder, and someone stepping forward to peer at the body might trample all over such vital evidence. So Mandy stood beside the river at the side of the towpath, like a mute sentinel guarding her hidden plunder, while pedestrians and cyclists passed by oblivious of her macabre vigil.

After a few moments she calmed down. Only then did it occur to her that she could have made a stupid blunder. What she had spotted in the water might be the arm of a life-sized khaki-coloured hand, or perhaps a mannequin from a shop window. But she had summoned the police, and it was too late to change her mind. She had given them her name and address, besides which they would be able to trace her from her phone number. All she could do now was wait for the police to arrive and if it turned out she had made an embarrassing fuss over nothing, that was just too bad. There was nothing she could do about it now. The police could hardly arrest her for making a mistake.

At last, a pair of uniformed police appeared and almost immediately the dreary quiet towpath erupted into a scene of bustling commotion. Within minutes, access had been blocked off to prevent members of the public from approaching, while white-clad officers began busily examining the river bank. Mandy was escorted away for questioning by a young policewoman who looked very smart and stern in her uniform.

'Is it a body?' Mandy enquired, although the teeming police presence had already confirmed her suspicion.

'I'm afraid so.'

'How did she die?'

'She?' the young policewoman repeated. 'How do you know the deceased person is a woman?'

Mandy shook her head, struck by a horrible thought. If the police thought she knew too much, they might suspect she was somehow involved in the death.

'I didn't – I don't –' she stammered. 'I just thought – it didn't look like something a man would wear. That bright blue, I mean.'

Miraculously, someone brought her a cup of tea and wrapped a silver sheet around her shoulders. Although she had not been aware of feeling cold, she realised that she was shivering and was grateful for their care. She sipped the hot tea and tried to control her shaking.

'I walk along here every morning, at about the same time,' she explained, when the policewoman asked her if she was ready to give a statement. 'It's important to get some daily exercise, and it's so lovely along here, watching the changing seasons. It's a really nice place to walk, well, most of the time. Anyway, this morning I was walking along, like I do every day, and I just happened to notice the blue jumper. I thought it was an unusual fish at first, or a bird, but when I looked, I saw there was a hand –' she broke off with a shudder. 'I realised it must be a dead body and called you straightaway. And that's all I know.' She hesitated. 'Do you think she meant to drown herself, or did she fall in by accident?'

'As yet we have no idea how the victim came to be in the river,' the officer replied quietly.

The policewoman's matter-of-fact tone calmed Mandy, and

she stopped shivering and tried to breathe deeply and slowly. The most likely explanation of the tragedy was that the dead woman had been drunk, and had stumbled into the water while staggering along the towpath in the small hours. It was a frightful way to die, but perhaps she had been too befuddled to grasp the danger she was in. If you were unconscious when you died, presumably you just stopped breathing without knowing anything about it. In any case, the shock of being immersed in freezing cold water might have killed her before she had time to realise what was happening.

'Let's hope we all go like that,' she said.

The policewoman looked surprised and Mandy realised she had spoken aloud.

'I mean –' she stammered, 'I mean I hope she was too drunk to know what was happening to her. I assume she was drunk, and that was why she fell in the river.'

'It seems likely,' the police officer replied with a noncommittal nod.

'I guess we'll never know for sure,' Mandy said.

The policewoman gave her a curious look. 'Maybe not,' she said.

Mandy nodded. 'I suppose finding out how and why she died is what you do. I mean, that's your job, isn't it?'

The policewoman nodded but did not reply. Feeling foolish, Mandy cleared her throat. 'I'd better be going then,' she said.

'If you're sure there's nothing else you can tell us?'

Mandy shook her head. 'There isn't anything else. Will you tell me what happened? How she died, I mean.'

The dead woman was a stranger, yet Mandy felt a strange sense of kinship with her. If it hadn't been for Mandy, the corpse might have lain in the river for weeks, slowly eroded by water insects and animals, prey to maggots and rats and other scavengers.

'I'm sure the media will report it,' the policewoman

responded, becoming brusque in her manner now that Mandy had concluded her brief statement.

'I wasn't being inquisitive,' Mandy tried to explain. 'I was just – concerned, that's all.'

The policewoman smiled and thanked her for her time before turning away.

# 2

GERALDINE HAD NOT LONG been at her desk when Detective Chief Inspector Eileen Duncan called a briefing. As the team listened, Geraldine stared at Eileen's ferocious expression with a mixture of admiration and concern. The senior officer's dedication to her work was unquestionable, but she had an unfortunate tendency to bark aggressively at the team. Everyone knew that complicated investigations could take time to clear up, and the Serious Crime Command in York had a reputation for solving crimes swiftly, so Geraldine was not convinced that Eileen's pushy attitude was actually helpful.

Scowling around the room, Eileen announced that a woman's body had been pulled out of the river. The consensus among the police officers present was that the woman had probably been drunk when she had stumbled into the river, while making her way home.

'Even sober you could trip on the towpath in the dark and fall in,' Eileen agreed, her large square jaw set in a determined line. 'She might even have been unconscious when she fell in the water.'

'That would have been a kindness,' Geraldine murmured to herself. 'Drowning must be a terrifying way to die.'

Although they had not yet determined that the woman's death had been anything other than an unfortunate accident, several unusual features at the scene meant that it was being treated as possibly suspicious.

'Until we know more, we have to remain open minded about the cause of death,' Eileen said.

'It's odd that no bag or purse has been found,' a constable said.

'And she had no keys or money on her,' someone else added.

'All of that could be lying on the river bed,' Ian said.

A search was under way along the river bank for the dead woman's bag, but it might have sunk without trace, weighted down with coins and keys. Leaving the room, Geraldine smiled at Ariadne, who sat opposite her. As detective sergeants working on a murder team, they were both accustomed to answering the summons to work at any time

'At least this report came in the morning when we were already at work,' Geraldine said as they walked along the corridor together. 'The older I get, the less I appreciate receiving a summons in the middle of the night.'

'It must be particularly annoying to be disturbed at night if you're sleeping with someone else,' Ariadne replied pointedly.

Geraldine did not answer. She and her colleague, Detective Inspector Ian Peterson, had so far held back from announcing to their colleagues at the police station that he was living with her. They had not yet admitted to anyone else that, after many years of friendship, they were now romantically involved. Since he had moved in with her, she had been trying to see as little of him as possible at work. When he smiled at her, she sometimes had to look away, afraid that her face would betray her emotions. A few of her colleagues must have noticed that neither she nor Ian went to the pub in the evening any more, but no one had commented on their absence, at least not to their faces.

Ariadne's eyes were as bright and black as Geraldine's and now they gleamed with barely suppressed curiosity.

'So tell me, what's going on with Ian?'

'I don't know what you mean. Nothing's going on.'

'Listen, I won't tell anyone if you'd rather it wasn't common knowledge, but I thought you two were –'

'Were what?'

'I thought you were an item these days?'

Doing her best to hide her irritation, Geraldine laughed. 'I don't know what gave you that idea.'

Ariadne sniffed and looked decidedly put out, and Geraldine turned away to hide her confusion. She was aware that she and Ian could not delay much longer before speaking to Eileen to explain their new relationship. But it was a long time since she had been romantically involved with anyone, and she was afraid of doing anything that might disturb their private happiness.

'You can tell me to mind my own business if you like, but don't lie to me,' Ariadne said.

'I thought I *was* telling you to mind your own business,' Geraldine replied quietly. 'Look, whatever's going on between Ian and me is just that, between Ian and me. If there *is* anything going on, and I'm not saying there is, then we're not ready to talk about it with anyone else yet. I don't want to fall out with you, so can we please leave it at that?'

By the time they reached their desks, a slight awkwardness had arisen between them. Geraldine regretted her brusque response to Ariadne's questions, and decided to approach her friend at the next opportunity and try to explain her reluctance to talk about her private life although she was not sure she understood her own attitude herself. Before agreeing to Ian moving in with her, Geraldine had insisted they remain discreet about their new relationship.

'You know how people gossip,' she had said. 'We have to remain strictly professional in our relations at work. Once we get back home, it's different, but at work, we need to continue as before.'

'You know we ought to tell the DCI,' Ian had replied.

'What we do outside of work is no one else's business.'

Ian had not been as concerned as she was to keep their relationship quiet, but he had accepted Geraldine's conditions cheerfully enough, and they settled easily into their new way of life. Still, Geraldine knew that they would not be able to keep their affair to themselves for long, and Ariadne's curiosity made it clear that their colleagues were already growing curious.

# 3

ARIADNE GAVE GERALDINE A sympathetic smile when she announced that she was going to the mortuary to view the body that had been retrieved from the river that morning.

'Have fun,' Ariadne called out to her as she stood up.

Grabbing her bag, Geraldine hurried away, relieved that her friend was no longer upset with her. She wondered if she was unnatural in caring more about her friend's opinion of her than the prospect of viewing a dead body but, unlike some of her colleagues, Geraldine had never been disturbed by the sight of cadavers. On the contrary, she found them fascinating, not out of some existential curiosity about death itself, although that was a question that troubled her when she had nothing else to occupy her thoughts. What she appreciated about attending a post mortem was the evidence a murder victim unwittingly revealed about how he or she had died.

The blonde anatomical technology assistant, Avril, greeted Geraldine with a weary smile.

'Looks like another one for you,' she said, handing Geraldine a mask. 'This one doesn't smell too fresh, I'm afraid.'

'Do they ever?' Geraldine replied.

Avril wrinkled her nose. 'She'd been in the water for a while when they found her.'

Geraldine nodded. The victim could have been in the water far longer if she hadn't chanced to be spotted by a passerby taking a walk along the towpath by the river. Still, it made no difference to the dead woman now. With a nod to Avril, she went in to see the pathologist. In her early forties, Geraldine was only a few years younger than Jonah Hetherington, yet she found him reassuringly avuncular. It could have had something to do with his being married, and the father of a teenage son, while she was single. He brushed a curl of ginger hair from his face with the back of a glove, leaving a faint red smear of a stranger's blood across his forehead. Had he been tall and blond, like Ian, the marking on his face might have given him the appearance of a warrior from a previous age, perhaps a Viking preparing for battle. As it was, he more closely resembled a clown, with his plump face and wispy hair, below which his blue eyes twinkled in greeting.

Geraldine waited good-naturedly for him to crack one of his usual jokes. 'We must stop meeting like this,' or 'What's a nice girl like you doing in a place like this?' or even, 'Of all the bloody joints in all the towns in all the world, she walks into mine.' But on this occasion, he merely nodded at her without speaking.

'Was this an accidental drowning, or do you think we need to investigate?' Geraldine asked.

Jonah raised his eyebrows, oddly orange against his pale freckled face. 'What would you say if I told you she didn't drown?'

'I'd ask you how she died,' Geraldine replied, with exaggerated patience.

The pathologist smiled before launching into his findings. 'There's no pulmonary oedema, and no sign of haemorrhaging in the sinuses or airways or lungs. If she had been conscious when she entered the water, she would have struggled to breathe, which would have caused pressure trauma in the sinuses, airways and lungs. There is no evidence of bleeding, and no debris from the water which would almost certainly have been sucked into her sinuses and lungs while she was attempting to breathe.' He paused.

'In other words, she was dead before she entered the water,' Geraldine said.

He nodded. 'Possibly some time before, probably long enough for the body to lose rigidity so that it would have been easier to transport.' He frowned. 'I'd say she was dead for at least thirty hours before she was deposited in the river, maybe longer. That's just an initial impression, but I'm confident further analysis will confirm my estimate.'

'Can you be more specific?'

'It's impossible to be more precise than that.' Jonah's tense expression relaxed into a resigned smile. 'Now if this was *CSI* or some such TV programme, I would pin the time of death down to the nearest hour for you. The nearest minute. And of course my own conclusion would be confirmed by her watch, smashed at the exact instant of her death. Unfortunately I'm not a glamorous star of fiction, but a tubby pug-faced pathologist working in the real world, and it's all rather messy and unsatisfactory. Don't blame me. I hate disappointing you like this, but I'm not responsible for reality.'

'So someone deposited the body in the water after she died?'

'Yes, and before you ask, cause of death was suffocation.'

Geraldine's eyebrows rose. 'Perhaps she was dumped in the river in an attempt to conceal signs that she had been suffocated?'

'I can only tell you what happened. Speculating about why it happened is your job, not mine.'

'But you're sure that was how she died?'

Jonah nodded. 'As sure as I can be.'

'So were there signs of suffocation that the killer failed to conceal?'

He nodded again, pointing to a small evidence bag. 'We found microscopic fibres in her sinuses and airways that she had inhaled, suggesting something was held over her mouth and nose before she expired, and there were a few of the same fibres still lodged under her fingernails. It's not absolutely conclusive but yes, that appears to be how she died.'

'Appears to be?'

'She might have covered her mouth and nose with a cloth of some sort herself, perhaps to protect herself from a noxious smell, or she could have been lying face down on something, and inhaled the fibres accidentally. But given that she was dead before she went in the water, and there is no other obvious cause of death, it seems fairly likely that she was suffocated by a killer who then disposed of the body. There is no conclusive physical evidence to confirm whether the killing was deliberate or accidental.'

'But if it wasn't murder, how did she end up in the river?'

Jonah inclined his head.

'So the killer thought that being immersed in water, the evidence of how she died would be washed away,' Geraldine concluded her train of thought.

'He might not have realised there *was* any evidence to destroy. Certainly nothing was visible. But it could be the killer dumped her in the river thinking she wouldn't be discovered for a while, and eventually even the microscopic evidence we found on the cadaver would have been obliterated.'

'He? You think the killer was a man?'

'He or she. We could be looking for a female killer. But the killer would need to be strong enough to carry a body.'

'How long was she in the water?'

He shrugged. 'A few days.' He stared down at the bloated body and heaved a sigh. 'She was quite young.'

He turned the body over and Geraldine studied the mottled grey cadaver lying in front of them, resembling a snake in human shape. The dead woman's fair hair was snarled and matted, making it look shorter than it actually was. When she had been alive, it must have reached down to her shoulders.

Individual features were difficult to visualise. Somewhere in the greying green oozing mess that barely covered her skull lay clues to her appearance, but an untrained observer could only speculate about what she had looked like.

'Her head was crawling,' Jonah said. 'She's not a pretty sight even now, but –' He grimaced. 'We've cleaned her up as much as we can for the time being, but we'll have to work on her before we can ask anyone to identify her.' He shook his head. 'You can't begin to imagine what she looked like.'

'I'd rather not try,' Geraldine replied.

The dead woman must have looked disgusting if even the pathologist had been repulsed.

'We haven't found her bag yet,' Geraldine went on more briskly. 'We don't know who she was. What about her clothes? Do they tell us anything?'

Jonah shook his head. 'I'm afraid not. She entered the water fully dressed in a blue jumper, jeans and trainers, none of which are in any way unique.'

Geraldine frowned. 'Had she been sexually assaulted?'

'Not as far as we can tell, although it's difficult to be sure of anything just yet,' Jonah replied solemnly, his customary good humour clearly shaken by the sight of the ravaged face lying on the table in front of them.

# 4

SHE WAS THE ONE he had chosen and, like a fool, she had allowed herself to believe they were happy. When he had told her he loved her, she had believed him without question. Now, seeing his arm around another woman's shoulders, a veil seemed to lift, as though it had been fluttering over her eyes ever since their wedding day. Remembering how happy she had been then, her eyes watered. She had convinced herself they had been married in the sight of God, even if her husband had refused to have the wedding ceremony in her church. Abandoning her faith like that, at least outwardly, was another change marriage had wrought in her life.

Her feet carried her across the wet pavement, seeming to act independently of her frozen will. The weather had turned chilly although it was not yet winter, and trees lined the street with burnished yellow and gold, the kerb littered with an early fall of brown leaves. Reaching the shelter of a shop front, she stood perfectly still, scarcely breathing.

Watching them.

It had been bound to happen again, sooner or later. Looking at them together, Bella realised she had been waiting for this moment for a long time. Waiting and fearing. Her husband's regular visits to the health club, and his occasional trips away from home staying out all night, had been obvious signs that she had refused to recognise.

One glimpse of them together changed everything, her carefully constructed life swept away by a single gesture. As she waited to see what they were going do next, her thoughts spun wildly. The scene playing out across the street, and her response to it, wouldn't only affect her own life. At thirteen, Zoe was going through what her teachers called 'a phase', whatever that meant. They assured Bella that her daughter was being a typical teenager and would 'grow out of it when she was ready', their comments so similar she suspected they had prepared in advance what they were going to say.

'It's all a natural part of growing up,' one of them had added, with a tinge of impatience.

Bella didn't remember having been so aggressive and secretive with her own parents at that age, but now it wasn't only her daughter's attitude she had to worry about. She wondered if Zoe suspected there were problems in her parents' marriage. Focused on what was happening just a few yards away, she barely noticed other people scurrying through the rain falling between her and the couple across the street. Holding his umbrella over her, he inclined his head to listen, and smiled at something she said. Anyone else watching them would probably admire his manners as the edge of the umbrella dripped on his shoulders, while she remained dry.

And all the time, out of sight across the road, Bella stood, huddled in a doorway, shock holding her physically upright. She felt as if she was under water, struggling to fight her way up to the air so she could breathe again.

There was nothing for it but to carry on as normal. Seething inwardly, she pulled herself together, finished her shopping and went home, bedraggled and stunned. As she was preparing the dinner that evening, she heard the front door slam. A few moments later John strolled into the kitchen, and dropped his sports bag on the floor.

'It's cold out there,' he grumbled. 'How long till dinner's ready? I'm starving.'

Her face felt like a mask, her smile was so rigid, but John

grinned at her as though nothing had changed between them. In a way, it hadn't. Certainly he had altered very little in the thirteen years they had been together. Nearing forty, he looked about ten years younger, the tinge of white on his temples barely noticeable against his fair hair. Other than that, the only changes in him were a barely perceptible thickening around his middle, and a few lines around his eyes that made him look as though he was permanently smiling.

What with motherhood, and losing both her parents, Bella hadn't aged so well. Her hair seemed to be thinner than when they had first met, so now she wore it short. Everyone said politely that it suited her. Only her mother had been honest, telling Bella that her new hairstyle made her look old. Her mother had been right. All the same, Bella kept her hair short because it was easier to look after. Gradually her mother had lost the power to speak. Probably she had continued to dislike her daughter's hair, but now the one person who had cared enough to tell Bella the truth was forever silent.

'What are you making for us tonight?' John asked, as though he was genuinely interested.

'Lamb hot pot.'

He leaned down to kiss her cheek, and she wondered if he had always been so oblivious to her feelings.

'It'll be ready in half an hour,' she said.

A moment later she heard him going upstairs. With a sigh, she carried her husband's sports bag to the washing machine and put his clothes and towel in to wash, before calling her husband and daughter down for supper. Zoe took her tray without a word and turned to leave. Bella had given up remonstrating with her for eating in her room.

'I need to do my homework,' was the only reason Zoe gave.

Zoe's figure told a different story. Beneath her baggy school uniform it was difficult to see quite how much weight she had lost, but any attempt to discuss it with her was met with a sullen glare. Every evening she would take her supper up to her room, and later she would bring her empty plate to the kitchen. Bella had checked her room furtively several times while she was out, but found no trace of the food Zoe had almost certainly not eaten. Bella suspected it had been flushed down the toilet.

'Where are you off to?' John asked with fake cheerfulness, as though he hadn't noticed Zoe no longer ate with her parents.

'As if you give a shit about what happens to her,' Bella thought, but she said nothing.

'I'm going upstairs. I've got homework.'

'Don't work too hard,' he told her.

John would have denied that was a deliberate dig at his wife but, at the very least, it was insensitive. For over six months Bella had done nothing, after spending four years visiting her mother every day in a care home and then the hospice where she had died a lingering death. In many ways the end had come as a relief, but it had left Bella's weekdays empty, with John out at work. Eventually she planned to look for a job, but after such a long break it was going to be difficult to find anything, and she kept finding excuses to put off registering with an employment agency. Instead, she scoured the papers for posts she wasn't eligible to apply for, and told herself it was impossible to find a suitable job. In the meantime, John insisted he was happy for her to stay at home.

'You're lucky your mother does such a good job of looking after you,' he told Zoe.

'I don't need looking after,' Zoe muttered. 'I'm perfectly capable of taking care of myself, and I always have been.'

'So we are a family of liars,' Bella thought.

After Zoe had disappeared upstairs, John and Bella ate in front of the television as they always did, the words of strangers shielding them from each other. It was easier that way. And all the while Bella was wondering how she was going to get through the night without betraying her feelings. Neither original nor inventive, the sole excuse she could think of was to say that she had a headache. Armed with a lie of her own, she went upstairs. She needn't have bothered to wrack her brains because as John climbed into bed beside her, he turned away.

'You don't mind, do you?' he mumbled. 'It's just that I'm dog tired tonight.'

Suspecting she knew the reason for his exhaustion, Bella welcomed the reprieve. Whatever happened, she could not bear him to make love to her when she knew what he had done to another woman only that day. Somehow she had to put an end to his life of sin and win back his affection, but she did not know how to go about it.

'You look tired,' John told her the following morning.

'I didn't sleep well last night,' she admitted.

That, at least, was true.

Brushing her hair off her face, she remembered that she hadn't cleaned her teeth that morning. Something else John hadn't noticed. But it was a while since he had kissed her on the lips.

'What are you up to today?' he asked.

Almost any answer would have served. He wasn't interested in her plans. She could hardly blame him. Between shopping and housework and looking after the garden, not forgetting the laundry, her life didn't exactly make for fascinating listening.

'Is everything all right?' He looked at her quizzically. 'You look – well, you don't look like your normal self.'

'It's nothing really, but I think I might have a bladder infection,' she said, preparing to fend off any attempt at intimacy.

'You should get that checked.'

'Yes, I'm planning to go to the doctor.'

'Well, make sure you do.'

'Oh, it's nothing. I've had it before. It just stings a bit, down there.'

He nodded. 'As long as it's nothing serious.'

Could he really be so obtuse? It never seemed to occur to him that she might be mourning for her mother. And he obviously had no idea that she had seen him with another woman. Instead of supporting her while she had been grieving, he had been off chasing someone else.

'Oh yes, they'll give me a course of antibiotics and it'll be sorted in a week or two.'

She fully intended to spin this alleged infection out for longer than a fortnight, after which she would tell him she had her period. That would get her through the next month, buying her enough time to find out exactly what her husband was up to. It was still possible she was giving in to groundless suspicion, but when she thought about what she had seen, there seemed only one explanation. Nothing could alter the fact that she had seen him with his latest victim, his arm slung casually around her shoulders in a gesture of intimacy.

Whatever happened, she had to save her husband from his evil compulsion, which had already cost more than one woman her life.

# 5

GERALDINE STARED MISERABLY AT a pile of papers on her desk. Nothing they did now could help the poor woman who had been sliced open, sewn up and stored in a drawer at the mortuary, awaiting release for burial. All the police could do for her was discover her identity so that her family could bury her with as much dignity as possible. Other than that, they would do everything in their power to track down her killer and bring him to justice. Someone had placed a piece of cloth – perhaps a pillow – over the dead woman's mouth and nose, pressing it down until she stopped breathing. It might have been any old rag that could have been boiled, discarded, buried or burned after carrying out its fatal operation. But if the murder weapon was impossible to trace, there had to be another way to trace the killer, and Geraldine would not rest until she found it and tracked him down.

By contrast to the elusive nature of the murder weapon, the means by which the body had been transported down to the river should have been easy to discover. It was hard to believe a body could be carried along the towpath and thrown in the river without leaving any tracks at all, yet so far scene of crime officers had drawn a blank. There were no unaccounted for footprints leading to the edge of the river bank near where the body had been found, and no signs of anything having been wheeled or lugged down to the water's edge. The fence on the far side of the path was solid. The only conclusion seemed to be that the body had been deposited in the water somewhere further along the river, or else had been transported to its final resting place by boat. In either case, it must have been thrown in the river in the night when there was no one else around to witness what was happening.

'Given that the body was in the water for a number of days,' Eileen said with an angry frown, 'it could have been dropped anywhere along that stretch of the river, quite possibly outside the built-up area, where no one was likely to be watching. There are stretches of water that are not overlooked from either bank, and if the body was deposited at night, there would have been almost no risk of being observed.'

'But whether it was in a boat or floating on the water, how could the body have travelled along the river without anyone seeing?' Ariadne asked.

Eileen scowled, as though the team were deliberately concealing evidence that might expose the killer. When she had first moved to York, Geraldine had been disconcerted by the detective chief inspector's flashes of temper. Before her own demotion from inspector to sergeant, Geraldine had been in line for promotion. In breaking the law to save her twin sister's life, she had risked her entire career, and was fortunate that she still had a job at all. She liked to think she would have treated her team, had she led one, with more respect than Eileen accorded them, but she would never find out how effective she might have been as a detective chief inspector. After a while she had come to realise that her colleagues accepted Eileen's irascibility as an expression of the frustration they all shared from time to time during the course of a murder investigation. No one took much notice of her outbursts.

'Well? Does no one have anything useful to add?' Eileen demanded, glaring around the room. 'Nothing at all? Are we all completely out of our depth here?'

No one attempted to crack a pun about the depth of the river where the body had been found.

'We need more information, not more chatter,' Eileen snapped, although no one had spoken. 'So let's get on with it.'

A team was set up to question everyone who lived or worked along the river, or belonged to one of the boating clubs nestling at the water's edge, and cyclists and pedestrians were questioned on the towpath. No one had noticed anything suspicious. Finally, a report was turned up that could be relevant. A woman who might match the description of the body had gone missing five days earlier.

'Reported missing five days ago, she could be our victim,' Eileen murmured thoughtfully.

Geraldine was sent to advise the missing woman's husband that there was a chance his wife's body had been found. While it was unlikely he would be able to identify her, they only needed a sample of her DNA to confirm or refute the identification. Greg Robinson was an electrician, employed in rewiring an old house. Before Geraldine could speak to him she had to get past the householder, a stout middle-aged woman who was reluctant to let her enter the property.

'He's here,' the woman admitted grudgingly, 'but he's rewiring the house and can't be interrupted. We've been waiting long enough for him to come, and now he's finally here, I don't want him disturbed.'

'I'm afraid I'm going to have to insist,' Geraldine replied quietly. 'We are looking into a serious matter, and no private concern can be allowed to hinder the investigation. I'm very sorry, but you're going to have to step aside or I will have to caution you for obstructing a police officer.'

Grumbling under her breath, the woman jerked her head in the direction of the kitchen where Greg was working. He turned when she called his name, his green eyes alert with alarm, and Geraldine saw that he was probably in his thirties, tall and thin.

'The police?' he repeated when she introduced herself. 'Is it about Angie? Have you found her?' His voice shook slightly. 'Is she all right?'

When Geraldine asked him to sit down, his demeanour altered. His shoulders drooped and he shook his head.

'What is it? What's happened? Tell me. I've been going out of my mind with worry. Just tell me she's all right.'

'Greg, we don't know if we've found your wife, but a body has been recovered from the river –'

'No, no!'

If he was putting on an act, it was certainly convincing. Hearing the cry, the householder came in. She looked furious.

'Is everything all right? What's the problem now? Don't tell me you're not going to get it done on time. I've got the decorator booked to start the day after tomorrow –'

'I'm sorry, but I'm afraid I'm going to have to borrow Greg for a while,' Geraldine said.

'What? But he's not finished. You can see for yourself, there are wires dangling all over the place.' She turned to Greg. 'You can't leave before the job's done.'

Greg followed Geraldine out of the house without a word, shrill complaints echoing after them as they walked down the path. Geraldine explained exactly what she needed from him. As he lived quite close to the police station, she followed him home and went inside with him. He left her in a small square living room, and she heard him bounding upstairs. Glancing around the living room as she waited, Geraldine's attention was caught by a wedding picture on the mantelpiece. She recognised Greg instantly in the smiling groom, but the beaming bride bore little resemblance to the bloated corpse that had been pulled from the river. She sighed, registering how happy they both looked.

'Here you are,' Greg said, clattering downstairs and entering the living room clutching a wooden hairbrush with fair hair caught in the bristles. 'I can give you her toothbrush as well if you want, but –'

'But if she comes home, she's going to need it,' Geraldine completed the sentence for him. 'I hope the woman we've found isn't your wife, Greg, but there's only one way to be sure. But this is enough,' she added, holding up the hairbrush which she had dropped into an evidence bag.

He nodded. 'It's her hair,' he muttered helplessly. 'It's Angie's hair.' He looked up at Geraldine. 'Please, please, don't let it be her.'

# 6

As usual, Zoe grabbed her plate without sitting down and turned to leave the kitchen.

'Where do you think you're going?' her father asked, eyeing her with a fake smile. 'Why don't you sit with us for once, and have your supper here?'

'Why would I want to do that?'

Zoe's mother was watching them fearfully, as though mutely begging them not to lose their tempers, but if her father was upset by Zoe's aggressive tone, he didn't show it.

'Because we're a family,' he replied evenly. 'We hardly seem to see anything of you these days. We never sit together, and it would be nice to talk to you once in a while.'

'What is there to talk about?'

'We could talk about you,' he replied patiently. 'About what we've all been up to.'

Zoe's mother let out a curious grunt, which he ignored.

'That won't take long,' Zoe replied. 'I've been bored out of my skull at school all day. You've been at work, probably bored too. Mum's been sitting around the house, bored. Nothing interesting ever happens and we're all bored. So what is there to talk about?'

She turned away.

'Just sit down,' he replied. 'Please. Just sit with us.'

'Why? What's the point?'

'The point is that it might be nice to sit together as a family, and talk to each other. So sit down.'

'Or what?' she replied. 'Are you going to shout at me?'

They both knew she was deliberately goading him. For a second, her father didn't respond. Then, with a sudden burst of energy, he sprang to his feet, his face flushed with anger. Zoe's mother reached out and put a restraining hand on his arm. Distracted, he glanced down and shook her off, but by the time he raised his eyes, Zoe had already reached the door. Her heart pounding, she dashed across the hall, raced up the stairs and slammed her door. Her bedroom was allegedly her own private space, but there was no lock on the door and her parents could walk in whenever they wanted. She knew her mother went in there while she was at school, because she often found her duvet straightened, and her clothes gathered up from the floor, but her mother seemed impervious to her protests.

'You say it's my room, but you just walk in whenever you feel like it,' she complained. 'You have no right to come in here when I'm out of the house.'

Her mother either lied outright and denied having gone in there, or else replied that she had every right to enter any room in her own house. So even her own bedroom didn't belong to Zoe. Whatever either of her parents said could not alter the fact that she was a prisoner in their home.

She sat down on her bed, listening, but there was no sound of anyone following her up the stairs. She picked at her food, eating a few peas without touching anything else. Finally she took her plate to the bathroom. At least there she could lock the door. Mashing up her food, she flushed it down the toilet. If there were rats living in the sewers, they must be growing fat on her mother's cooking. Having finished her nightly ritual, she slumped on the floor, leaned back against the side of the bath, and considered her situation. Whichever way she looked at it, her life was intolerable. Worse than endless pestering from teachers was the claustrophobic atmosphere at home. There seemed to be no end to it, and there was no let-up. Day after day life stretched ahead of her until she was finally old enough to leave her parents' house. That day couldn't come soon enough, as far as she was concerned. In the meantime, she had to endure her current circumstances for years and years, feeling as though there was a volcano inside her head, waiting to explode. She had nothing to look forward to, and her life and youth were slipping away. She was already a teenager, and she had nothing to show for the time she had spent in so-called living. The other pupils in her class at school were all idiots or bullies or swots, and there was no one she could talk to honestly about her intolerable existence.

From downstairs came the sound of raised voices. Her parents were arguing again. All at once, she knew what she had to do. Her father had yelled at her for the last time. With a snarl of frustration, she grabbed her wash bag, dashed back to her room, and closed the door. Seizing her rucksack, she shook it upside down, letting her school books drop on to her bed. Sweeping them to the floor, she began stuffing clothes into her bag. Satisfied she had as much as she could carry, she ran lightly downstairs. Through the small window in the hall she could see it was drizzling outside, so she grabbed her school coat and an old knitted hat that was lying on the floor in the hall and ran out of the house, closing the front door quietly behind her. It would soon be dark and she hurried along the street, slowing down only when she was out of breath from running. At last she reached her school friend's house and rang the bell. There was no answer. She knocked on the door, but still no one opened it. It had not occurred to her that her friend might be out.

She had been thinking about walking out of her parents' house for a long time, but when she had finally acted on her plan, it had been entirely spontaneous, more a reaction against them than a properly thought-out strategy. She was already regretting her impulse, but it was too late to change her mind. If she went home now and her parents spotted her returning with her bag, they were bound to realise what was going on. They might already have noticed her absence and searched her room, in which case they would have spotted that her bag was gone, along with some of her clothes, and other personal items from the bathroom. The missing toothbrush alone was a giveaway. She had to find somewhere to hide where her parents would never find her. Only then would they understand how miserable she was, and how much she hated them. They might even be sorry. And they would no longer be able to dismiss her feelings as trivial.

She had often overheard them talking about her.

'All teenagers go through a rebellious phase,' her father had said. 'It doesn't mean anything.'

He could hardly have been less respectful of Zoe's feelings.

'Yes, I know you're right,' her mother had replied, in another devastating betrayal. 'But it's hard to put up with her when she's like this.'

Well, now they no longer had to put up with her at all, and if that made them regret the way they had treated her, it served them right. Overcome with self-pity, she sat on the step and began to cry. After a while, it began to rain so she set off to look for shelter, wiping her eyes as she scurried along the pavement. She passed several shops that were closed for the night, but just as she was resigning herself to huddling under a bridge, which would at least offer some protection from the rain, she spotted a café that was still open. Her clothes were damp and she was beginning to shiver. Keeping her hat pulled down over her ears, she addressed the girl behind the counter in as gruff a voice as she could muster, bought herself a hot soup and sat down to sip at it slowly. Hopefully her friend would have returned home by the time Zoe went back there.

In the meantime, she had something hot to drink, there was a grubby toilet at the back of the café, and she was safe for a few hours. She wondered if the café would stay open all night.

Zoe had only once been out at night without her parents, when she had gone to a club in the centre of town with a group of her classmates from school. If the café closed, she would try and find her way back to the club which she knew remained open until late. She might even see someone from school there and go home with them for the night. With that idea in mind, she finished her soup and sat, waiting for the café to close. She was in no hurry to leave, while it was still raining outside and she had nowhere else to go.

# 7

AT THE END OF her shift, she hurried across Lendal Bridge towards home. The bridge was busy with people going home or out for the night, even on a Tuesday. Not only was the road packed with traffic but the pavement was crowded with pedestrians, in spite of the rain. Keen to avoid colliding with anyone or losing her footing, she hurried on, taking care on the slippery pavement. It seemed to take her a long time to cross the bridge but at last she arrived at the junction where she turned left, away from the station, and walked along the side of the huge Grand Hotel.

It was quiet once she left the main road, and she hurried between high buildings away from the station. However careful she was, her feet were soon drenched because puddles were difficult to spot in the glimmering lights. The street was virtually deserted in the rain, and the few people she passed took no notice of her as she hurried on. As she reached the end of the road where she turned right into Tanner Row, she had a creepy sensation that someone was following her. She walked faster, along Toft Green towards another hotel, this one on her right on the opposite side of the road. Ahead of her there were two pubs, and an apartment block, and after that the disused brewery next to her own block of flats

On a wet evening the area was deserted, and she felt a faint sense of unease. The street which she had traversed many times seemed unfamiliar in the gathering darkness until, wherever she looked, strange creatures seemed to be lurking in the shadows. Hearing footsteps behind her, she glanced over her shoulder to see a stranger, striding along. She couldn't see his face beneath his hood, but she had a suspicion he was looking at her. With an effort she reassured herself that she was worrying about nothing. The rain grew heavier again, and she walked more quickly, cursing herself for having left her coat at home.

Nearly tripping on an uneven paving stone, she cursed aloud as one of her trainers sploshed in a deep puddle. Her soles were reasonably waterproof, but water soaked through the top of her shoe, cold and clammy. The rain had eased off, but her foot remained wet and uncomfortable, squelching every time she walked on it. Indoors, the first thing she would do was take off her socks and shoes and dry her feet, rubbing them until they were warm again. As it was, all she could do was continue trudging, doing her best to avoid stepping in any more puddles. Not that it would have made much difference if she did, except that at least so far only one of her feet was soaking wet. It was little enough to feel gratified about.

Preoccupied with her feet, she barely registered a faint noise behind her. It reached her again, a soft sound like someone sniffing gently. She stopped abruptly and listened. All she could hear was a faint plopping as rain dripped from nearby window sills and gutters, and a distant whispering of wind overhead. But when she walked on, listening, she heard it again: a faint snuffling, like a small dog casting around for a scent. Only the noise made by a small dog would come from somewhere below her knees and this sound came from above her head. She stopped again, poised to run, and heard only the spattering of water and the whisper of the wind.

She scurried on, moving as fast as she could without stumbling in the darkness. Behind her she heard footsteps on the cobbles, or it could have been the pounding of her heart that she heard. But this time there was no mistaking the sound of someone sniffing close by. With a low cry, she spun round. A figure was standing behind her, close enough to touch her. One arm was raised as though to strike her with a fist wearing a leather glove. Over her attacker's shoulder, she could see a massive building site where a new block of flats was being constructed. The neighbours were pleased about it, as they said it would improve the area and increase property values in the street. But at this time in the evening, the site was deserted, and there was no one to witness what was happening. She turned to run, but before she could move, a hand was slapped across her mouth from behind, pinching her nose so tightly that she could think only of the pain. It felt as though her nose was being wrenched off her face.

One moment she was vexed about her soaked foot, the next she was unable to draw breath. If she did not free herself soon she was going to suffocate, but the realisation came too late. While one hand prevented her from breathing, her assailant grabbed her arm and shoved her forwards, off the street, propelling her through a high wooden gate. She stumbled over a brick that was propping the gate open, into an alley beside the disused brewery. In her panic she barely had time to catch sight of a riot of plants growing wild along the centre of a stony path. To the side of the path, more weeds reached halfway up a brick wall. The weeds flourished undisturbed, but her life was under threat.

A rusty old bicycle was leaning against the wall. Unable to move her head, she stared helplessly past it to the buildings at the far end of the cul-de-sac. They were too far away for anyone to see what was happening in the alley below, even if someone happened to look out of the window. The horror of what was happening was too stark to comprehend and, for an instant, time seemed to hang suspended. A huge void opened in her mind and she understood that she was going to die.

'Why are you doing this?'

Her words sounded like a muffled whimper at the back of her throat, barely louder than the rustle of leaves in a tree, or the gentle drip, drip of the rain. No one would understand that she was asking a question.

She tried again. 'Who are you?'

Even if her attacker felt the shuddering movement in her neck and understood what she was trying to say, there would be no answer for her.

# 8

THE FOLLOWING MORNING THEY learned that the DNA found on Angie Robinson's hairbrush was a match for the body found in the river. There was a faint murmur around the team when that information reached them, along with a few tentative smiles. Recalling the foul remains of the victim, and Greg's anxiety about his wife, Geraldine could not share the general feeling of relief that they had at least established the identity of the dead woman. Although of course if the body had not been that of Angie Robinson, another family would have been grieving the loss of a different woman, and in the grand scheme of things it made no difference whether the victim was Greg's wife or someone else's loved one. Whoever it was, a life had been taken, and the killer had to be brought to justice. But Geraldine's recollection of Greg's apprehension and the image of his wife's putrefied body made the investigation feel somehow personal for her.

Looking into Greg's history, Ariadne had come across something that was potentially interesting. When he was seventeen, Greg had been prosecuted for the alleged rape of a young girl. His version of events had been that the girl had not only been willing to have sex with him, but she had been the one to initiate intercourse by kissing him. The defence alleged she had stripped off and unzipped his trousers. Ariadne circulated the report before the next briefing, and Geraldine read it carefully. When questioned under oath, Greg had insisted that the girl had approached him in a club.

She had appeared in court in a knee-length navy skirt and a blue polo neck jumper, wearing no make-up and with her long hair tied in a high ponytail. If anything, she had looked younger than her sixteen years, but she had lost credibility when the defence showed a photograph of her wearing heavy make-up and skimpy clothing, and adopting a seductive pose, in the company of several young men. Whether or not there was any substance to it, Greg had been cleared of the rape charge.

'This could be significant,' Eileen commented at the morning briefing.

'He was acquitted,' Geraldine pointed out.

'True, but we need to consider him carefully,' Eileen said. 'Geraldine, you met him, didn't you?'

Geraldine nodded.

'I suggest you go and bring him in. We need to find out what he was up to when his wife went missing. Ian, you can go with her in case he objects,' Eileen added.

Geraldine forced herself to appear impassive. After all her training, and her years of experience, she was professional in her work, regardless of who her partner was. Across the room, she glimpsed Ian's face, drawn and stern. His expression could have been a result of the investigation, but Geraldine suspected that, like her, he was finding working together was more of a strain than he had anticipated. She nodded at Eileen again, without looking directly at Ian.

'We're on our way,' she said, although as her senior officer it was Ian's place to respond to the instruction.

'Your car or mine?' Ian asked, as they walked out of the incident room.

'I'll drive if you like,' she replied.

Sitting behind the wheel gave her an excuse to keep her eyes on the road ahead. Their affair was so wonderful, it had transformed her life, but they could not allow it to interfere with their work. They drove in silence until they reached the house where Geraldine had seen Greg the previous day. Seeing who was calling, the woman who lived there scowled. Geraldine promptly pushed her way inside, before the woman had a chance to slam the door.

'This is the second day in a row you've turned up here uninvited and stopped him from getting on with the job,' the woman fumed. 'I've already had to phone the decorators and postpone them once. I'm not going to put up with another delay. I want you to leave right now, and not come here bothering us again.'

While Geraldine apologised for the intrusion and the woman blustered and issued idle threats, Ian went inside and emerged a moment later with Greg at his side.

'Where are you taking him?' the woman demanded, her round cheeks red with indignation.

'We're asking Greg to accompany us to the police station,' Ian replied.

'Not in my time, you're not,' the woman replied. 'I'm paying for a job to be done. Look,' her voice changed and she began wheedling. 'He's nearly finished. Can't you just let him complete the job? He can't leave it unfinished.'

Greg walked out without a word, and a moment later he was sitting in the back of a police car, with Ian at his side.

'This is about Angie, isn't it?' Greg asked in a flat voice.

In her rear-view mirror, Geraldine glimpsed his face, pale and twisted with the effort not to cry. When they arrived at the police station, they sat Greg down and a constable brought him a cup of tea while Geraldine confirmed the terrible news that his wife was dead. At first he merely nodded. He didn't break down in tears as she had feared, but looked sadly down at his long white fingers which were fidgeting with the handle of his mug of tea. He had not drunk it.

'In a way it's almost a relief,' he muttered. 'I mean, I wish she was still alive, of course I do, more than anything in the world. I'd give my right arm to have her back –' He broke off and bit his lip. 'But at least I know what's happened to her, and she's not somewhere... suffering... I was so afraid she was in pain...' He looked up and stared directly at Geraldine. 'Did she – was she – did she suffer much before she died?'

Geraldine sighed, but there was no point in delaying telling him the terrible truth.

'Her body was pulled out of the river. Do you know what she was doing along there?' Ian asked.

Greg shook his head. 'I already told your colleague, I haven't seen her since I left her at home a week ago. She's been gone a week... I didn't know what had happened to her... and now you're telling me she fell in the river? How did that happen? Why was she there?' His voice rose as he asked his next question. 'Who was she with?'

'I'm afraid we don't know what happened. We were hoping you might be able to help us,' Geraldine replied.

'Help you? What do you mean?' Greg asked, looking bewildered. 'You said she drowned. You told me just now.'

'I said her body was found in the river.'

'Are you sure she's dead?' he asked with a pathetic desperation that convinced Geraldine he had not killed her.

'Or he's a good actor,' Eileen retorted sharply when Geraldine shared her impression.

Geraldine had no answer to that.

# 9

ONCE GREG HAD BEEN told that his wife was dead, Eileen wanted him questioned more closely.

'I'm not convinced he was surprised. I know you said he appeared to be shocked, but we can't be sure. You can tell him it's to eliminate him from our enquiries,' she said. 'Even if we are all convinced he did it.'

They all knew that a spouse was, statistically, the most likely suspect in a murder case.

'Greg, we need you to help us trace Angie's movements on the night she died. Where was she going?'

Greg shrugged. 'I don't know,' he muttered. 'I've no idea what she was doing down by the river. There's no point asking me, because I don't know.'

'What you were doing last Wednesday night?' Geraldine said.

'You can't think… No, no.'

Geraldine questioned him as gently as she could, but he became increasingly distraught and incoherent. At last he seemed to realise that the police suspected he knew more than he was telling them about how his wife died.

'That's why you're taping every word I say, isn't it? Oh my God, you think I killed her. She was murdered, wasn't she? Wasn't she?'

Greg's face turned even paler than before, and he pressed his lips together with a wild expression in his eyes. He folded his arms with forlorn bravado, and refused to continue until he had a lawyer present.

51

'I've seen enough cop shows to know my rights,' he added.

None of them mentioned his previous prosecution for sexual assault.

'You haven't arrested me, have you? So you can't question me like this without a lawyer to defend me. Otherwise you have to let me go. And you can't keep me for more than a day, not without evidence that I'm guilty. I'm not saying another word until I have a lawyer here to defend me. I know my rights and I'm taking the fifth amendment right now.'

Without bothering to correct his confused understanding of the law governing the treatment of suspects, Geraldine agreed to his request. They heard him protesting loudly as he was led away to wait in a cell until the duty brief arrived, and they could continue the interview.

'It's a pity we don't have enough on him yet to arrest him and be done with it,' Ian grumbled as they walked along the corridor together.

Geraldine frowned. 'Apart from the fact that he was the victim's husband, we have nothing at all against him. He reported her missing the day after she disappeared and, if he's telling the truth, he hasn't seen her again since then.'

'*If* he's telling the truth,' Ian repeated. 'We can't take anything he says at face value.'

'We have no reason to suspect he's lying. Although he was accused of rape,' Geraldine said thoughtfully.

'That was years ago, and the case was thrown out.'

'That doesn't mean he didn't do it.'

'Even if the jury were wrong,' Ian said, 'we have to believe the justice system works, more or less, or everything degenerates into a chaotic free for all, where the powerful can flout the law with impunity, and the poor and disadvantaged go to the wall. That's what we spend our lives fighting to prevent. But in any case, there's nothing to suggest there was a miscarriage of justice in this instance. And even if the jury *were* wrong – and we have no reason to believe they were – he wasn't violent towards the girl.'

'Rape is always violent,' Geraldine corrected him sharply.

'Yes, yes, I know that, of course, but what I'm saying is, he had sex with a promiscuous sixteen-year-old when he was seventeen. There were several witnesses willing to swear in court that she had slept with other men. Just because the girl later thought better of what she had done and changed her mind, and wished she hadn't had sex with him, and cried rape, that's hardly relevant now.'

'It hardly points to him being a murderer,' Geraldine agreed.

'No. Killing his wife would make him a murderer.'

'And so far we have no evidence to suggest he killed her.'

'You don't think he did it, do you?' Ian asked.

'Honestly, Ian, I don't know what to think. That's what we're trying to find out. But if you press me to say one way or the other then no, I don't believe he's guilty of killing his wife.'

'What makes you say that?'

'It's just my impression of him, but that isn't relevant either. Whether or not he's guilty, until we find evidence that condemns him, we have to think of him as innocent. I could equally well ask what makes Eileen suspect he did it?'

'Because he's the victim's husband, and all husbands want to kill their wives, sooner or later.'

'Ian, don't be flippant. This is a woman's life we're talking about, and a man's liberty.'

Ian strode away, leaving Geraldine feeling unsettled by the suspicion that Ian's response had been influenced by his feelings towards his ex-wife. It was impossible to discuss a case sensibly with a colleague who allowed their personal experience to influence their assessment of the facts. As she busied herself tidying her desk, she wondered whether she was being unfair. She was probably never completely disinterested when forming an opinion. At least she tried to be detached, but perhaps that was worse, believing she was objective, while allowing her personal opinions to shape her views without realising it. Maybe she ought to recognise her bias, rather than deny it. Still irritated with Ian, she switched her attention to her iPad, and began a desultory search through recent reports pertaining to the case. But her thoughts kept wandering back to Ian and his cynical remark.

She was shocked to discover how bitter he had become. When they had first met, years before, he had been relentlessly cheerful, but since his divorce, he seemed to be increasingly cynical. She understood he had been disappointed in his failed marriage, but she wished he would stop thinking about his fickle ex-wife. With an effort she forced herself to focus on the potential suspect, Greg. She was still rereading his statements when she was summoned. The duty brief had arrived and was ready for Greg's interview to resume.

The lawyer was a slender blonde woman, immaculately dressed in a tailored trouser suit. In some ways she reminded Geraldine of Ian's beautiful ex-wife, Bev, and she wondered if he would have noticed any similarity. The interview seemed to drag on interminably, with Geraldine and Ian repeating their questions in various ways, while the lawyer responded so slowly it was hard to believe she was speaking her mother tongue. At length Greg grew fidgety, and demanded to know when he would be allowed to go home.

'The police have not charged you with anything,' the lawyer drawled in her laboured manner. 'You are free to go whenever you like.'

'That's it then,' Greg announced, rising to his feet. 'I'm out of here.'

'Not quite yet,' Ian said.

'You just told me I can go,' Greg whined at his lawyer. 'I

want to go home. They can't stop me, can they? You said I can go.'

Heaving an exaggerated sigh, Ian pointed out that refusal to co-operate with the police investigation into his wife's murder might in itself be sufficient grounds for suspicion. The accused man stared at him for a second, looking baffled. Then he turned to his lawyer.

'You said I could go home. You're supposed to be defending me. What the hell's going on?'

'I said you were free to leave as long as the police haven't charged you with a crime,' the lawyer replied. 'They have no legal power to detain you, but that doesn't mean they won't want to question you, to eliminate you from their enquiries.'

'Please tell your client that if he continues to refuse to answer any questions we will hold him here overnight, and perhaps that will persuade him to talk to us,' Ian added with grim satisfaction.

Geraldine glanced at Ian, but he did not look at her.

'Very well,' the lawyer said. 'I need to talk to my client.'

'What's going on?' Geraldine blurted out when Greg had been led away and she was alone with Ian.

'We have to put pressure on him,' Ian replied. 'If he confesses he killed her, we'll be putting him behind bars where he belongs.'

'What if he's innocent?'

'Then he won't confess. But if he did it, I think he'll crumble.'

'I don't think he did it,' Geraldine replied.

In the meantime, a team had been studying CCTV footage from the area closest to the river where Angie's body had been found. There was no camera in the immediate vicinity, but officers were searching for sight of her on the bridges leading down to the river path, and passing by the boat club that had security cameras in place to film anyone who approached the building. Another team was investigating Angie's contacts on social media, trying to find out where she had gone on the night she died. So far, no new information was forthcoming, but the work continued. Someone had killed Angie, and it could have been her husband. As the dead woman's spouse, there was a weighty balance of probabilities against Greg being innocent. All Geraldine had to persuade her of his innocence was a gut feeling that he hadn't killed his wife.

# 10

'SHE WENT MISSING YESTERDAY?' Eileen repeated, red-faced with outrage. 'Why the hell didn't her parents report it at once? Why did they wait? What sort of parents are we looking at? A teenage girl was out all night? Should we be looking at her parents?'

'They probably thought she'd come back today,' Ariadne said. 'We don't know that she hasn't run off before. She might just have gone to visit a friend and forgotten to tell them. Teenagers can be thoughtless like that.'

A few middle-aged officers with teenage children muttered darkly.

The constable who had taken the call shook her head. 'Apparently they were under the impression they couldn't report a missing person for twenty-four hours.'

'She's thirteen, for Christ's sake!' Eileen protested. 'If they had any sense, they would have called us straightaway. Perhaps we shouldn't have waited to let the media loose on the recent murder.' She sighed. 'It's time to issue a press release about Angie Robinson.'

The decision had been made to keep Angie's death quiet for forty-eight hours, in hopes of concluding the investigation before the media caught on to it. Now it was going to be exploited as a sensational item of news, and no doubt used as an opportunity to attack the police for failing to apprehend a dangerous murderer promptly enough, as though an efficient police force should be able to track down an elusive killer within hours of the victim being discovered. In addition, a sensational item of news about a murder inevitably resulted in a host of false accusations, which wasted many hours of police time, and even raised the spectre of a copycat killing. The decision to keep the situation under wraps had not been taken lightly.

Geraldine understood why Eileen was incensed about the parents' delay in reporting their thirteen-year-old daughter missing. Had the police known about it at once, they could have initiated a search straightaway, instead of twenty-four hours later. The fact was, the missing girl could be at greater risk than her parents had realised, because Eileen had chosen not to share news of Angie Robinson's murder immediately with the public. It was a tough decision, and Geraldine was glad she had not been called on to make it. On balance, she would probably have done the same as Eileen, governed by her reluctance to spark a media frenzy as soon as Angie Robinson had been pulled from the river. They were not to know that only a day later another young woman would disappear.

'There is absolutely no reason to suppose this missing girl has anything to do with Angie Robinson's murder,' she said. 'The chances are the girl will turn up, safe and well, oblivious to her parents' concern. It's true, teenagers are often thoughtless. And she might have deliberately decided to pull a vanishing stunt just to worry her parents. There's nothing to suggest her disappearance has anything to do with our investigation.'

Eileen grunted.

In general, a report of a missing girl might not be acted on immediately, but in this instance Eileen was keen to investigate the disappearance without delay. In the unlikely event that the two cases were linked, the second victim might help them to track down the killer they were already looking for.

The couple who had reported their daughter missing lived only a couple of miles from the station.

'Where they live isn't far from the river,' Ariadne said.

'Nowhere's far from the river in York,' Eileen replied brusquely.

'And we don't know that Angie Robinson was killed anywhere near the river,' Geraldine added, 'only that her body was dumped in the water some time after she was killed.'

'That's true,' Eileen chimed in. 'The body could have drifted quite a long way before it was spotted. She might have been killed somewhere further up, outside the city.'

Geraldine was sent to question the parents of the missing girl. She did not need Eileen to remind her not to mention that a woman had been murdered only two days earlier, the body having been discovered close to where they lived. As yet there was nothing at all to connect the murder to the missing girl, who in all likelihood would turn up, unharmed.

'In this job we have to be optimistic,' Geraldine agreed.

Glancing up, she happened to look at Ian, whose face relaxed in a grin. Geraldine looked away quickly, but not before their eyes met fleetingly.

'Well, I for one am going to take that advice to heart,' he said.

Geraldine suppressed a smile, pleased that he seemed to have recovered his good spirits.

Bella and John Watts lived in a small brick-built terraced house in Milner Street, along Acomb Road. Geraldine had to drive past to find a parking space. Walking back along the road to the house she was looking for, she thought about the missing girl. A woman opened the door as soon as Geraldine knocked. With her pale face and light blue eyes, she looked almost spectral in the dim light.

'Have you found her?' she asked, without even waiting to hear that Geraldine was a police officer.

A dark-haired man joined them and Geraldine followed them into a small living room furnished with a settee and three chairs upholstered in maroon, and a low coffee table in the centre of the room. Since all the pieces were too large for the room, it seemed to be crammed with furniture. Geraldine wondered if they had moved to their house from somewhere larger. The man, who looked about forty, had blue eyes that contrasted strikingly with his dark hair, and seemed to gaze at her with a disconcerting kind of rapture that was quite seductive. She noticed he looked at his wife with the same attentive expression. Clearly he was an accomplished charmer. With his dazzling good looks and beguiling voice, she guessed he was a salesman of some kind. His wife was equally attractive, in a fragile way. She had wispy blonde hair, matched by eyebrows and eyelashes that looked white above her pale blue eyes. Her arms and legs were long and slender and she had a remarkably narrow waist. Geraldine was slim, but compared to Bella she was robust, even bulky.

Geraldine listened as John and Bella went through their account of the last evening their daughter had been at home. After checking Zoe's age and confirming that it was out of character for her to stay out all night without telling her parents where she was going, she enquired about the circumstances under which the girl had left home.

'Circumstances?' Bella echoed with a puzzled frown. 'What do you mean?'

'Had you had an argument with her?'

'We didn't even know she'd gone out,' Bella said, reaching for a tissue and wiping her eyes. 'She took her dinner upstairs and that's the last we saw of her.' She let out a sob.

'She didn't eat with you?' Geraldine asked.

'She preferred to eat in her room,' John explained, with a faint moue of regret. 'She's a teenager. We tried to give her as much freedom as we could, in the house, where she was safe.'

'Did you feel she wasn't safe outside the house?'

'Well, yes, of course, hopefully she was, but these days you hear all sorts of terrible stories, don't you? We weren't keeping her here against her will or anything like that,' he went on, with a smile that contrived to be both concerned and endearing. 'She was happy here. We liked her to stay in on school nights, to do her homework, but she was free to go out with her friends at weekends, and she never complained about her situation. Well,' he added with a regretful smile, 'not more than any teenager might. But we negotiated with her, the time she had to be home, and so on, and we never laid down the law. There was nothing like that, no conflict. She was very amenable. If we were at fault it was in being too lenient, so it was easy for her to co-operate. Teenagers these days don't like to be told what to do.'

Geraldine suspected Zoe's father of putting a positive spin on the operation of the household, but she made no comment, instead taking down the names of the missing girl's friends, before asking to see her bedroom.

'Is that necessary?' Bella asked. 'I mean, she didn't even like us going in there.'

'Let the police officer do her job,' John said. 'We want Zoe found, don't we?'

Zoe's room yielded little of interest, other than that she had left her phone on the bed, presumably to prevent anyone from tracking her location. Her parents had already said that she had taken her school bag packed with clothes and a wash bag, including her toothbrush. Geraldine explained that an officer would come round to look at Zoe's phone and computer, in case she had left any clues as to where she had gone.

'If she's still not returned tomorrow, we'll ramp up the search,' she said.

'Ramp it up how?' Zoe's father asked. 'Shouldn't you be doing everything you can right away?'

'We'll begin at once with questioning your neighbours in case they saw anything, and speak to her friends, and do everything we can to discover where she might have gone,' she said with what she hoped was a reassuring smile. 'In the meantime, if you can think of anything at all that might help us to find her, please do get in touch straightaway.'

As Geraldine was speaking, Zoe's mother glanced almost fearfully at her husband, who kept his eyes fixed on Geraldine and paid no attention to his wife.

# 11

FIRST THING THE FOLLOWING morning, Geraldine and Ian drove to the café where Angie had worked. Ian went to speak to the shopkeepers on either side of the café: a betting shop and a hairdresser. There was a slim chance one of them might have seen or heard something suspicious happening in the café, or outside on the street. Geraldine questioned the manager of the café, who was only able to tell her that Angie had been punctual, hardworking, and polite with customers.

'She will be a great loss,' he added gravely.

'How well did you know her?'

The manager shook his head. 'Not at all, I'm afraid. She turned up for work and did a good job, but our conversation never strayed beyond the customers' orders. We're generally too busy here to stop and chat. If there was ever a slack period, she would chat to the other waitress. I think she might be able to tell you more about Angie than I can.'

Geraldine sat at a table in the corner, waiting for the manager to send a skinny dark-haired girl over to speak to her. The odd mustard colour of the tables should have complemented the brown chairs and pale yellow walls, yet somehow the décor and furniture all seemed to clash. Geraldine stared at the plastic table top, and tried not to think about Ian.

The waitress came out from behind the counter, looking like a child, with a flat chest and virtually no hips. She claimed to be twenty-four, although she looked half that age. She spoke English fluently with a marked foreign accent, and seemed happy to chat about herself. Geraldine learned that Klara had left Poland when she was eighteen, coming to England as an au pair. She had met her partner and moved in with him six months later, after quitting the family she was living with.

'I am happy to leave house,' she said. 'They are not nice people. Not kind. They treat me like servant. I am slave to horrible children.' She pulled a face. 'Now I work here. Is good job for me.' She grinned. 'No more slave to horrible children.'

Klara had been working at the café for five months. She didn't know how long Angie had been employed there, but she had the impression her colleague had been working at the café for quite a while. Geraldine nodded, aware that Angie had been a waitress there for nearly three years.

'What was Angie like?' Geraldine asked.

Klara shrugged, and answered with a question of her own. 'Why she not here? Please to tell me what is going on.'

When Geraldine explained gently that Angie was dead, Klara looked startled. Her lower jaw dropped so that her mouth hung open for a second.

'She dead?' she repeated in a shocked whisper. 'How that is possible? She not sick. Is she killed by car? Oh my God!'

Geraldine explained that Angie's body had been discovered in the river.

'So she drowns and not… not…' Klara said, struggling for the word she wanted. 'How very sad is this. My poor friend.'

Geraldine questioned the girl gently, but Klara knew very little about her dead colleague. They had never socialised, and most of their time together had been spent working. All that Klara could say was that on the rare occasions they had time to chat, Angie had seemed very nice, and very happy.

'You called her your friend just now,' Geraldine reminded her. 'How well did you know her?'

'Yes, she nice to me. I think we can be friend. But I think

she have husband,' she told Geraldine. 'He now very sad. I sorry.'

Klara had never met Greg, and was unable to pass on anything specific that Angie had said about him.

'She say she have husband. She say her man clever, very good looker, this what she say. And she happy with her man.'

There was no reason to doubt the girl's sincerity, and Geraldine left soon after. Ian's questioning had proved similarly fruitless.

'None of the staff in the shops on either side knew anything about the waitresses here. They seemed to know the manager by sight, but that's about the extent of it. One of the hairdressers claims she regularly saw two girls coming in and out of the café, but that's about all I could gather, and her description was extremely vague.'

'Yes, I had the impression she was just trying to be obliging,' Ian said.

'Angie's colleague was no more helpful,' Geraldine replied and proceeded to tell him the little she had managed to elicit from Klara. 'This whole trip has been a complete waste of time,' she added.

'It would be good to feel we were actually getting somewhere,' Ian replied. 'The DCI seems a bit down in the dumps.'

'She's like a bear with a sore head, but as long as she gets the job done, who cares?' Geraldine answered testily.

She had no wish to gossip about her colleagues. All she wanted to do was find out who had killed Angie.

They drove back to the police station in silence. Actually, Geraldine reflected, the DCI's personality did matter. An effective team leader encouraged her officers, and commanded respect and loyalty. Undermining other people's efforts, while intending to spur them on to work harder, could be counterproductive. She suspected that beneath her gruff façade, Eileen lacked faith in her own ability to lead the team. But it was easy to judge others, and Geraldine had never been called on to lead a team herself.

'We each have to do our best,' she said aloud, and Ian grunted.

She glanced at him but he was staring straight ahead. She hoped she had not been curt in dismissing his attempt to air his concerns about Eileen. Geraldine had insisted she and Ian keep their relationship quiet, but now she wondered what other officers might say to him about her, not knowing about their relationship. She already had a reputation for being cold and detached. Such personal qualities were not necessarily inappropriate in an officer working on murder investigations, but they did make it more difficult for her to form friendships. Ariadne was the only close friend she had on the local force, apart from Ian.

With a sigh, she turned her attention to the case. It was easier to focus on the death of a stranger than to brood over her own shortcomings. She was mulling over everything Angie's boss had told them, and his reaction on hearing about her death, when they arrived back at the police station. Ian smiled at her before he jumped out of the car, and she wondered if she had misinterpreted his apparent chagrin. Probably he too was preoccupied with the case. Having checked in at the police station and written up her report, Geraldine's next visit was to Angie's neighbours. She wanted to find out as much as she could about the dead woman's relationship with her husband. It was ironic that she should be reluctant to listen to tittle-tattle in general, when her work necessitated prying into the circumstances of strangers.

# 12

As she drew into the kerb, Geraldine wondered whether it was a coincidence that Greg lived only a few blocks away from Zoe's house. His home was in the middle of a row of terraced York stone cottages, most of which would have benefited from some renovation. A few had new UPVC windows, but most, like the property where Greg lived, had old-fashioned sash windows with rotting wooden frames which must have been draughty in the winter. In the absence of a bell, she knocked and waited. When Greg finally opened the door, she noticed his hangdog expression and bloodshot eyes straightaway. Either he had been crying, or else he had rubbed his eyes to give that impression. Geraldine felt a stab of pity for him, and wished she did not have to approach the bereaved with such relentless suspicion. He had been allowed home, but as Angie's widower, he remained first in the line of potential suspects.

'Well?' he asked, in a dull monotone that barely sounded like a question. 'Do you know how it happened? Not that it makes any difference now, but I'd like to see the sick fucker who did this and smash his bloody face in.'

The words sounded robotic, as though he had rehearsed them so often they no longer held any meaning for him.

'We're following several leads,' Geraldine assured him blandly. 'I just called to enquire whether you had remembered anything else that might help us, and to let you know that a team will be here shortly to search your house.'

'What?' he burst out, momentarily startled out of his

dejection. 'What for? You already took her DNA. You know it's her – Oh God!'

He broke off, seemingly overcome with emotion. Geraldine was inclined to believe his reaction was genuine, but it was impossible to determine whether he was overwhelmed by grief or guilt; possibly both. Before Geraldine could continue, the search team arrived. They set to work briskly, removing any electronic devices for scrutiny, and sifting through the house looking for evidence.

'What are they hoping to find? Some kind of murder weapon?' Greg asked Geraldine. 'Why not just arrest me and have done with it? You've made up your minds I'm guilty. What makes you think I care a toss about what happens to me now?'

She shrugged. 'It's possible your wife had a friend you didn't know about,' she suggested.

Greg shook his head. 'No way.' But he didn't sound convinced.

'And there might be something that could lead us to investigate a contact who doesn't appear on the list of friends you gave us.'

'You think she was having an affair!' he snapped. 'Angie wasn't like that. We were happily married. I'm telling you, we were happy.'

Leaving the search team to their work, Geraldine went to speak to Greg's neighbours. There was no response to her knock at the house on the left, but when she tried the house on the other side, the door was opened almost at once by a white-haired woman with a youngish face. Geraldine judged her to be in her fifties.

'What's this about?' the woman demanded, glaring at Geraldine's identity card. 'Are you here about Angie next door? I saw something on the news. It's her, isn't it? She's dead. Is that why you're here?'

'What can you tell me about Angie?'

'I haven't seen her for about a week. I asked him if she was all right, and he just said she'd gone.'

'Gone?'

The woman nodded. 'That's all he said.'

'Please, think very carefully, when did he say that?'

The woman shrugged. 'I can't remember. It was at the weekend, Sunday morning I think. I saw him going out and asked because he was on his own and I hadn't seen her going to work for a few days. I thought she might be ill. I only wanted to help. Just being a good neighbour,' she added, as though concerned that Geraldine might think she was a busybody.

By Sunday, Angie had been missing for four days and Greg had already reported her absence. His admission to his neighbour that Angie had 'gone' proved only that he wasn't keen to share his concerns with his neighbour. If that was the case, Geraldine could sympathise with him.

'What sort of neighbours are they?' she asked.

But the woman had become circumspect, and began demanding answers to questions of her own.

'What's going on? Who are all those people? They can't all be police.'

'We're looking into what's happened to your neighbour,' Geraldine replied.

She tried to say as little as possible, while still avoiding antagonising the woman by refusing to tell her anything. Since a press release had gone out, she could hardly deny what had happened to Angie.

'Is she really dead?' The woman pulled her cardigan more tightly around her waist and took an involuntary step backwards into her house. 'Did he kill her?' she asked in a dramatic whisper.

'What makes you say that?'

'She's dead, and the police are looking into it, so what other explanation could there be? That's why you're asking about him, isn't it?'

'We have no evidence to suggest her husband has killed her,' Geraldine said truthfully. 'Now, it would help our investigation into her disappearance if you agreed to answer a few questions.'

The woman nodded.

'Can you tell me what they were like as neighbours?'

Geraldine waited.

'They argued a lot,' the woman said finally. 'He was always raising his voice, and probably his fists too.'

There had been no indication on the body to suggest that Angie had been physically abused before she was killed, so Geraldine was inclined to dismiss that allegation. All the same, she followed it up with a question.

'Did you ever see Greg hit his wife?'

'No, of course not. He wouldn't have done it outside, where anyone could see, would he? But they were always shouting at each other. We hear them – we used to hear them – at it in the summer, when the windows were open, yelling and screaming like they were at each other's throats.'

Along with repeated accusations of violent arguments, she indulged in wild supposition about how Greg could have lashed out at his wife with a kitchen knife, or hacked her to death in the garden with an axe.

'You need to search the house and garden for blood,' she suggested. 'He probably did it at night, as there were no witnesses, but the evidence must be there in the garden, under the earth, right now.' She shuddered. 'You need to find out what happened to that poor woman and then give her a proper Christian burial. It's only right.'

After listening to some more wild speculation and inappropriate advice, Geraldine took her leave.

'And you will keep me updated, won't you?' the neighbour asked eagerly.

Geraldine wondered whether it was worth requesting her not to speak to any reporters about Greg and Angie, but decided it would be a mistake to introduce the idea of media interest to a neighbour who was likely to welcome such attention. She left, after thanking the woman for her assistance.

When Geraldine was back at her desk and had completed her report, Ariadne suggested popping along to the canteen for a coffee.

'So I take it there's nothing new about Angie yet,' Ariadne said, when they were seated with their drinks.

'Not that I've seen.'

'Well?' Ariadne went on, leaning forward in her chair and lowering her voice. 'Have you got anything else to tell me?'

'Like what? I can't say the neighbours were very helpful, although it does seem that Greg and Angie argued a lot. But that's hardly unusual, is it?'

'I'm not talking about the case,' Ariadne replied impatiently, glancing around to make sure they could not be overheard. 'I'm talking about Ian.'

Geraldine frowned. 'What about Ian?'

Ariadne grinned, her eyes shining mischievously.

Geraldine took a sip of her coffee. 'What about him?' she repeated.

'Geraldine, don't be coy. It's obvious you like him.'

'He's a nice guy,' Geraldine answered cagily, adding, 'and we've been friends for a long time.'

'He's divorced, isn't he?'

'Listen, Ariadne, if you're suddenly so interested in Ian's marital status, why don't you ask him about it yourself? I'm sorry to sound dismissive but really, you seem to know as much about it as I do, and right now I'm not thinking about

71

anything much unless it has something to do with the case we're investigating.'

'Ooh,' Ariadne replied, still grinning. 'That's a very feisty response to a simple question!'

Ariadne laughed, but Geraldine did not join in and the conversation turned to Angie and her relationship with her husband. The search team had finished looking around in the house, and both Angie and Greg's laptops had been removed for examination, along with Greg's mobile phone, despite his angry insistence that he needed it for his work. Angie's phone had not been found, and the river was being dredged in hopes of recovering it. That evening Geraldine returned to speak to the neighbours on the left side of Greg's house. A young couple lived there. Although they seemed willing to help, they knew little about their neighbours.

'We only moved in three months ago,' the man explained.

'We did introduce ourselves when we first arrived, but since then we haven't really spoken to them, have we?' his girlfriend added.

'Have you ever overheard them at home?'

'Overheard them?'

'Yes, any loud music, raised voices, that kind of thing?'

'No, we keep ourselves to ourselves and they seem to like to do the same. But, like I said, it's only been three months. It's not as if we're deliberately being unfriendly, but we've been busy moving in.'

Geraldine thanked them for their time, asked them to contact her if they thought of anything that might help the police enquiry, and went home slightly irritated. It seemed the first next-door neighbour she had questioned had exaggerated the rows she had overheard between Greg and Angie.

# 13

DURING HER LUNCH BREAK the next day, Geraldine stepped outside to phone her twin sister, Helena. It was difficult to call her privately from home now that Ian was there, and she suspected he disapproved of her relationship with her twin. It was chilly outside and she had left her coat behind, but their calls never lasted for more than a couple of minutes, so she would be back inside soon, and well before she had to return to her desk. Despite being identical, she and her twin could not have been more different. When Geraldine had been adopted by a prosperous professional family, Helena, a sickly baby, had remained with their birth mother. Against all expectations, the delicate baby had survived. It was not until she was an adult that Geraldine had traced her birth mother. To her horror, Geraldine had discovered not only that she had a living twin, but that Helena was a heroin addict. Worse, Helena was in debt to her dealer who was threatening to kill her if she did not pay up.

Helena had been too terrified to face her dealer again, so Geraldine had reluctantly agreed to meet him in her place. As Helena's identical twin, she had planned to pay the dealer off masquerading as Helena, and so free her sister from his clutches. In exchange for Geraldine rescuing her, Helena had promised to go into rehab. But in the event, Geraldine had been arrested handing a substantial amount of money over to a known drug dealer. She had been released without charge, but had sacrificed her own career prospects. Although Geraldine had done everything in her power to help her destitute sister, their relationship remained rocky.

'What's up?' Helena's gruff voice came down the line.

'I'm just calling to see how you are.'

'My saintly sister checking up on me. How nice,' Helena replied, her voice heavy with sarcasm. 'I'm still clean, if that's what you want to know.'

'I just called to see how you are,' Geraldine repeated quietly.

In the background she heard a man's voice, and Helena remonstrating.

'Got to go. I'll speak to you later,' Helena said suddenly.

'Sorry, have you got someone there?' Geraldine asked, but Helena had already hung up.

Shivering, Geraldine went back inside and even a mug of soup in the canteen failed to warm her.

'Are you all right?' Ariadne asked when she returned to her desk.

'Just got a bit cold going outside for a breath of air,' Geraldine replied.

Ariadne looked faintly puzzled, but Geraldine turned her attention to her screen, with a pretence of being focused on a document, and was soon genuinely engrossed in her work.

Later that afternoon, Eileen summoned the team together for a briefing so that the family liaison officer, Susan, could update them on Zoe's disappearance. Her impression of Zoe's parents did not match Geraldine's.

'I didn't see the father on this visit,' Susan said, 'but mother was clearly very distressed. She told me she had been to speak to Zoe's best friend, Laura, but she had not been able to learn anything new from her. We went over the list of belongings Zoe took with her, and she confirmed that it seems to be complete. So there's nothing new to report from her home.'

'We just have to hope there'll be a sighting of her soon,'

Eileen said. 'It's time to alert the media and find out if any members of the public have seen her.'

'Missing persons have heard nothing from any of the shelters or hospitals,' Susan said, 'and there's no record of her using public transport. As far as we can tell, she disappeared voluntarily and completely.'

'We have no reason as yet to think her missing status might be in any way related to our murder enquiry,' Ian said. 'Without any evidence she's been done away with, the chances are she's just hiding out at a friend's house, as teenagers do.'

'Done away with?' Eileen echoed, her eyebrows slightly raised.

Ian seemed impervious to the implied criticism of his choice of words, and Geraldine warmed to him. His self-assurance stopped short of arrogance, and his confidence was somehow reassuring. Eileen questioned Susan about Zoe's parents, and seemed satisfied there was no reason to suspect them of anything untoward.

'I thought Bella seemed a little in awe of her husband when I went to speak to them,' Geraldine hazarded.

'How do you mean, in awe of him?' Eileen asked. 'Do you think there was anything going on that we should know about?'

'She seemed afraid, not of him, perhaps, but of what he might tell me, almost as though she couldn't trust him, as though there was something they didn't want me to know.'

Susan shook her head. 'I didn't get that impression of them at all,' she said firmly. 'Do you have any reason to suspect them of not being straight with us about Zoe's disappearance?'

'It's just a hunch,' Geraldine conceded. 'And in any case, their uneasy relationship might have nothing to do with their daughter.'

'It probably has,' Susan replied. 'I'm guessing they may have had a few arguments about the way they've been behaving towards Zoe. Teenage girls are notoriously difficult to handle, and parents don't always see eye to eye about how to treat them. More often than not, one parent is in favour of imposing strict rules, and the other thinks they should give their child greater freedom. With the pressure of their current trouble, they're quite likely to be at loggerheads. But, like I said, that's just a guess in this case. They struck me as caring, concerned parents.'

'Yes,' Geraldine agreed, 'I'm sure there's nothing more to it than that. She's a teenager, which is bound to be causing some perfectly normal friction in the household.'

She still had a feeling that Bella and John had been hiding something, but there was nothing she could say to substantiate her impression, and she was beginning to regret having mentioned it.

'Susan has seen a lot more of them than I have,' she conceded, 'and they must be stressed about their daughter.'

'Well,' Eileen said cautiously, 'Susan is the family liaison officer, and she has spent more time with them than anyone else. But let's keep an eye on them all the same.'

With a brisk nod, Eileen turned her attention to the murder enquiry. The search team had completed their scrutiny of Greg's house and had found no leads to anyone who might have held a grudge against Angie. Greg remained the only suspect for Angie's murder.

'Just because we can't find anything to incriminate someone else doesn't mean he did it,' Geraldine pointed out once the meeting was concluded and Eileen had returned to her desk. 'We can't accuse a man of murder merely because his wife is the victim and there are no other obvious suspects.'

# 14

On Friday morning, Geraldine got up early to make breakfast which they ate on the balcony, bundled up in warm clothes. It was a sunny day in late autumn, with a faint breeze blowing up from the river. There would not be many more such bright fresh mornings that year, when it would be mild enough to sit outside. They sipped fresh coffee and crunched toast, as they sat watching the dark grey river below them, and by an unspoken agreement neither of them mentioned work until they had finished. Geraldine wanted to be at her desk early, so Ian offered to clear the breakfast things away.

Leaving him on the balcony, Geraldine walked to the underground car park where she kept her car overnight. She reached a bend in the stairs that led beneath her block of flats when, without warning, a hood was flung over her head, her bag was snatched from her shoulder, and her hands were tied behind her back. The smell of stale cigarette smoke inside the hood made her retch. It flashed across her mind that whoever was assaulting her knew the exact spot on the stairs where there were no CCTV cameras. Endeavouring to control her panic, she yelled and tried to kick out, and nearly lost her footing. Her alarm increased when she felt her phone being taken from her pocket. Struggling and shrieking inside her muffled hood, she felt herself lifted bodily off her feet, carried rapidly down the last few steps and shoved on to a hard surface, hitting her shoulder and hip as she fell.

She realised she had been thrown into the back of a van

which had been waiting at the foot of the stairs, concealing her descent from the nearby cameras in the car park. The engine started up and the vehicle jolted into motion. As she lay trussed up on the floor, she wondered whether her abduction could possibly have been spotted on any CCTV camera, but the slick operation had been conducted swiftly and discreetly enough to avoid leaving any trace. Doing her best to remain calm, she tried to work out the direction in which they were travelling, but her mind was in turmoil and the vehicle seemed to be driving round in circles. Her first task was to free herself from her handcuffs, but the metal was unyielding. However hard she tried, her hands would not fit through the bracelets, which cut into her flesh when she tried to force herself free. At last, exhausted and bleeding, she gave up. There was nothing she could do but conserve her energy and focus on keeping her wits about her. That was challenge enough in her present circumstances. She hoped it would not be long before Ian noticed she was missing, and discovered her car was still in the car park, but by then she might be miles away.

A long time seemed to elapse before the van drew to a halt. Geraldine heard several male voices, although she could not make out anything they said. A moment later, the door creaked open. Through the fabric of her hood she was faintly aware of light outside, as rough hands grabbed her upper arms and dragged her out of the van and on to her feet. Her legs felt stiff, her hip ached from where she had fallen on it, and her head throbbed. One of her wrists was smarting, but she could not tell whether she had hurt herself in attempting to escape her shackles or if she had sustained an injury when she fell. More than anything, she struggled not to break down in tears. A faint breeze fluttered across the backs of her hands as, blind and terrified, she was dragged across rough ground. After a few seconds, the smell inside the hood grew ranker, and the slight breeze she had felt on her hands vanished, while the sound of several feet on the ground altered from a dull thudding to a sharper clacking and she realised they must be indoors. They had not climbed any steps so were on the ground floor. Behind her a door clanged loudly. She guessed they were in a garage or a storage container of some sort.

She tried not to cry out as she was suddenly shoved down on to a chair, her ankles were secured, and the hood was tugged off her head. Blinking in the sudden onslaught of light, she struggled to remain calm. She knew she ought to memorise as much about her environment as she could, and tried to dismiss the possibility that she might never have an opportunity to describe the location to her colleagues. After the terrifying darkness to which she had been subjected, the brightness of a naked bulb suspended from the ceiling seemed to pierce her eyeballs; it cast long shadows across the grimy floor. As her eyes grew accustomed to the light she saw that she was seated in a large, empty brick shed of some description. The windows had been painted over and the metal door was shut. Somewhere in the distance she could hear whirring, but she was unable to determine whether the sound came from machinery or traffic. That was the kind of detail which could result in identifying her abductors' hideout, if she ever escaped. Endeavouring to memorise her environment helped her to control her panic. At least she felt as though she was able to do something, however futile it might be. The place stank of mildew. It could have been a large garage anywhere in the country. But she had no idea how far they had travelled, and was unable to see the time to estimate how long she had been locked in the van, speeding along the streets. She could have been anywhere in the country. Despair threatened to overwhelm her as she realised the futility of any attempt to work out where she was being held.

'Is she wired?' a hoarse voice called out.

Nervously, Geraldine turned her attention to her captors. The man who had spoken was seated in front of her, his eyes blazing at her through holes in a black balaclava.

'I don't think so,' another man answered, in a slightly higher rasping tone.

The second man was standing behind her, out of her line of vision.

'I'm not wired,' she replied loudly. 'Why would I be? It's not as if you sent me advance notice you were going to attack me. Or do you think I routinely wear a wire in case someone decides to kidnap me?'

She was pleased to hear that her voice sounded confident and strong, the very opposite of how she was feeling. However difficult it was, she knew she had to force herself to join in their conversation; the longer they discussed her as though she was not present, the easier it would be for them to objectify her.

'Why would I be wearing a wire?' she repeated earnestly. 'I was going to work when your gorillas grabbed me. Do you think I wear a wire at the police station?'

It would not do any harm to remind them that she was a police officer. It was even possible they were unaware of her identity and might think twice about assaulting her, once they knew who she was.

'Are you sure?' the seated man asked his companion, as though she had not spoken.

'The only way to be sure is if we get her to strip,' the other man responded with a deep throated laugh.

He stepped forward from the shadows, and she was not surprised to see that he too was wearing a balaclava. Their facelessness, combined with their casual verbal exchange, was chilling, as was their continued conversation about her as though she was not a sentient human being. She struggled to commit the sound of their voices to memory, although she was aware it was hopeless. She would never be able to identify them just from hearing them speak. In any case, she suspected they were disguising their voices because they both sounded curiously hoarse.

'Who are you?' she demanded, speaking as forcefully as she could.

'Take off her shirt,' the seated man said.

He continued to ignore her when she spoke, in what she realised must be a deliberate ploy to unnerve her. He seemed to be in charge. Resolutely, Geraldine stared at him. His age was difficult to judge without seeing his face, but he was sturdily built, and he spoke with an air of authority. All she could observe of him was that his eyes were dark. The second man was slimmer and more excitable, and he appeared younger than the seated man. His eyes were lighter, blue or hazel in the strange light of the single bulb. He stepped forward and tore her shirt open. Several buttons ripped off and bounced on the floor. The young man studied her body, grinning, before feeling carefully down her legs, checking her ankles and removing her shoes.

'Who are you?' Geraldine asked. 'Tell me what you want.'

She addressed her question to the seated man, doing her best to ignore the man who was manhandling her.

'She's not wired,' the younger of the two men announced, stepping away from her at last.

'Who are you?' Geraldine repeated, barely managing to control her voice.

'*We* know who *you* are,' the seated man replied. 'And that's all that matters.'

# 15

ZOE HAD BEEN MISSING for nearly two days, and the police did not seem to be making any attempt to find her. Someone from the school called to say they were contacting social services about Zoe's continued unauthorised absence.

'Please do,' Bella snapped. 'We told you she's missing and we've reported it to the police. The more people there are looking for Zoe, the better. So please, tell everyone you like.' She slammed the phone down and turned to John. 'We need to look for her ourselves. Anything could have happened to her. She could have been knocked down, or assaulted, or – or anything...' Bella said, her blue eyes stretched wide with concern. 'Why haven't the police found her yet?'

A plump blonde police officer called Susan was acting as their family liaison officer.

'We're doing everything we can,' Susan reassured her. 'A team is talking to all of Bella's friends from school and one of them may well know where she's gone.'

'She's probably perfectly fine, and just visiting a friend,' John replied, a trifle impatiently. 'Listen, Bella, I know you're going out of your mind with worry. Believe me, so am I. But there's nothing we can do. We have to let the police do their job.'

Bella lowered her voice and gestured to John to follow her into the kitchen so that Susan could not hear them talking.

'The police aren't doing anything. We can't just sit around and do nothing. I'm going to speak to Laura when she gets home from school. She might know where Zoe's gone. They were inseparable before Laura started going out with that boy.'

'How is Laura supposed to know where she is?'

'If she can't tell us where Zoe is, at least she'll know who Zoe's friends are now, won't she? They're supposed to be best friends. Or they were.'

John gazed at his wife, frowning. 'I can't see what we can do that the police aren't already doing.' He paused on seeing the resentment in his wife's expression. 'Well, if you think it will help,' he conceded. 'Would you like me to come with you?'

Bella shook her head. 'One of us should stay here, in case –'

'She'll be back soon, you'll see,' John said. 'She won't stay away forever.'

'But where is she?'

John couldn't answer.

Laura's mother looked surprised to see Bella standing at the door.

'We're looking for Zoe,' Bella said, without a greeting or any other preamble.

'Zoe? She's not here.'

'Can I speak to Laura?' Bella asked.

'Laura?'

'Yes, only you see – we don't know where Zoe is, and we thought – we were hoping Laura might know,' Bella stammered.

Laura's mother frowned. 'I don't see –' she began.

'Please,' Bella interrupted her urgently. 'We don't know who else to ask. She's been gone since Tuesday night.'

'Tuesday?' Laura's mother looked shocked. 'And you don't know where she is?'

Bella shook her head.

'You should report it to the police.'

'We've been to the police and they've said they're looking for her, but so far they've drawn a blank.'

'They can track her phone, can't they?'

'She left her phone at home.'

Laura's mother frowned. 'Wait here.'

She disappeared into the house and Bella heard her yelling to Laura to come downstairs. A moment later Laura appeared, looking sullen. Her expression barely altered when she heard the reason for Bella's call.

'I've no idea where she is,' she replied promptly. 'How should I know? I haven't seen her for ages. She was at school on Monday, I think, and she's been off ever since. No, she was there on Tuesday because it's PE on Tuesday and she was definitely there, but she wasn't in yesterday or today.' She shrugged her thin shoulders. 'I thought she was ill or something. She didn't say anything to me about bunking off.'

'Bunking off?' Laura's mother repeated, sounding vexed. 'This is more than just bunking off school, Laura. Zoe's disappeared and her parents are very worried that something might have happened to her. It's no joke, her going off like this without telling anyone where she's gone.' She stared closely at her daughter. 'Are you quite sure you don't know anything about this?'

Laura glared at her mother. 'I said so, didn't I? Why can't you believe anything I say? Do you really think I would lie to you about something like this?' She turned to look at Bella. 'If I knew where Zoe was, I'd tell you, but I don't know where she's gone, so there's nothing more I can say.'

'I'm sure she'll come home when she's ready,' Laura's mother said helplessly. 'I hope she doesn't stay away too long. They have no idea how much we worry about them.'

With a sniff, Laura turned away and they heard her feet pounding up the stairs.

'I'm sorry,' Laura's mother said. 'I'm sure Laura doesn't mean to be rude. Teenagers aren't easy, are they?'

With a sigh, Bella turned away. She had more important

matters on her mind than Laura's manners. There was no word from Zoe, and that evening they had another visit from their family liaison officer. Susan sat down with Bella and went through everything the police had so far done to find her daughter. It didn't seem to amount to much, and Zoe was still missing. Bella explained that she had gone to see Zoe's friend, Laura, who had known only that Zoe had been absent from school that week.

'And the school have been on to us to say they're going to involve social services to investigate Zoe's absence,' she added with a scowl.

Susan shook her head and said a team would be visiting the school to speak to Zoe's classmates. Bella nodded. Laura knew about it, and by the next morning all of Zoe's classmates would be aware that she had run away from home.

'The more people we can speak to who knew Zoe, the greater the chance that we'll find her without any further delay,' Susan said.

'What are the chances that she's...' Bella began but broke off in tears, unable to complete the sentence.

Susan gave a reassuring smile. 'The likelihood is that we'll find her alive and well and staying with a friend,' she said. 'It's encouraging that she packed a bag. That shows she intended to run away. If she had disappeared unexpectedly on her way home from school, for example, it might suggest that she'd met with an accident, or been abducted. But from what you told us, she left home deliberately, and presumably she had a plan in mind. Now, can we go over exactly what she said to you on the evening before she left home, and everything she took with her? Please don't leave anything out.'

'Is there any point in going over it all again?' Bella asked.

'We won't know until we finish.'

# 16

AWARE THAT HER CAPTORS were doing everything they could to intimidate her, Geraldine told herself that if they intended to kill her they would have done so already. She tried not to give way to panic when the hood was pulled over her head again, and she heard footsteps retreating. A few seconds later, a metal door clanged shut. She was alive, and her injuries were relatively minor, but the silence was terrifying.

'Hello?' she called out. 'Hello? Are you there? Is anyone there?' Her voice sounded oddly muffled inside the dark hood. 'Hello? Are you still there? Is anyone there? We need to talk.' No one answered. 'I may be able to help you. Tell me what you want.'

It was not clear whether she was alone, or in the presence of a taciturn guard. She tried to stand up but her legs were tied to the chair. If she tipped her seat over, she might be able to release her legs, but she had no way of knowing whether there was a bar preventing her from slipping her shackles off the legs of the chair. Besides, without being able to move her arms, she might injure her head if she succeeded in rocking the chair violently enough to make it fall over. On balance, she decided it was not worth the risk. Not yet at any rate. It took all her powers of mental control not to cry as she contemplated her predicament. Doing her best to ignore her physical discomfort, she focused on the rescue operation that was doubtless already under way. By now Ian would have noticed her absence and a search would be in place.

Reassuring herself that she would soon be found, she did her best to wait patiently.

A very long time seemed to elapse before she heard footsteps approaching. Her momentary flicker of hope was extinguished as soon as her hood was removed and she saw the older of her two captors standing in front of her, staring at her through the holes in his balaclava.

'What do you want?' she asked. 'I can't help you if you don't tell me what you want.'

'A friend sent us to question you,' he replied quietly, in his oddly hoarse voice.

From the way the skin around his eyes creased, Geraldine had the impression he was smiling.

'A friend? What friend? What are you talking about?' All at once, a wave of anger swept through her. 'Whatever you want, you won't get it, and if you kill me, you'll be killing a police officer. Do you really think you can get away with that?'

The man spoke so softly she had to strain to hear the words. 'You have a sister living in Hackney.'

As she listened, Geraldine's fortitude deserted her and she stared at the speaker, no longer making any attempt to conceal her apprehension.

Relentlessly the voice continued. 'She's teetering on the edge. Once an addict... well, you know how it ends.' Once again she had the impression the speaker was smiling. 'We've left her alone, for now. It would be so easy to slip a needle in her arm.'

As he spoke, he mimed injecting himself. Without seeing his facial expression, his guttural laughter sounded strange, as though he was choking.

'What do you want from me?' she repeated in a hollow voice.

'We heard you would do anything to save your sister from, well, people like us.'

'What do you want?' she repeated, her voice shaking.

Behind her, Geraldine heard someone stir and guessed that the younger man had also returned. It sounded as though he was spitting on the floor.

'What do we want?' the older man asked. 'You know what we want.'

'What do you mean?'

'You know what I mean.'

'I've no idea what you're talking about. If you're planning to do away with me, just get it over with,' she blustered. 'But you'd be throwing your own lives away along with mine, because my colleagues will hunt you down if you kill me. And it would all be for nothing. I don't know anything that could possibly be useful to you.'

'You're a police officer.'

'I'm just a detective sergeant. I don't have any influence, and I don't know anything.'

'You're a police officer. You know enough.'

'You're making a mistake. You have nothing to gain by bringing me here.'

She hoped it was not obvious she was terrified they might torture her.

'I tell you what,' she went on, growing desperate, 'let me go, right now, and I won't report this. You don't really want to murder a police officer, do you? You'll never get away with it, and you'll be banged up for life.'

Her captor burst into raucous laughter. 'Report it? Report what? Do you seriously think you're in a position to threaten us? Listen, you're the one in trouble, not us. You don't call the shots here.'

'What do you want from me? What's this about? You wouldn't risk abducting a police officer if you weren't after something. But you won't get anything out of me, and if you threaten to kill me, you know as well as I do that won't get you anywhere.'

'No one's threatening to kill you, for fuck's sake. Did anyone mention wanting to kill you? Has anyone even hurt you? Now just shut up and listen. Here's the deal.'

Tempted to retort that she would never make a deal with criminals, Geraldine hesitated. Her only priority right now was to get away. Once she was back with her colleagues, any promises she had made under duress would be void.

'Go on,' she said.

The man grunted. 'You do exactly what we want, or your sister's back on the smack. And this time you won't be able to save her.'

'You won't get anywhere by threatening me like that.'

'Maybe we won't get anywhere with you, but do you really want to stand by and see your sister lose everything?'

'This has nothing to do with my sister.'

'On the contrary, this has everything to do with her.' He stared at her. 'What did you expect to hear me say?'

'I didn't think you had brought me here for a picnic.'

He laughed. 'You can't afford to refuse my offer, not if you care about your sister.'

'What offer?' she asked, hoping he might reveal something about himself.

'You follow my orders, to the letter, and we leave your sister alone. Otherwise –' He shook his head.

'What orders? You haven't told me what you want me to do.'

He shrugged. 'Whatever I need when the time comes.'

'I can try to help you,' she lied, 'but I won't break the law.'

'Sod the law. The law doesn't come into it. It's very simple. All you have to do is follow my orders. And no messing around or you're –' He made a gesture miming a gun shooting himself in the head. 'Only it won't be you. No, it'll be your precious sister.' He held out his arm and mimed injecting himself inside his elbow.

'You have to tell me what you want me to do,' Geraldine said.

Her voice sounded thin, like a wire about to snap.

'We'll be in touch and when we are, you'll do exactly as I tell you. And in the meantime, not a word to anyone. You know how to keep your mouth shut, don't you? And you know what will happen if you don't.'

She watched as he repeated his sickening mime of injecting himself. A moment later, she felt her ankles being untied. With an effort, she resisted the temptation to leap up and give the man behind her a strong kick. There was no point in antagonising her captors. For the time being she had to put on a show of co-operating with them, until she had worked out what to do. If it proved impossible to retain her integrity as a police officer and still protect Helena, she was not yet sure whether she would sacrifice her sister or her principles. Somehow she had to find a way to safeguard them both.

The older man spoke again. 'Your sister won't be touched if you do as you're told. But you have no idea what she's going to suffer if you let us down.' He stood up. 'Think about it.' He lowered his voice until Geraldine had to strain to hear what he was saying. 'If you mention a word of this to anyone, we'll find out soon enough, and before she knows what's happening, your sister will be experiencing her favourite rush. Only this time you won't be around to help her to get clean, because you'll be behind bars where you can't get to her. Yes, poor Helena's going to be all on her own with her addiction. How long do you think she'll last? And we'll make sure she knows who abandoned her this time.'

Without warning the hood was thrust over her face from behind. In suffocating darkness she was hoisted to her feet and shoved forward. Terrified, she stumbled along blindly, powerless to resist as she was forced forwards. Once again she was bundled into the back of a van which jolted into gear, and they drove off. After a while they stopped and she was pushed out on to the road, her hands swiftly released and her hood yanked off. With a roar, the van sped away and she found herself on the road under Skeldergate Bridge, not far from her apartment. Grabbing her bag, which had been slung out after her, she realised she was not wearing her shoes. Out of immediate danger, she began to tremble violently.

# 17

BLINKING AND SHAKING, GERALDINE picked up her bag and made her way home, dashing tears from her eyes as she stumbled along, and talking to herself crossly. Breaking down in tears was no way for a detective sergeant to behave.

'Where have you been all day?' Ian asked as he came out into the hall. 'I tried to call you at lunch time.' His eyes widened in alarm as he caught sight of her. 'What the hell happened to you? You look like – Were you knocked down? What happened? Are you hurt?'

Geraldine ducked her head. 'I'm fine, I'm fine. I just need a shower.'

She attempted to push past him before he could see how distressed she was.

'No!' She paused at the urgency in his voice. 'Tell me what happened. Have you been attacked?'

She nodded uncertainly. 'It was an accident,' she mumbled.

She would have to admit the whole truth at some point, but was not yet ready to talk about her ordeal.

'I just need a few minutes to myself,' she said by way of explanation, as she made another attempt to pass him.

'Geraldine, the last thing you want to do is take a shower.'

She nodded, understanding his drift, and burst into tears.

'I'll put a plastic bin liner on a chair in the living room so you can sit down,' he said. 'I'll make you some tea and then you can change out of those clothes and tell me exactly what happened, while it's all still fresh in your mind.'

He fetched a bin liner, spread it on a chair and Geraldine obediently took a seat and waited while he made the tea. Placing a steaming mug on the table in front of her, he questioned her gently, and gradually she regained her equanimity sufficiently to give him a brief outline of what had happened, taking care to leave out any mention of her twin sister, Helena.

'So you're saying a criminal threatened you in an attempt to force you to protect them?' Ian asked her, when she had finished her account. 'Scum!'

'It sounds crazy, I know, but –' She broke off, aware that her voice was wobbling.

She wondered whether she would find it easier to maintain her composure if she spoke to someone else. She still did not know what to do, and needed time to think. It was difficult for her to lie at the best of times and almost impossible when she was talking to Ian. He knew her too well.

'We've most likely got the DNA of at least one of your attackers on the database,' he was saying.

'They were wearing gloves and they put a hood over my head. I don't think they touched me or breathed on me, and I never laid a finger on either of them. I wish I had now.'

'Yes, if you'd managed to scratch one of them –' Ian paused. 'But then they might not have let you go.'

She nodded and her first lie slipped out. 'That's what I thought.'

Instead of being annoyed with herself for failing to acquire vital evidence that might lead to her assailants' arrest, she was relieved to have so far protected their identity. Until she had devised a way out of the situation, she could not afford to take any steps that might antagonise her captors.

'You said your hands were secured behind your back and that's why you couldn't defend yourself, so there could be DNA on your wrists.'

'They were both wearing gloves.'

'So you're sure there'll be no DNA?'

Geraldine went over what she had seen and heard, as sketchily as she could, omitting to mention any details about the shed where she had been held.

'Did you see anything?'

'No,' she lied. 'I was blindfolded the entire time.'

'And did you hear anything at all other than the two men's voices?'

'Nothing. And their voices were disguised.'

Ian looked faintly puzzled, but didn't question her response. Instead, he nodded briskly.

'I'll note down everything you said, and you can check it, and then I'll drive you to the station to make a formal statement. Don't worry we'll get these bastards, even though you haven't given us much to go on. You can't say how far away their hideout was, or describe anything about the place or the two men who abducted you. Nothing at all?' He ended on an interrogative note which Geraldine ignored.

'I need a shower.'

'You need to go to the station first. They'll want to swab you for DNA whatever you think.'

'You can take my clothes, but they didn't touch me,' she lied, with a faint shudder as she recalled how she had been checked for a wire.

'What about your shirt? How did that tear?'

She shook her head. 'I think I stumbled when I was pulled out of the van. It must have caught on something. No one's going to believe what happened,' she added, with a faint laugh.

After her shower, she saw that Ian had put on gloves before slipping her clothes into a large evidence bag. She did her best to stall him, but he became annoyed when she refused to make a statement, and she was afraid that she would be unable to prevent him from taking matters further.

'Ian, I can't report this,' she said firmly. 'Not yet. I need time to think.'

'What are you talking about?'

'And you can't report it either.'

'Geraldine, you're not making any sense. What else happened? Did they threaten you?'

Finally she broke down and told him the truth.

'They told me that if I mention a word of this to anyone, they'll visit Helena. They threatened to make her start using again. I can't do that to her, Ian, not after all she's been through. I may have to accede to their demands, at least until I can discover who they are.'

Ian stared at her, horrified. 'Geraldine, you're not thinking clearly. What about what *you've* been through? You've been demoted, and had to leave your home, and nearly lost your job altogether, all to protect your sister. Are you seriously saying you'd be prepared to break the law to keep her from going back on heroin? And what guarantee do you have that she wouldn't slide back into it anyway, whatever you do?'

Geraldine shrugged miserably. There was no guarantee. For a drug addict who had kicked the habit, every day held a risk of relapse. Only Helena's continuing determination stood between her and addiction.

'Listen,' Ian went on, 'nothing that happens to your sister is your responsibility. She's made her choices. What if you sacrifice yourself and she starts shooting up again? Do you really think you can prevent her doing it? And don't you think the guilt she'd feel if you were caught protecting a criminal gang because of her would drive her to it? What difference does it make who gets her back on it? She might give in to irresistible temptation regardless of what anyone else says or does. If she wants to do it, you can't stop her, Geraldine. No one can. The stark truth is, you can't protect her, and you have to start accepting that before both your lives are ruined. And mine,' he added softly.

'So you're saying I should turn my back on her and leave them to destroy her? It's as good as murdering her.' She shook her head. 'I can't do it, Ian. I just can't.'

'Then I can't do what you want,' he said. 'I won't sit by and watch you throw your life away like this. I can't do that, and you can't demand it of me.' He stood up, and hovered for a moment as though he was waiting for her to tell him she had changed her mind. 'If you won't go to the station and report what happened, I will.'

Geraldine nodded. 'All right,' she replied. 'I'll do it. But first you have to give me time to warn my sister.'

'One week,' he replied sternly. 'You have until next Friday and then I'm going to the DCI myself.'

'Give me until midnight next Friday,' she said. 'I'll go to see her as soon as I can get away. I need to see her one last time. Give me that, at least. Don't force me to tell her this over the phone.'

# 18

THIS TIME THE PLANNING had been meticulous, and the disposal of the body had been carried out with consummate skill, bordering on genius. It was truly brilliant, because there was absolutely no way the corpse could be traced back to the location where the execution had taken place. The death itself was history, all but forgotten by the time the corpse was deposited in the open air to be found by a stranger.

The delay in moving the body was not the sole reason the killer's identity would remain hidden. Sooner or later, of course, someone would come across the body. No doubt they would be shocked, but that was too bad. Speculating about the finder's reaction was curiously diverting, but it was ultimately unimportant, because the discovery of the dead woman's physical remains was utterly insignificant. What really mattered was that nothing could possibly link the two key locations: the site of the death and the discovery of the body. In that respect, the plan had worked perfectly. Admittedly the body would be found not far from the scene of the murder, but that was of no consequence, since the killer could not be traced.

What had made the operation particularly tricky was that the body had to be transported along a crowded pavement, in full view of anyone passing by. If moving the body had not been so difficult and stressful, it would have been entertaining. In retrospect, it was actually quite hilarious. So many stupid people – no doubt all regarding themselves as intelligent –

had walked past the body, completely oblivious to what was happening right in front of their eyes. People were blind when it came to noticing what was in front of them. So the body had travelled along the street, unobserved. That had been challenging. After that, there had been nothing to do but slip away without attracting attention, and wait. Before long, there would be an announcement in the news. The police would start scurrying around, searching for evidence to lead them to the killer. They wouldn't find any, for all their forensic examination of the scene, and teams of officers questioning potential witnesses. As it happened, there had been witnesses, and plenty of them, only none of them knew what been going on right under their noses.

In the meantime, he had returned to his daily routine as though nothing had happened. For all that anyone else knew, nothing *had* happened. But for one woman everything had come to an end, and for those close to her, nothing would ever be the same again. In a way, that made it all seem desperately sad. If only he could stop pursuing other women, no one else would need to suffer. Somehow there had to be a way to banish the devil from his heart. But before that happened, he had to want to walk away from the path of sin. Only if he truly repented, could he receive divine pardon from a forgiving God.

# 19

THE MUSIC WAS SO loud Jamie couldn't hear what any of his friends were saying, although they all seemed to be shouting cheerily to each other easily, as though they were having a normal conversation. He found it hard to believe they could possibly make out what was being said above the noise of a roomful of people yelling to make themselves heard above the din the DJ was making. The bass alone was enough to drown out any other sound. After less than half an hour, he was beginning to feel more than a little nauseous. He wasn't sure of the exact time, but it was certainly past midnight and his head was throbbing in time to the beat. If he didn't leave soon, he was in danger of throwing up all over the girl dancing right in front of him. She was slim and energetic and under any other circumstances he would have made a move, but as it was he had to get out of there. Fighting a passage across the crowded dance floor, he made his way towards the neon exit sign. It seemed to take forever. His head was spinning by the time he finally reached the door.

A bouncer with a square face nodded at him as he stepped outside. 'You going to be all right?'

'I think I'm going to be sick,' he replied thickly.

'What have you been taking –' the bouncer began.

'No,' he interrupted quickly, shaking his head. 'It's the noise.'

Bright spots of light darted across his field of vision with the movement, and he froze.

'Too many beers,' he said, speaking as clearly as he could.

He staggered away from the bouncer who immediately lost interest. Drugs on the street were not his concern. With one hand on the wall for support, Jamie made his way around the corner of the building into a narrow alley where the light was gratifyingly dim. His nausea subsided as he stood in the alley, away from the glare of neon lights. Rummaging in his pocket for his cigarettes, he pulled one out with his lips. Cupping one hand around the tiny flickering flame of his lighter, he barely noticed a bundle lying at his feet which he had accidentally kicked. Inhaling deeply, he leaned back against the wall and felt the pressure in his head ease. He wondered whether it was worth returning to the bar to try again. The girl he had been eyeing up earlier might still be there, if he could find her in the throng. If not, there were plenty of other girls displaying themselves, any one of whom would do. Finishing his cigarette, he tossed the butt away and retraced his footsteps.

No sooner had he entered the bar again than he felt a strong hand seize him by the arm.

'What's this?' a voice shouted in his ear.

Turning, he stared at the bouncer who had spoken to him earlier.

'I told you, it was just the beer,' he protested.

'Your feet,' the bouncer replied.

'What? What about my feet?'

Without relaxing his grip on Jamie's arm, the bouncer glared at the floor.

'What? What?' Jamie stammered. 'What are you doing? What's wrong?'

He glanced down and stared, his eyes riveted to a black footprint just behind where he was standing.

'What's that?' he asked.

'You tell me, wanker.'

Jamie shook his head. 'Whatever it is, it's nothing to do with me.'

'Take off your shoes.'

'What?'

'You heard me,' the bouncer said, leaning forward and glaring at Jamie. 'Take off your shoes.'

A second bouncer had joined them and Jamie complied with a sigh. Turning his shoes over, he was surprised to see a dark glistening on the bottom of both his shoes. The first bouncer touched one of the souls and grunted.

'What the hell have you been walking in?' he asked.

'You can't bring that shit in here,' the other one said.

'It's not my fault if –' Jamie began and fell silent as the second bouncer shone a bright torch on the shoes to reveal that the sticky substance was not black after all, but dark red. 'Is that –' Jamie stammered. 'What is that?'

'You tell me,' the first bouncer said with a nasty leer. 'You been up to no good while you were out there?'

He began to frisk Jamie, demanding to know where the knife was.

'I haven't got a knife,' Jamie protested. 'I don't know where that came from. I just went out for a fag. Give me back my shoes.'

'Where's the victim?' the second bouncer demanded. 'He's going to need assistance. Where is he?' He was shouting urgently.

'I went out, and round there,' Jamie replied, pointing wildly in his panic. 'It was in the alley. I just had a smoke, that's all. I didn't see –'

The second bouncer ran outside, his phone in his hand. In his socks, cursing and complaining, Jamie was forced to accompany the square-faced bouncer through an internal door which led along a corridor into a small office. A small man seated behind a small desk looked up when they entered.

He was wearing a black T-shirt and jeans, and a gold chain hung around his neck.

'What have we here?' he asked with a weary grimace.

The square-faced bouncer held out Jamie's shoes, upside down, so the dark red substance that covered the soles and heels was clearly visible in the electric lighting.

'What the hell is that?' the man behind the desk asked.

'It looks like blood,' the bouncer said grimly. 'This bloke went outside, he says for a cigarette, only when he came back in he appeared to have been wading in blood out there. He won't say whose it is but it doesn't look like his own. Robbie's gone out to see if he can administer first aid, in case the victim's still out there and in trouble.'

The manager swore. 'That's all I need,' he said. 'Oh well, nothing for it.'

'I don't know –' Jamie stammered. 'I've no idea – I just went out for a smoke.'

'Save it for the cops,' the manager replied wearily. 'Here's hoping they don't shut us down.'

'It was outside, boss. He went out. There wasn't any action in the bar.'

'That's something, at least.' The manager nodded and picked up his phone. 'Still, a stabbing on our doorstep is all I need right now. You couldn't have done your filthy business somewhere else, could you?'

'I haven't done anything,' Jamie protested. 'I just needed some fresh air, that's all. Whatever happened out there, it was nothing to do with me.'

'Save your breath… Hello? I need urgent medical assistance and then I need the police.'

# 20

GERALDINE WOKE AND STRETCHED. Ian was already up and she could hear him clattering around in the kitchen. She had decided to request leave for a day to visit her sister in London. It was rare for her to ask for time off when they were involved in a murder investigation, but she needed to speak to Helena urgently. With luck she would be able to persuade Eileen to grant her request, without going into too much detail. While she was rehearsing what to say, Ian called out to say that breakfast was ready. But as they sat down at the table, their phones pinged simultaneously. Glancing at his screen, Ian swore. Geraldine leapt up and ran to the bedroom to dress quickly and followed Ian out of the flat. They drove to the police station in separate cars, as usual. When she drew into the car park, Geraldine saw his car already parked. She hurried to the incident room where the briefing began a few minutes later.

'We don't have a name for this latest victim yet, but we're treating the death as murder,' Eileen said, glaring at the assembled officers.

It was less than ten days since Angie had been killed, and they had a second victim to investigate.

'According to the assessment team, it's going to be difficult to establish an identity, but we're hoping forensics will be able to come up with something. In the meantime, let's get to the scene and see what we can find out before the body's moved.'

'There's a good possibility this was an accident,' Ian said.

'If the assault took place outside a bar in the early hours of Saturday morning, as we've been led to believe, surely it's more likely to have been the outcome of a drunken brawl than a deliberate murder. It's unlikely to have anything to do with the case we're working on.'

'Yes, it's possible this was the result of a fight, or an assault, that got out of control,' Eileen conceded, 'but the assessment team seems to think it was rather more than an inadvertent stabbing. In any case, whatever happened, a woman is dead and we need to look into it.'

With the whole team bustling into action over the report of another fatality, it was hardly the right time to request a day off, but Geraldine was desperate to speak to Helena and explain what had happened. In a week's time, Ian had promised to arrange for Helena to be sent to a safe house. By the time Geraldine handed in her delayed report, Helena would have a new identity in a different location, somewhere untraceable. After that, Geraldine would be unable to track Helena down without threatening her sister's safety in her new life.

'Eileen,' she said, 'would it be possible to take a day's leave?'

Eileen turned to her in surprise. 'Geraldine, this isn't the time. Ask me later.'

'But I need –'

As Geraldine hesitated to explain that she needed to take time off straightaway, Eileen turned to talk to someone else, and the moment was lost. Helena's future was uncertain, but the latest victim was dead, and Geraldine had to get to work. She still had a week in which to speak to Helena. With a sigh, she switched her attention to her allotted task which took her to the bar adjacent to the scene where the body had been discovered. Safely wrapped in protective clothing, with her shoes covered, she walked along the common approach path along a narrow cobbled alley, where a woman's body had been dumped beside a row of large rubbish bins. One side of the alley was bordered by a high white wall covered in red and black graffiti. Several large rectangular blue garbage bins stood nearby, beside a row of smaller bins.

A forensic tent had already been erected over the site. Several white-clad scene of crime officers were working silently, gathering minute scraps of litter that might yield crucial evidence: cigarette butts, matches, bottles, gum, condoms, anything that could be examined under a powerful lens for hairs and fibres and skin cells too small to discern with the naked eye. If they found any trace of Greg's DNA at the scene, two murder cases might be solved in one day.

Entering the tent, Geraldine looked down at the body and drew in a sharp breath.

'Not a pleasant sight, is she?' a scene of crime officer said. 'I've never seen anything like it, and I've been at this job for years.'

The dead woman was wearing jeans and a T-shirt that had once been white. Blood had splattered over her arms and legs as well as drenching her T-shirt, and she lay spreadeagled on her back, with a brown shoe on her left foot. The other shoe lay a short distance away where it had fallen off, perhaps during a scuffle. Her long hair appeared to be black, but nothing else about her was in any way recognisable. What had once been a face was now a shapeless mire of bloody pulp, the features indistinguishable. Her nose had been flattened, her eyes and mouth crushed beneath a mess of congealed blood and splintered bone. Only the position of her head, and her hair, indicated where her face had once been.

'Someone wanted to conceal her identity,' the scene of crime officer commented.

'Or they were angry,' Geraldine replied. 'Are her teeth intact?'

'All smashed, along with her skull. There's not much left of her head. Even parts of her brain are unrecognisable. What monster did this? Let's hope we find him soon.'

'We'll do our best,' Geraldine replied.

'It's enough to give you nightmares,' he went on. 'And it's not like we're not used to dealing with corpses.' He drew in a breath. 'Oh well, I'd best get on, I suppose. The mortuary van will be here soon. Good luck with getting anyone to confirm this one's identity.'

'It looks like someone was keen to obliterate anything that could be recognised, so I'm guessing there was no handbag, and nothing in her pockets?' Geraldine asked.

'Nope, nothing on her at all. Pockets empty, no jewellery, no watch or rings, no piercings or tattoos, and no handbag anywhere along the alley. We're still hunting for it but it looks as though whoever attacked her took any identifying evidence away with him. It's a quiet alley. He probably had time to search her after she was dead, and go through her pockets.'

'Was she killed here in the alley?'

The scene of crime officer shrugged. 'We're not absolutely sure about that yet. Once we move her, it's going to be easier to establish whether she was placed here after the event, but from the amount of blood on the ground, it looks as though she was killed right here. In fact, I'd put money on it. But don't quote me on that.'

With a final look at the gruesome mask of blood that had replaced the victim's face, Geraldine left the tent. She did not often feel nauseated by the dead, but there was something singularly horrific about the faceless woman abandoned in an alley that usually concealed only litter and rubbish bins. For once she was relieved to leave the crime scene. There was no point in her lingering there. Any evidence that might be found would be discovered by the forensic team tasked with scrutinising every inch of the place. Geraldine's time would be more usefully employed talking to potential witnesses.

Peeling off her outer layer of protective clothing, she took a deep breath to clear the stench of death from her lungs, before turning her attention to the living.

A team of trained constables had already started the long drawn-out process of speaking to everyone who had been in the bar the previous night. Many of the guests had now gone home, having answered an initial set of questions and given their contact details. None of them had seen the body, but they had all been informed that a murder had taken place outside the bar. They were all being asked whether they knew of anyone who had gone missing. So far, no one was unaccounted for.

Leaving the team to continue working through the guests, Geraldine focused on the staff. She started with one of the bouncers. He was a tall, strapping youth of about twenty, dark haired, with a broad pale face.

'We're paid to sort out drunken scraps, you know,' he said, jittery with shock. 'We're trained to break up brawls, and deal with obnoxious creeps and drunks and shit heads, that sort of thing. We're not paid to look at things like that, out in the alley.' He grimaced. 'Bloody hell, have you seen what he did to her? Some sick bastard he must be.'

'I see from your initial statement that you went to investigate because someone came into the club with blood on his shoes?'

The bouncer nodded, frowning. 'He told my colleague he'd just gone out for a smoke, but I went to take a look outside, because the soles of the bloke's shoes were covered in blood, like he'd been walking in it. He was leaving dirty marks all over the floor.'

Geraldine nodded. 'You did well to take his shoes off him straightaway.'

'Yes, well, we were thinking of the carpet as much as anything,' he admitted. 'Anyhow, my colleague took the guy straight to the manager and I went to check on the victim and call for medical assistance. I just assumed it was a stabbing, you know, and we're trained in emergency first aid so I thought I might be able to stop the bleeding and save the guy who'd been stabbed. Only of course it was too late.' He shook his head, with a miserable scowl. 'I tried to check for any signs of life, but it was obvious she was dead and I didn't want to touch her.' He shuddered. 'I mean, she wouldn't have been able to breathe, would she, even if she hadn't bled to death. She couldn't breathe without her – I was relieved when I heard the sirens, and the paramedics arrived, I can tell you. I mean, even though I knew she was dead, it was still awful having to try and do something, although there wasn't anything I could do, was there? The first aid course didn't prepare us for something like this.'

# 21

THE MANAGER OF THE bar was a small man in a plain black T-shirt, and black jeans, with a gold chain around his neck. His face was drawn with tension beneath his designer stubble, but when he spoke he sounded irate rather than fearful.

'When is the body likely to be moved?' he demanded in strident tones, once Geraldine had introduced herself. 'You do realise it can't stay out there much longer. And anyway, surely you can examine it more thoroughly in the mortuary than out there in the alley? They're telling me the van hasn't even arrived to take it away yet. What I want to know is what the hell is going on out there? This isn't *CSI*. We don't want a lengthy drama made out of a tragic incident. You don't seem to appreciate the bad publicity something like this could generate for us.' By the time he finished speaking, he was almost shouting in his agitation.

'No one wants any drama,' Geraldine assured him. 'And the media are being kept well away, although of course we won't be able to prevent your customers from talking to them. All we can do is tell the public as little as possible, and request their discretion, but we have no control over them.'

'Listen,' the manager went on in a more measured tone of voice, 'I know we were heaving last night, and I get it that you want to speak to everyone who was here, in case anyone saw anything kick off indoors before they took it outside. We agreed to co-operate with your enquiry as far as we can, and I made it perfectly clear your team of constables were welcome to speak to everyone here on the premises. But you must understand we can't allow this situation to continue indefinitely. It's the weekend, and tonight is one of our busiest nights of the week. We have to open as usual and that means I need you all gone, or,' he added, seeing Geraldine's expression, 'at least out of sight. You can carry on nosing around in the alley, if you must, but I can't have a police presence inside the bar. It would be an absolute disaster for us. We'd be ruined. I just can't allow that on a Saturday night. You do understand, don't you? If this had been a week day we could have been more relaxed about it and allowed you to remain here longer, but on a weekend I'm afraid it's just not possible. So I'd very much appreciate it if you would ask your officers to leave. If you don't, I'll have to tell them myself, but I'm sure it would be better coming from you.' He gave her a strained smile as he finished speaking.

Geraldine drew up a chair and sat down, uninvited. 'Mr Collins,' she began.

'Jeff,' he interrupted her. 'It's Jeff. No one calls me Mr Collins.' He gave her another forced smile.

'Mr Collins,' she repeated firmly, 'there is no way you are going to be able to open your bar to customers this evening, and probably not for another week, at least, until we've made a thorough forensic search of the premises.'

The manager half rose to his feet, his face turning red with pent-up fury. The gold chain at his chest swung slightly with the movement.

'But – you can't expect me to –'

'I hope you are not intending to obstruct us in our murder investigation?'

'Murder investigation? What are you talking about? What the fuck is going on here? Aren't you getting a bit carried away? Someone got accidentally killed in a fight and you're closing the club for a week? You can't do that. It's insane.'

'You didn't see the victim, did you?'

'I don't care if her arms and legs were sliced off, you're not closing the club on the weekend, and that's final.'

'Her arms and legs were not "sliced off" as you put it,' Geraldine replied quietly. 'But the front of her head was. Although her face was obliterated by being crushed by repeated vicious blows, rather than sliced off, I'd say. If you don't want to take my word for it, perhaps you would like to see for yourself? I can show you photos of the victim if you like, but I should warn you, it doesn't make for pleasant viewing. She is completely unrecognisable, not just as an individual, but as a human being. So no, this was not a fight that got out of hand, nothing like it, and you are going to have to be very discreet about what really happened out there, unless you want your bar to remain closed for a lot longer than a week.'

While she was speaking, the manager sat down and bowed his head. He had a small bald spot on his crown, about the size of a two penny piece. When she fell silent he looked up, his cheeks no longer flushed, and his eyes were weary.

'I see,' he said, his voice drained of any indignation. 'I had no idea you were investigating a murder.'

'I'm sure you'll attract plenty of ghoulish customers once the investigation is over,' she suggested with a disapproving scowl.

'And do you know when that is likely to be?'

'I'm afraid I can't say for certain, but we should be finished searching your premises and the alley outside before too long, hopefully within a couple of weeks, maybe less.'

'Very well.' He frowned. 'You said you'll be searching the premises? Is that really necessary?'

'We'll be looking for anything that might help our enquiry, nothing else.'

He nodded and licked his lips nervously. 'Some of our guests like to pep themselves up when they're dancing.'

'We are not the drug squad, Mr Collins,' she replied, 'although I can give no undertaking that they will not be interested in seeing the results of any forensic examination of your premises we consider necessary in the course of our investigation.'

'If you find any trace of illegal substance abuse anywhere on the premises, I assure you the management and staff here know nothing about it. We can't be held responsible for what goes on in the toilets, or outside in the alley, and we routinely search customers' bags and pockets when they enter the club. We check for weapons and illegal substances, but you know as well as I do that drugs are easy to conceal, and there's a limit to what we can do to stop people bringing them in. We have bouncers on the doors whenever we're open, and security guards patrolling inside, but we can't observe everything that goes on in the toilet cubicles. Customers are entitled to some privacy. We do what we can. The last thing we want is any trouble with the law.'

'Thank you for agreeing to co-operate with the search of your premises which, as you must be aware, is already under way. Now we've cleared that up, I'd like to ask you a few questions about what happened last night, and then I and my colleagues will need to finish speaking to your staff. I assure you we would be happy if there was any way we could complete this process quickly, but talking to people takes time and we have to be thorough.'

The manager nodded wretchedly. 'Of course you must do what you have to do. What is it you want to know?'

# 22

WHEN SHE HAD FINISHED questioning the manager about the events of the early hours of the morning, Geraldine proceeded to the next member of staff on her list. The second bouncer was broad-shouldered, short and stocky. His lank hair hung low over his forehead, and he had a long nose and a very square chin. He had a habit of twitching his head sideways, to flick his hair out of the small grey eyes that peered at her from beneath his heavy brows. He seemed far more composed than his fellow bouncer, and answered Geraldine's questions concisely. She suspected he had rehearsed what he needed to say before the interview. When he had finished describing what had happened, she quizzed him on his version of the events leading up to the discovery of the body in the alley.

'What made you suspect foul play?' she asked.

The bouncer raised his shaggy eyebrows, seemingly surprised by the question. 'The guy had blood on his shoes,' he repeated. 'It must have come from somewhere, and since he didn't appear to be injured, I figured someone else must be hurt. But I never suspected it was anything other than a violent brawl.'

'If you thought someone was injured, why didn't you go outside to investigate straightaway?'

He nodded, as though this was a question he understood. 'I thought the man who'd come back in with bloody shoes had probably been involved in an altercation. I didn't want him to skedaddle, so I hung on to him. That's why I sent my colleague to have a look around outside, while I took the suspect off to the office.'

'If this man was guilty of stabbing someone, as you suspected, do you really think he would have come back into the club?'

The bouncer shook his head. 'I had no idea he'd killed anyone, and I don't suppose he realised what he'd done either. He came back in, so I assumed he'd cut another guy in a scrap, and didn't know how badly he'd injured him. He must have thought there was no real harm done. Otherwise, like you said, he'd have done a runner. I assumed he'd shivved someone in a scrap, and thought it was nothing too serious. If I'd thought about it at all, I probably would have suspected he'd come back in for a girl. That's often what these fights are about. But I was concerned enough to hold on to him and contact you,' he added quickly.

'There was a lot of blood,' Geraldine pointed out, watching the bouncer's reaction closely.

He nodded. 'Yes, I was worried the other guy might be in need of medical assistance, and that's why I sent someone out there to take a gander immediately. Of course, it was too late. He wasn't in need of any medical assistance by then, but I wasn't to know that, was I? In any case, my main concern was to protect the club. That's what I'm paid to do. We're not responsible for making sure people are safe on the streets. That's your job, isn't it?'

Geraldine did not answer, but continued with a question of her own.

'What can you tell me about the man who came into the club with bloody shoes? My colleague has been speaking to him, but I'd like to make sure your account confirms what he's told us.'

The bouncer nodded and repeated what he had already said

about the customer leaving, allegedly to have a cigarette, and returning with blood on his shoes.

'Did you believe him?' Geraldine asked when he had finished.

The bouncer shrugged. 'He looked like he was about to throw up when he went out, so I think he was telling the truth about that.' He paused, frowning. 'If you're asking for my opinion, he didn't seem like the kind of guy who would assault anyone. He struck me as the type who comes to the club hoping to pull, because he's too nervous and twitchy to get his hands on a girl anywhere else. He certainly didn't have a blade on him when he arrived. We search everyone who comes in. So if you ask me to think about it, I'd say that if he did stab someone in the alley, he'd have had to have hidden a knife somewhere outside and, honestly, I don't think he was the type. He was more likely to be the victim of an attack than the aggressor. But of course you can never be sure. When he came back in, he insisted he'd just gone outside for a cigarette and he claimed to know nothing about any blood on his shoes until we showed it to him.'

'Did he smell of cigarette smoke when he returned?'

He shook his head. 'I didn't notice. Honestly, I wouldn't bet on whether he was the type to stab someone or not because, like I said, you can never tell, can you? But I don't remember getting the impression he had been in any sort of a fight before he came back in. You can tell when a guy's been roughing someone up because he's juiced, but this guy looked just the same as when he went out.'

'And how did he look?'

'Twitchy and pathetic, and like he might throw up. The only difference was that he had blood all over the bottom of his shoes when he came back in, and he didn't even seem to be aware of it until we pointed it out. I'm not sure there wasn't something wrong with him. At any rate, I don't think he was the sharpest tool in the box.'

Geraldine thanked the bouncer for his help and returned to the police station to write up her notes. Her most pressing concern was the identity of the body. There was no reason to suppose the victim was Zoe, the thirteen-year-old who had gone missing from her home five days earlier, but it was possible.

'It doesn't really make any difference who she was,' Ariadne pointed out. 'If she's not Zoe, then she's some other girl. Whoever she is, she was horribly murdered.'

Geraldine nodded. Ariadne was right. It made no difference if the victim had been thirteen or ninety, she had still been a living breathing human being whose life had been violently taken away. But somehow the death of a young girl seemed worse than that of an older woman.

'I know it's not logical,' she told Ariadne, 'but it just feels worse. I don't know why.'

'Because she hasn't yet had a chance to live yet, I suppose,' Ariadne replied.

'And she isn't old enough to know how to keep herself safe.'

'I know what you mean. Rationally it doesn't make any difference, yet it seems far worse.'

Reading through Ian's report of his interview with Jamie, Geraldine was inclined to agree with the bouncer's impression of him. Jamie had no record for assault, and had never been questioned by the police for anything at all prior to this. There was nothing in his history or present circumstances to suggest that he might be easily provoked to violence. Not only that, but his cigarette butt had been identified near the body. It had been smoked down to the filter, and he had not left the club for longer than about five minutes, a time frame that had been confirmed by the club's CCTV. It seemed virtually impossible that he could have smoked a cigarette and battered a girl to death within so brief a period of time.

'Even if he had smoked while hitting her, he wouldn't have had time,' Ariadne agreed with Geraldine's conclusion.

'And the idea of his beating someone so violently, all done with a cigarette stuck between his lips, somehow doesn't seem likely,' Geraldine added.

Ian's impression of Jamie had coincided with the bouncer's view. Taking all of that into account, along with the fact that no blood at all had been discovered on his clothing, he seemed an unlikely suspect. Geraldine would not have been surprised to learn that the victim was already dead by the time Jamie had walked out of the club for a cigarette. The evidence against him was circumstantial but, all the same, he remained on the list of suspects. Until they had established the identity of the dead woman, they could not rule out her connection with anyone who had been at the club that evening.

'She might turn out to have spurned Jamie earlier on that same evening,' Ariadne suggested.

It was idle speculation in a case where so far just about anything was possible.

# 23

IT WAS LATE BY the time Geraldine was finally able to leave York. Only by borrowing time from her few hours of sleep could she fit in driving all the way to London at such an early stage in an investigation. As it was, she was not going to reach Helena's flat before midnight. On her way she tried to call Ian several times to let him know where she was, but he did not answer. She had no luck calling Helena. Staring at the road ahead, she put her foot down, hoping she would find her sister at home. As she drove, she did her best to remain positive. Her only concern should be to focus on the case, and missing a night's sleep to visit her sister wouldn't help, but she had no choice. The following day she determined to talk to Ian so that together they could work out a plan to trap her abductors, while continuing to protect Helena. She had no idea when the criminal gang would contact her about helping them, but she suspected it would be soon.

She understood why her sister had to be spirited away, but she wanted to speak to her in person first to explain what had happened, and convince Helena that she was not abandoning her. At last she reached the street where Helena lived in East London, found a parking place, and rang the bell. There was no answer. Helena was probably asleep. She rang again. Still no one came to the door. If Helena was out, and Geraldine had driven all this way for nothing, it would be galling. But far worse was the prospect that Geraldine might not see Helena before she was relocated. She tried Helena's phone but it went straight to a generic voicemail. As she rang off, her phone rang. She answered it at once, and was disappointed to hear Ian's voice.

'Geraldine, where are you? Do you know what time it is? Come home for goodness sake, and get some sleep.'

'I'm not in York,' she replied.

'What?'

He sounded startled, although he must have realised where she had gone. Geraldine told him she had driven to London to speak to Helena, who was not at home.

'Where is she, Ian? Where have they taken her?'

There was a slight pause before he answered. When he spoke, she had the impression he was irritated with her, but she didn't care.

'I told you I would give you a week, so you have time to speak to her before she is relocated.'

'Then where is she?'

Down the phone line she heard Ian sigh. 'I have no idea. She must have gone out.'

'Ian, if you ever cared for me at all, tell me where she is.'

'I can't tell you because I don't know,' he said. 'If I did know I would contact her and tell her to go home right away and see you, but I don't know where she is and I have no way of contacting her.'

'If she's already been taken into witness protection, I won't be able to find her. I'm her sister, Ian. I have to see her.'

'Geraldine, come home now and at least get a couple of hours' sleep tonight. You're behaving irrationally because you're too tired to think sensibly. What you're doing is insane, and it isn't helping anyone. Helena isn't there and nothing you or I can do is going to magically make her appear.' He paused. 'Listen, Helena's safe for the time being, and so are you, and that's what matters. Nothing's going to happen tonight.'

'No,' Geraldine wailed, 'that's not the only thing that

matters. I have to say goodbye before she's taken away.'

Crying too hard to speak, she hung up and returned to her car, afraid she might never see her twin sister again. They were dead to one another, and it was all Ian's fault. He had no right to insist that Helena be spirited away like that against Geraldine's wishes.

Slowly she made her way back to York. After stopping for an early breakfast on the way, she went straight to work without going home. A few of her colleagues were already there and she spent a fruitless half hour trawling through images of villains implicated in drug deals, vainly hoping to spot someone who might match the appearance of the men she had seen concealed by balaclavas. They could have been just about any of the images she saw on her screen. When her colleague Ariadne arrived, Geraldine reciprocated her cheerful greeting, and turned her attention to her allotted tasks for the day. Halfway through the morning, Ian passed her desk. He stared morosely at her as he walked by, but he said nothing.

'You look exhausted,' Ariadne said, frowning at Geraldine across the intervening desks. 'Are you all right?'

Geraldine nodded. 'Just focused,' she replied a trifle curtly, keen to end the conversation.

'Let's go for a coffee,' Ariadne suggested.

'I'd rather crack on,' Geraldine replied, declining the invitation.

A team had been occupied questioning all the guests who had been at the club on the night of the murder, and it was a mammoth task to read through all the statements. So far none of them had revealed anything of interest, but Geraldine pressed on.

'You know how it is,' she added, 'the very last report is going to be the one that has some significant detail.'

Ariadne nodded without answering, but she looked concerned.

'Are you sure you're all right?' she asked again towards the end of the morning.

'Yes,' Geraldine replied without looking up from her screen. 'Why?'

Ariadne shook her head and her long, dark curls bounced on her shoulders. 'Nothing, it's just that you look terrible. What's wrong?'

Geraldine gave a half-hearted smile. 'I've got a bit of a headache,' she replied.

'Late night?'

'Something like that. I didn't sleep well, that's all.'

Ariadne gave a sympathetic grunt before turning her attention back to her work.

# 24

BELLA GLARED AT JOHN. 'You can't,' she blurted out, 'you just can't.'

'I'm sorry, Bella,' he replied. 'I'd rather not go, but you must see that I don't have any choice in the matter. I've already been off work for four days and I can't stay away indefinitely.'

'I get it that you have to go back to work, but you can't go away. You can't leave York, not now. John, our daughter's missing! Surely you can tell them you can't leave York until she comes home. We have to be here, both of us. We need each other. And what about Zoe? We have to be here together when she comes home.'

'And I need to earn a living,' he replied. Far from repentant, he looked smug. 'They want me to visit the London office, and I can't back out at this late stage, not when the meeting was arranged months ago. There are meetings all tomorrow, and all the regional managers will be there. I can't refuse to go, so don't make a fuss, please. It's only for two nights. If the boss says I have to be there, that's the end of it. You know I'd stay here if I could, but I'm not going to risk losing my job over this.'

'This?' she repeated furiously. 'By "this" I take it you mean our daughter's disappearance?'

'Besides,' he went on, ignoring her outburst, 'a girl who runs away from home is more than likely going to end up in London. Who knows? I might even find her while I'm there.'

'Don't be ridiculous,' she snapped. 'London is vast. There's no chance you'll find her there. What? You think you're just going to spot her in a crowded street somewhere and bring her home?'

'No,' he replied with exaggerated patience, 'but I can take photos of Zoe with me and show them to the local police while I'm there.'

'Her picture will already have been circulated to the police nationwide,' Bella said. 'If she'd gone to London, the police would have told us. What? Do you think they wouldn't know about it? She couldn't have travelled there without being spotted. There are cameras everywhere on the trains and buses. She wouldn't be able to leave York without being seen. You don't really think you could find her when they can't?'

'If they're actually looking for her,' he muttered.

The notion that John might be responsible for Zoe's disappearance kept forcing its way into Bella's thoughts, but she dismissed it fiercely. Such a possibility was too horrific to contemplate. It could not be true. John adored Zoe, and Bella could not believe he would ever do anything to hurt her. With a sob, she turned to glare at him but he was already leaving the room. A moment later she heard his footsteps pounding up the stairs. She was not prepared to drop the subject and dashed after him. She dared not admit that she could not trust him on his own at night in London; she was afraid of what he might do. At least in York she could try to keep an eye on him and hopefully prevent him from giving in to his evil impulses. He did not know that she was aware of his vicious tendencies, but knowing she was nearby must surely help him resist temptation. It must be more difficult for him to go out and chase women knowing she was at home, waiting for him. Once he was away from her, in London, he would be alone and anonymous, and she would have no influence over his behaviour. Somehow she had to stop him going.

She found him in the bedroom, packing his case. Cautiously

she sat on the bed and approached the subject in a roundabout way.

'You can't wait to get away from here, can you?' she said. 'Not that I blame you.'

He did not answer straightaway, so she repeated herself.

'What are you talking about?' he asked her wearily. 'I've already told you, I'm not going because I want to. And now this discussion is over.'

He turned away from her and zipped up his case. 'I'll tell you what, I'll only stay overnight and be back late tomorrow.'

'What if something happens while you're away?' she asked in a low voice.

'Then you'll phone me immediately. I'll keep my mobile on, even in meetings, I promise. I'll have it silenced in my pocket all the time, so I'll feel it vibrating if you call.'

'What if they find her and you can't get back in time?'

'In time for what?'

'I don't want to be left alone here, not while –'

'Nothing's happened to Zoe, and no one's going to "find her", because she's going to come home of her own accord. She's not going to stay away forever, is she?' he asked, with a forced smile. 'If something *had* happened to her, we'd know about it already. She's hiding somewhere, and she'll come home when she's had enough of this foolishness.'

But she could tell he was as worried as she was.

'I mean,' she said miserably, 'what if they find her? What if they're too late?'

'What do you mean, too late?'

'You know what I mean. If anything's happened to Zoe I want you to be here, with me.'

'Nothing's happened and nothing's going to happen,' he said.

'You don't know that.'

'Oh do stop worrying. She's a teenager and she's gone off with a friend, that's all.'

In spite of his efforts to sound reassuring, he looked really anxious. Bella was furious, but there was nothing she could do about it. John grabbed his case and walked out of the room, and a few moments later she heard him call out and the front door slammed. She had an uneasy suspicion she knew exactly what he was planning to do in the buzzing metropolis once his meetings were finished. He had assured her that he and the other regional managers would be spending the evening together, but once he slipped away there were bound to be numerous women out on their own on the streets alone in London, any one of whom might become his next victim. She could imagine the scene. It kept replaying in her mind, over and over again.

John would wait until his first colleague went to bed, to avoid drawing attention to himself by leaving the table early. Then he would take the opportunity to excuse himself on the grounds that he too was tired and wanted an early night. But instead of going straight up to his hotel room, he would step outside for a breath of air before retiring for the night. And once he had left the hotel, or the restaurant, wherever they were having dinner, he would vanish and claim his next victim.

She did her best to reassure herself that there were far too many CCTV cameras everywhere in London for anyone to be able to move around without being captured repeatedly on film, but that did little to dispel her fears. Had she known where he was staying, she could have followed him, but she had not thought to ask for the address, and now it was too late to find out without seeming to make a fuss. John would not thank her for calling his office to find out where he had gone. There was nothing she could do now but wait for him to come home, and pray that he exercised restraint while he was away from home. And then the thought that he might be involved in Zoe's disappearance resurfaced. With a low moan, she flung herself down on the sofa and wept. At first she did not hear the doorbell, but it rang again, insistently. Wiping her eyes on her sleeve, Bella hurried to answer, praying fervently that she would see Zoe on the doorstep. But when she opened the door, Susan was standing there, with a concerned smile on her face.

'Hello, Bella,' she said. 'I just came to see how you are.'

'How do you think I am?' Bella snapped, unable to suppress a sob. 'Go away, just go away. I don't want to talk to anyone until Zoe is home.'

# 25

GERALDINE WAS FEELING WORN out. Along with Ian and a team of officers, she had spent the best part of two days questioning a stream of staff and customers who had been at the bar on Friday night. When she had not been interviewing people herself, she had been reading statements taken by her colleagues. Most of the people questioned had been eager to help, and many of them had spent a long time gossiping about encounters that had no bearing on the murder investigation at all. A lot of the remarks seemed to focus on a particular member of the bar staff who had done nothing to attract suspicion beyond being rude to many of the customers.

'He was just mean, you know,' one girl claimed.

'He was on some kind of power trip,' another girl said.

To the question, 'Did you see him leave the bar at any time?' all the guests who disparaged him shook their heads.

'No, that's the thing,' one of them said. 'He was there all night, just standing behind the bar ignoring people who had been waiting an age to be served. It's not as if he had anything else to do. He was just a complete dick.'

Geraldine was not interested in staff inefficiency. That was the manager's problem. As far as she was concerned, a man standing behind the bar all evening could not be responsible for battering a girl to death in the alley outside. All the complaints had achieved was to provide the abrasive barman with a watertight alibi. Other customers grumbled about trivial incidents where someone had pushed ahead of them in the queue and then sworn at them for protesting, or about people engaging in sexual activities or taking drugs in the toilets.

'Perhaps I shouldn't be surprised to hear so much was going on at the club that night,' Geraldine said ruefully to Ian. 'I think I'm showing my age.'

'I can't imagine you had sex with many strangers in public toilets, even when you were younger,' he replied.

Geraldine laughed. 'I'll take that as a compliment.'

There was a chance a few comments from different sources might combine to form a picture of events leading up to the attack, so every statement was recorded and cross-referenced for inconsistencies. It was a time-consuming task and so far they had not come across anything significant. Along with customers eager to gossip, quite a few others had been reluctant to co-operate, insisting the crime had nothing to do with them, and demanding to know why they were being questioned at all. No one noticed that anyone had gone missing, and nothing suspicious was reported.

Geraldine only had three more people to question. The first was a sullen girl who had been at the bar while Jamie was outside.

'What's going on?' she demanded before Geraldine had opened her mouth.

Patiently Geraldine explained yet again the reason for the investigation.

'Well I never saw anything that happened outside because I was in here, wasn't I? Can I go now?'

Geraldine's next potential witness was a thin, young girl who had started working at the bar that week.

'I don't know anyone here,' she stammered nervously, 'and I don't know anything about what happened. I was just focused on trying to remember what I was supposed to be doing.' She was nearly in tears.

Geraldine assured her that the questions were routine, and there was little expectation she would be able to pass on any information, but they had to question everyone, just in case they had happened to spot anything unusual.

'I'm not sure I'd know if anything was unusual,' the girl replied. 'I mean, everything seemed unusual to me, because I'm new here. All I can remember is that it was noisy and there was a lot of jostling to get to the bar, and some people were dancing.'

'Did you notice anyone acting suspiciously?'

'What do you mean by suspicious?' the girl asked.

Geraldine did not detain the girl for long. It was pointless talking to her. There was one more person to question and Geraldine was struggling to concentrate on the task. Her final interviewee was a girl who had a part-time job handing out tickets in the cloakroom near the entrance to the bar. She was unlikely to have seen anything of interest, but in a murder enquiry even the most obscure avenues had to be explored. The girl, who was in her mid-twenties, was well built, with pencilled eyebrows and a mop of curly, dark hair. She took a seat when invited to do so and waited respectfully for Geraldine to begin, a welcome contrast to some of the obstreperous customers who had been answering questions all day.

'I never go out there in the alley,' the girl said in answer to Geraldine's first question.

Geraldine gave a noncommittal nod.

'I mean, why would I?' The girl shrugged her broad shoulders. 'It's probably nothing, but –'

'Yes?' Geraldine stifled a yawn.

'There was a man acting suspiciously.'

Geraldine was instantly alert. The witness seemed to be a sensible woman and, being staff, was more likely to have been sober than most of the guests.

'What was he doing that looked suspicious?'

'For a start, he was older than our average punter. He looked about fifty. Maybe more. Old, anyway. I saw him following a girl who was young enough to be his daughter, if not his granddaughter. But it wasn't just his age. I remember noticing him because she seemed scared of him.'

'Scared?'

'Yes.'

'Are you sure?'

'Yes.'

'Where did you see them?'

'In the foyer.'

'And what happened?'

'She was telling him to leave her alone. That's why I noticed them. She wasn't that polite about it. She swore at him, calling him an arsehole and worse things, and told him to leave her the fuck alone. That was more or less what she said. She was drunk, or high, or both, because her speech was slurred, and she was staggering on really high heels, you know, like so many girls wear. Anyway, she left and he went after her. I didn't really think much more about it until now.'

'What was she wearing?'

'I can't really remember. Jeans, I think, and some sort of skimpy top. It was her face I noticed more than anything else, because she looked so frightened.'

Usually crucial, a description of the girl's face was the one detail that would not help in the current investigation.

'What about her hair?'

The woman frowned with the effort of remembering. 'She had it tied back in a ponytail. It was mousy coloured, I think.'

The description was vague, but it could fit the dead girl.

'Can you describe the man?'

The woman nodded. 'We're expected to be aware of our customers, so I'm used to observing faces,' she replied with a touch of pride. 'He was fattish, bald, about fifty I'd say, maybe older, clean shaven and sweaty, and he was wearing a grey T-shirt with some kind of image on it, I can't remember what – no, wait, it was a picture of Marilyn Monroe.'

'And you say he followed the girl outside?'

The woman nodded solemnly.

'And what time was that?'

'I didn't make a note of the time. I'm sorry. I didn't realise it might be significant.'

Geraldine assured the woman she had been extremely helpful and let her go after making a note of her contact details. She wasn't sure, but she had a feeling they might be making progress at last.

# 26

BELLA BELIEVED IN THE power of prayer, but lately everything had been going wrong in her life and her prayers didn't seem to be helping at all. She felt as if God had abandoned her. Ever since she had stumbled on her husband's dark secret she had been praying for him to give up his sinful ways, but he seemed resolved to continue along his chosen path. And now, not only had she discovered her husband's wickedness but her daughter had gone missing, and even Zoe's friends didn't seem to know where she was. The school assured her they had contacted all the parents who had pupils in Zoe's year group, and Bella had been to see Zoe's few friends herself to question them, begging them to tell her if they knew anything about her daughter's disappearance. None of them did. There was nothing more Bella could do to find Zoe, except pray for her safe return.

But there was something she could do to prevent another poor soul from falling prey to her husband's evil ways. If she could have reported him to the authorities she would have done so, but in the absence of proof her allegations were bound to be dismissed as spiteful nonsense, and she dreaded to think what John might do to her if he learned that she had discovered his terrible secret. In the meantime, no one was going to believe a wife's accusations against her husband. They would conclude that she was suffering from stress over her missing daughter. She had to take action to control him herself.

On a memo she had found on his desktop, she had seen an entry about his meeting, and in the notes there were details of the hotel where his conference would be taking place, as well as the nearby Travelodge where he was booked to spend the night. It was only five minutes' walk from King's Cross station. Once he had left the house, she packed a hold-all and set off for the station, determined to follow him, only to discover that the train to London cost a small fortune at such short notice. She would have to pay for a ticket in cash so that she could hide her purchase from John, and at King's Cross she would have to find the conference hotel. Once there, she would not be able to enter the hotel itself in case he noticed her. All she could hope to do would be to find a table in the window of a café on the opposite side of the road, if there was one, where hopefully no one would take any notice of her as she sat all afternoon and evening over one mug of coffee.

Even as she was formulating her plan, she knew it was hopeless. If there was a café in sight of the hotel, she might sit there until it closed and John would probably still be at dinner with his colleagues, out of sight inside the hotel. He might even find his next victim while he was in there, but that would probably be too risky. Whatever else he was, John was no fool. She shivered, considering the repercussions if he was caught. It would be terrible for Zoe to hear about the sin her father had committed, not once but several times. Perhaps, after all, it would be better if he met with an accident so that he could no longer carry out his atrocities. She tried to dismiss the idea, but found herself planning what she might do to put an end to his activities. He would have to be immobilised in such a way that no one would ever suspect she was responsible. Somehow she would have to carry out her assault without betraying her identity. He must believe the attack had been carried out by a stranger. Either that or he would have to be silenced as well as incapacitated. She was not sure how that could be achieved, unless it was by killing him, and that was the last thing she wanted to do.

John arrived home late on Monday afternoon, dishevelled and tired from travelling.

'I came straight back,' he told her. 'I didn't stay on with the other guys. They all understood that I wanted to come home, in the circumstances...'

He broke off and gazed at her anxiously, as though Zoe's disappearance affected her alone, and he was worried about how she was coping.

'How are you bearing up?' he went on, as if to corroborate the impression.

'I'm all right,' she replied, asking almost as an afterthought, 'How was your trip?'

He shrugged. 'It went OK, I suppose. I can't say I was really taking in what anyone was saying.'

'I don't know why you went,' she said bitterly.

She understood only too well why he might be drawn to spending a whole night away from home. He had no doubt had dinner with his colleagues and then slipped away, ostensibly to his hotel. Once he was out on the streets of London, alone, he could have gone anywhere. She wished now that she *had* gone to London, and watched for him leaving the hotel. Like a private detective, she could have followed him. She pictured herself jumping in a taxi and instructing the driver to 'Follow that cab!' But of course that would have been impossible, not to mention outrageously expensive.

'I went because I had to go,' he replied crossly. 'We've been through all this before. It's not my fault I have to go to work.'

A moment later, she heard his feet thundering up the stairs, and the bedroom door slammed.

'Welcome home,' she muttered. 'Although I don't know why you bothered.'

It was true. He might as well have stayed away for all the support he gave her. He barely spoke to her all evening, and left early the next morning for work, still maintaining a sullen silence.

# 27

A TEAM HAD BEEN tasked with trawling through the bar's security cameras, searching for an image of the fat man described by the coat check woman. The team was led by a constable who had been drafted in from Northallerton to help with the double murder investigation. Tall and slim, with dark hair and eyes and a ready smile, Andrew Wilder was an attractive man who specialised in surveillance and VIIDO assessment. When he asked if he might sit with Geraldine in the canteen, she was happy to be friendly towards a new member of the team.

'Eileen seems tough,' he remarked quietly, after glancing around to check they could not be overheard.

Geraldine smiled. 'She is tough,' she agreed, 'but she gets things done.'

He nodded. 'I'd rather have a severe senior investigating officer than a wishy-washy one who can't make decisions.'

Geraldine wondered whether he had a particular SIO in mind, but she said nothing and the conversation moved on to the less controversial topic of the canteen. The following day, perhaps by chance, Andrew turned up in the canteen queue just behind Geraldine so they naturally sat together for lunch again. She did not mind. He was pleasant enough company. Only when he had invited her to join him for a drink after work did she become slightly distant and he took the hint at once. After that, he stopped coming to sit with her at lunchtime.

Andrew spotted the fat man entering the club at around

ten thirty on Friday evening, reappearing in the entrance hall around half an hour later. He stood there for a moment conversing with a young girl, exactly as the witness had described. The girl teetered outside, and the man left straight after. It was difficult to be certain, but he could have been following her. At that time, there was a queue to enter the premises, and the camera did not record where the young girl or the fat man went after they left the bar. They simply vanished into the small crowd of people outside. It was possible they had disappeared into the alley.

Eileen was understandably eager to trace the man as quickly as possible, and an image was broadcast on the local news, asking the man to come forward to help them with an enquiry, or for anyone recognising him to contact the police. The request provoked the usual deluge of calls, and officers were drafted in from other police stations to help answer the phones. None of the callers claimed to be the girl who had been harassed at the bar, but several callers claimed to recognise the man as someone who worked as a local butcher. On Monday morning Geraldine went along, accompanied by a constable, to speak to Richard Ellis who was alleged to have been seen following a young girl out of the bar.

There was a customer ahead of her, and Geraldine waited while the woman discussed the merits of sausages as opposed to burgers with the older of the two men serving behind the counter. Around fifty, balding and clean shaven, with a plump face and round shoulders, his appearance matched the description they had been given by a witness at the bar.

'Can I help you?' a young man behind the counter asked Geraldine.

'No, thank you, I'm waiting to talk to Mr Ellis.'

As soon as the customer left, Geraldine nodded to the constable who turned the 'open' sign round on the door.

'Hey,' the stout butcher cried out. 'What do you think you're doing?'

His face went slightly red, but he looked puzzled rather than frightened when Geraldine held out her identity card and introduced herself.

'What can I help you with, officer?' he asked.

As he spoke, he cast an anxious glance at the constable blocking the doorway.

'Were you at the Livewire Bar on Friday night?'

'I went there, yes,' he replied cagily. 'What's wrong with that?'

'A girl's body was discovered in an alley beside the bar in the early hours of Saturday morning.'

'Oh yes, of course, I read about that. Shocking. Just shocking. It could have happened to anyone, couldn't it?'

That seemed a strange comment to make, but Geraldine did not respond to it. Instead, she asked the butcher to accompany her to the police station as they had reason to suspect he might have witnessed something useful. He agreed cheerfully enough to go along to the police station when he finished work.

'We'd rather like you to come along with us right now.'

'Can't it wait?'

'No, I'm afraid it can't.'

'Oh, very well. I can see that this is an important matter, but I'm afraid I'm not going to have anything very helpful to tell you. I was only there to take my daughter home.'

'Your daughter?' Geraldine repeated in surprise.

'Oh, I know what you're going to say.'

'What?'

'That I shouldn't have let her out. But I can hardly lock her in her room at night, can I? I know there are parents who ground their teenagers but I have to say I've never understood how that works. If I tell Tilly not to go out, she'll go out anyway, just to spite me. I mean, she's not a spiteful girl, don't get me wrong, she's just a bit troubled, you know how it is with kids. And since her mother died a year ago, she's been angry with the whole world, especially me.' He heaved a sigh that made his round shoulders rise and fall. 'Everything would have been different if her mother was alive.'

'What were you doing at the Livewire Bar?'

'Looking for Tilly, of course. Didn't I just tell you? She was determined to go out on Friday night and I strictly forbade it. She's only fourteen for Christ's sake. Anyway, we had a massive row about it. Half an hour later, when I called her down for supper, I discovered she'd left the house. So I went to look for her. To be honest, it was only by chance that I found her. I know the kinds of places she goes to with her friends.' He shuddered and the folds of skin beneath his chin trembled. 'Some friends! She's in with a crowd of older girls. They go clubbing at the weekends, so I set out to visit the clubs and bars in town and found her in the third one I tried. It was a long shot because I could easily have missed her, but once I saw her I insisted on taking her home with me. She didn't want to leave but she was afraid her friends would see me nagging her, so in the end she agreed, if only to save face in front of these friends of hers. She was furious with me for turning up like that.' He frowned. 'That murder, it could have been Tilly bashed to death in an alley, couldn't it? She's only fourteen. I have to say it's helped to make her see that she's not safe going out on her own like that at night, but it's a shocking thing to happen. Shocking.'

'We're interested in tracing anyone who was at the club on Friday evening,' Geraldine said.

Richard nodded his understanding and she asked whether he had noticed anything untoward at the club on the night of the murder.

'A lot,' he replied promptly. 'The whole place was a den of

iniquity. It's a foul place. I mean, I'm as broad-minded as the next man,' he amended his statement, 'and I don't suppose there was anything illegal going on. That is, I didn't see any sign of drugs, although I'd put money on it that some of the people there were high on something or other. No, what I mean is, they let girls in without checking their ID properly.' He sniffed. 'I think the trouble is they all know how to get hold of fake ID these days. My daughter's only fourteen and she had a student card on her that said she was eighteen. It didn't even have her own name on it. I had a go at the bouncer but he just said that if a girl looks eighteen, and is carrying ID which says she's eighteen, he's not to know she's only fourteen, and how is he supposed to know it's not her name on the card? I can see it's a problem, and they can't refuse her entry, but all the same –' He shrugged helplessly. 'I honestly don't know what to do. She's only fourteen and she was in there, prey to goodness knows who or what. It could have been her stabbed to death in that alleyway. It doesn't bear thinking about. What am I supposed to do? I've tried talking to her but she just won't listen. All she wants to do is go out with her friends until all hours. It's a terrible thing to say, but I'm hoping this incident may help her to appreciate the danger she puts herself in when she goes out at night.'

Muttering sympathetically, Geraldine thanked him for his help and nodded to the constable, who turned the sign around on the door. She left, aware that she was wrong to feel disappointed that far from pursuing a young girl for nefarious purposes, Richard had gone to the club as a concerned father looking out for his young daughter. But it meant they were no closer to finding the killer.

# 28

JONAH SIGHED AND SHOOK his head mournfully. 'She could have been suffocated,' he said. 'It's really impossible to say.'

Geraldine frowned. 'I don't understand. Surely her injuries make it clear that she was battered to death?'

'Unfortunately the state she's in doesn't make anything clear. My guess – and it is just a guess – is that she died like the other girl, the one who was fished out of the river.' He nodded at the mutilated corpse on the table. 'She's been dead for about a week, I'd say.'

'A week? No, she was killed two days ago, out in the alley. I saw her lying there.'

Jonah smiled sadly. 'But you didn't see her die there, did you? What you saw was a body that had already been dead for at least two or three days, probably longer, that had been dumped in the alley.'

'No, I'm telling you, she was killed in the alley. There was so much blood. She couldn't possibly have bled that much in the alleyway if she'd been killed somewhere else.'

'Yes, there was a lot of blood, but none of it was hers.'

'Whose was it then?' Geraldine failed to conceal her sudden flicker of hope.

Jonah shook his head. 'It wasn't the killer's, if that's what you're thinking.'

'How can you be sure?'

'Apart from the fact that there was an awful lot of it, the blood she was lying in wasn't human.'

'What do you mean, it wasn't human?'

'The body in the alley was lying in a pool of animal blood, dog's blood, to be exact. The killer must have brought it with him to throw us off the scent.'

'You mean the killer wanted to make it look as though the victim had been killed where the body was found?'

Jonah's lips twisted in a contorted semblance of a smile, but his eyes betrayed his dismay. It was rare that he was lost for words

'So she was killed elsewhere,' Geraldine said thoughtfully. 'And all this was carefully planned to fool us.'

'Not carefully enough.'

'Do you think she was suffocated?'

'Well, that's certainly possible, but it's hard to say, given the nature of the post mortem mutilation.'

With nothing more definite to go on, Geraldine returned to the police station, where Eileen was as perplexed as Geraldine.

'How the hell did someone deposit a dead body in the alley in front of all those people?'

That particular mystery was solved when one of the brown wheelie bins in the alley was found to be splattered in blood, along with hair that matched the victim's. DNA soon confirmed that the body had been transported inside it, together with a bag containing blood.

'But the club was busy, and the bin must have been wheeled there from somewhere,' Eileen said. 'Surely it couldn't have been pushed along a crowded pavement? The lid only had to flip open and its contents would have been on view to a host of witnesses. What if someone wanted to throw their rubbish in it? Anyone could have seen inside it. A killer as careful about escaping detection as this one would never have taken that risk. And how come it's not shown up on any CCTV?'

'If the victim was killed a few days before the body was deposited in the alley, the bin might have been wheeled there at any time, maybe one night during the week, when the place is less busy,' Geraldine replied. 'Wearing a rubbish collector's jacket and gloves, the killer wouldn't have attracted any attention. Then all that would have remained for him to do on Saturday night would be to slip into the alley, tip open the bin, and disappear into the crowd.' She paused, considering the idea. 'It would have been risky, but it's perfectly feasible.'

Eileen nodded. 'Yes, it's possible that was how it was done. Get all the CCTV film in the area for the past week downloaded and arrange a team to study it. We need to find whoever it was wheeled that bin into the alley, and we need to find him quickly.'

Geraldine hurried off to carry out Eileen's instructions. She was pleased that they seemed to be making some progress, not least because it helped her to keep her mind off her own troubles, and her fear that she would never see her sister again. While they were waiting for the results of the scrutiny of the CCTV footage, Jonah submitted his report. They had no match for the victim's DNA on the system, and no means of identifying her. A message was circulated among dentists, searching for a match for her partial dental records, but they all knew that was a long shot. Apart from any other consideration, the victim's teeth were too badly damaged to be recognisable. Geraldine went to see Eileen again, this time to suggest that they attempt to come up with a digital image of the dead woman's face in the hope that someone might recognise her. Eileen agreed, and asked Geraldine to implement the idea. An expert in facial reconstruction was contacted and, within a few hours, Geraldine was staring at an image of features that could conceivably match those of a faceless corpse.

'It's only an approximation,' the digital reconstruction expert warned Geraldine when they spoke on the phone. 'The process of recreating an individual face from skeletal remains is no more than a rough combination of expert deduction and sheer guesswork. It's inevitably subjective, and that's why it's so controversial. People want our work to be an exact science, but it's more a question of artistry. We're making advances all the time, but I'm afraid for now what I've sent you is the best we can do, given the state of the skull.'

'It's brilliant,' Geraldine replied.

'But you need to bear in mind that it's not necessarily accurate.'

The image the police had produced was broadcast in the media and circulated online. The Missing Persons Bureau was contacted, and after that there was nothing to do but wait. Eileen summoned the team to a briefing in the Major Incident Room, to review the investigation so far.

'Our victims so far are Angie Robinson, twenty-four, husband Greg, pulled from the river. And then we have a second unidentified victim found in an alley outside the Livewire Club on Sunday morning.' She paused. 'There's no evidence to suggest that the missing girl, Zoe Watts, is in any way linked to the two murders, but she went missing at around the same time, and in the same vicinity, so we're keen to find her. Hopefully alive,' she added almost under her breath.

Ian cooked steaks that evening, and opened an expensive bottle of Claret, but Geraldine struggled to respond to his tentative advances.

'Geraldine, I know you're still angry with me,' he said, looking wretched. 'Believe me, if there was anything I could do to make the situation better, I would do it like a shot. You know I'd do anything to make you happy.'

Painfully aware that she was being unfair, Geraldine bit her lip and turned away so that he would not see the tears in her eyes. She and Ian loved one another, and she knew he had acted for the best in removing Helena to a safe location, where no one could force her to relapse into her lethal addiction. Yet somehow Geraldine could not forgive him for the enforced separation.

'Geraldine, talk to me,' he said. 'Tell me what you're thinking.'

She gazed at his familiar face. Much as she hated causing him distress, she resented her own anguish more.

'We are identical twins,' she whispered. 'Helena is the only surviving blood relative from my immediate family.'

'I'm your family now,' he replied.

For years she had dreamed of hearing him speak to her like that, but the words sounded meaningless. How could she explain that without the twin sister she had barely known, she felt alone in the world?

'I'm sorry,' she muttered, and she truly was. 'I can't help how I feel.'

# 29

Nearly a week had passed since Zoe had run away from home. Despite being exhausted from lack of sleep, she was feeling pleased with herself for having managed to stay out of sight for so long. It would serve her parents right if she never went home. It was their fault she had left, and she hoped they blamed themselves for driving her away. Fortunately, when Zoe had finally contacted her friend, Laura had agreed to help her without any hesitation.

'This is going to be fun,' she had responded, her voice bright with excitement, when Zoe explained she needed somewhere to hide out.

'It's just for a few days,' Zoe had said, 'just until I sort myself out.'

Now she was regretting her optimism. To begin with, when she had first arrived at Laura's house, everything had gone like a dream. The two girls had hurried up the stairs to Laura's bedroom without anyone seeing them.

'It's all right,' Laura had assured her. 'They're both out at work all day. No one else ever comes here.'

Hearing Laura's parents moving around in the house, Zoe had been solemn, but Laura had giggled helplessly, spluttering at the audacity of their plan. In the safety of her own home, she seemed to have no sense of caution.

'Shh,' Zoe had whispered angrily. 'Your parents will hear us.'

Shaking her head, Laura had put her finger to her lips to

warn Zoe not to talk any more. But they had not disturbed Laura's parents, and with Zoe safely up in Laura's room, it had been easy to remain hidden. Laura's parents were both out at work all day, and she had the run of the house until they returned in the evening. Going to the toilet once Laura's parents were home was risky, but other than that the situation presented no problem. Laura went out to the shops for food, and filched more from the kitchen, and for a change Zoe ate hungrily. Away from her parents, she seemed to have recovered her appetite. Besides, she had spent hours not knowing when she might next be able to eat, which helped her to appreciate whatever supplies Laura brought her. She was feeling comfortably ensconced in Laura's room, when her friend dropped a bombshell.

'So what are your plans?' Laura asked.

Her parents had gone to bed, and the two girls were whispering together in the darkness. Laura was in bed, and Zoe was lying on a thick fur rug on the floor, inside a sleeping bag. It was quite cosy.

'What do you mean?' Zoe replied.

'Well, you can't stay here forever.'

'Of course I realise that,' Zoe said, hiding her dismay. 'You don't think I *want* to be stuck here hiding like this, do you? But I need to stay with you until we work out what I'm going to do. I can't just leave, with nowhere to go, can I?'

'You could go home,' Laura pointed out.

'No, I already told you, I can't. I'm never going back there. It's just not possible.'

'Well, you have to go somewhere. People are going to start asking questions.'

'What people?'

'Well, school for a start. This is serious, Zoe. You know I lied to the police when they came to school? You can't keep this up much longer. Once they speak to your parents and find out you're not actually sick, they'll want to know where you are, and then everyone will know you're missing.'

'Who's everyone?'

'The school must have reported your absence by now. Why else were the police there? Besides, my parents are bound to find you, sooner or later, and then I'll be for it. And anyway, it's beginning to smell in here.'

'And I suppose you think that's my fault?'

Admittedly, Zoe hadn't showered for days. She thought about what Laura had said.

'Laura?'

'What?' Laura replied sleepily.

'Can I use the bathroom tomorrow? As in, use the shower?'

'No.'

'Why not?'

'Because I don't want you abusing my parents' hospitality.'

'What are you talking about? What hospitality?'

'You're staying in their house, aren't you? Eating their food.'

'Yes, but they don't even know I'm here!'

'Shh, keep your voice down. They'll hear you. If they find out you're here, I'll be in real trouble.'

'So, you'll let me stay as long as I keep quiet and don't let them find me?'

'No, I already said, you can't stay here. For fuck's sake, you've already been here for a week. That's long enough. I want you to leave.'

'But I haven't got anywhere else to go.'

'Go home.'

'If you won't let me stay, I'll tell your parents,' Zoe said in desperation.

'If you don't go, I'll tell them myself. Seriously, Zoe, I've had enough of this. It was a lark to begin with but it's gone on for long enough. I can't keep nicking food from downstairs, and I've spent my entire allowance for this month on buying stuff for you. You've got no money, and I can't keep on supporting you like this. I'm not your mother. Just bloody well go home, will you? And now shut up, I'm trying to get some sleep.'

Zoe lay awake for a long time, fuming. Not only furious with her parents for being so horrible, now she was angry about her friend's betrayal as well. It was hardly her fault she was homeless.

'I would have let you stay with me,' she muttered, but Laura was either asleep or else ignoring her.

In a sudden temper, Zoe clambered out of the sleeping bag she was lying in and began to shove her few belongings into her backpack. She was startled when a light was suddenly switched on. Blinking, she looked round. Laura was sitting up in bed, staring at her.

'What the hell are you doing?' she demanded in a furious whisper.

Zoe scowled at her. 'What does it look like I'm doing? I'm packing. I know when I'm not wanted.'

'I never said you had to go right now,' Laura protested.

They both knew that was not true.

'You don't want me here,' Zoe replied.

'You don't have to leave tonight.'

Zoe grabbed a T-shirt and stuffed it in her bag.

'Hey, that's mine,' Laura said.

Zoe retrieved it and flung it at her friend. 'Here you go,' she muttered crossly.

'Listen,' Laura said, leaning forward. 'Why don't you stay for another week? You must see that in the long run, it's going to be impossible. Apart from school interfering and asking questions, and getting on to social workers and truancy people and everything, my mum's bound to come in here sooner or later. I've done my best to warn her off, and after that she's usually all right for a while, but then she has these fits when she's like a complete control freak and insists on coming in here and cleaning everything. I can't do a thing without her breathing down my neck. You have no idea. She can be a right pest.'

'So I can stay here for another week?'

'Yes, that's what I said, isn't it?'

'Awesome.'

A week was a long time. Zoe was sure she could think of somewhere else to go.

'I might go to London and get a job,' she said, but Laura had fallen asleep again.

# 30

BY THE FOLLOWING DAY, a number of responses had come in from people claiming to recognise the image of the dead woman. Some of them were easily dismissed, but others were credible leads. Geraldine decided to focus on the handful of local reports first, and requested DNA samples to be taken for each of the possible missing persons. With that work in progress, she checked on the team who were examining CCTV looking for someone pushing a large brown wheelie bin into the alley. After that, she could only wait for the results of the various investigations.

'It must be awful, waiting and thinking it might be your missing wife or mother or daughter whose body was found,' Ariadne said. 'I always think the uncertainty would be the worst part of it, not knowing whether to grieve or keep on hoping. This must be torment for Zoe Watts' parents.'

It struck Geraldine that she would never know if her own sister went missing. Perhaps the criminal gang had already abducted Helena and were intending to use her to coerce Geraldine to do whatever they wanted. She felt uncomfortable distrusting Ian, and, on reflection, was sure he would not have lied to her about what had happened. Her anger towards him had already begun to fade. She had been nearly ready to relent, understanding that he had only acted in her interest, until the appearance of an unidentified victim outside a club. Of course the dead woman wasn't her sister, but she could have been. With the reminder that she had no idea where her sister was, or whether she was safe, her anger against Ian returned.

That afternoon, the forensic lab called to report that a match for the unknown victim's DNA had been found. There was no longer any doubt that the dead woman's remains belonged to a twenty-seven-year-old woman called Leslie Gordon. Geraldine went to see the family with the sad news. Leslie had lived with her husband in a small semi-detached house round the corner from the station. Parking nearby, Geraldine tried to prepare herself mentally for the task ahead. Dealing with the remains of the dead was never as painful as coping with the grief of the living. She rang the doorbell and a grey-haired man came to the door. He stooped slightly as he gazed at her with a worried frown.

'Mr Gordon? Mr Robert Gordon?'

'Yes, is this about my wife? Has she been found?'

Older than his twenty-seven-year-old wife, he looked as though he was in his fifties. Stifling a sigh, Geraldine introduced herself and suggested they went inside. As she spoke, Robert's anxious expression turned to one of despair and his shoulders drooped even further.

'Something's happened to her, hasn't it? Is she going to be all right?' he asked.

'Please,' Geraldine replied gently, 'let's go in and sit down.'

It was not easy telling him that not only was his wife dead, but she had been so horribly mutilated after her murder that her face was no longer recognisable as human, let alone as his wife. She shared the news as sensitively as she could and he broke down, dropping his face in his hands and sobbing. When she was able to make out what he was saying, she heard him mumbling that he was to blame for what had happened.

'What do you mean?' she asked. 'How was this your fault?'

It was hard not to ask a leading question.

'I'm responsible for what happened to her,' he blurted out, still sobbing. 'It's all my fault she's dead.'

When he had calmed down sufficiently to speak coherently, he explained that he and his wife had argued on the night she disappeared from home.

'She was younger than me,' he explained apologetically. 'Twenty-five years younger, to be precise, but she assured me the age difference wasn't a problem for her.' He sighed. 'I wasn't sure, but she was adamant she wanted us to get married.' He sighed. 'As it turned out, the age difference was a problem after all. Leslie was always wanting to go out, have fun, you know. Fun,' his voice broke and he sobbed again. 'What fun is she going to have now? We thought – we both thought I would go first. It never occurred to either of us that I might outlive her. I'd made provisions for her after my death.' He broke off, too overwhelmed to carry on.

'What happened the last time you saw her?'

'She was all dressed up to go out. She said she was meeting a girlfriend.'

'Can you give me her name?'

He shook his head. 'I don't know. Leslie didn't say. All she told me was that she was going out with a colleague from work. She left the house about nine and didn't come home. I never saw her again.' He stifled a sob and drew in a deep breath before continuing. 'I waited up for her all night and the next morning I went to the police station to report her missing. They weren't very helpful. If they had found her sooner, she might be alive now.'

Geraldine told him that they believed his wife had probably been murdered on the night of her disappearance, but he shook his head as though he didn't believe her.

'You would say that, wouldn't you?' he replied, with a flash of anger.

But he immediately broke down in tears again. Repeating her commiserations, Geraldine left. There was nothing more to be learned from Leslie's widower, and she had work to do.

Leslie had worked as a waitress in one of the many coffee shops in York. This one was near Lendal Bridge. Geraldine went straight there on leaving Robert, and found a small café bustling with customers. Having arrived at tea time, she waited patiently in a queue at the counter where a middle-aged woman, two girls and a young man were working and waiting at the tables. Geraldine held out her identity card.

'I'd like to speak to each of you in turn,' she said quietly.

The older woman answered her. 'Please, come and take a seat,' she said, leading Geraldine to an empty table in a corner. 'What is this about?'

'Did Leslie Gordon work here?'

'Leslie? Yes. But she hasn't been here for a week.'

'Didn't you find it strange that she just stopped coming into work?'

'I called her and her husband told me he didn't know where she was.' The woman shrugged. 'There was nothing I could do about it if she'd run off and left him. I mean, I don't know where she is, if that's what you're asking. It wasn't as if she took me into her confidence. Oh, she was pleasant enough to work with, and she did her job all right, but we weren't what you might call friends. We had a good working relationship. I was going to wait until the end of the month before looking for someone to replace her, just in case she came back. But even if she turns up again after a month, she can hardly expect to walk back into her job, can she? I'll have to check her rights, but I don't see how she can think I'm going to keep her job open when she's just taken off. How do I know if she's ever going to come back?'

'She won't be coming back,' Geraldine said gently. 'Leslie's been murdered.'

The woman's jaw dropped and she stared at Geraldine in consternation.

'Murdered?' she repeated in a stunned whisper.

She gazed around the café, as though she expected all her customers to stand up and walk out.

'I'm afraid so,' Geraldine replied.

'How did it happen?'

'I'm sorry but none of the details can be shared with you yet, but we do need to find out as much as we can about Leslie, any enemies she might have had, and what happened on the night she died.'

She quizzed the manager and the other employees, but none of them had known Leslie very well, or was able to reveal anything about her, and what was more significant, none of them admitted to having gone out with her on the last night of her life. Unless one of them was lying, none of her work colleagues knew anything about where she had gone that night. Geraldine was inclined to believe them, not least because they all concurred that Leslie had not formed any particular friendships with any of them.

'Not that she wasn't sociable or anything like that,' one of the young girls at the café told Geraldine. 'She had loads of friends.'

She was the most relaxed and the most loquacious of the employees there, and did not seem at all dashed by what had happened to her colleague. On the contrary, she seemed slightly excited. Geraldine spent the most time with her, hoping she would come up with something to shed light on what had happened to Leslie.

'What makes you say that?' she prompted the girl.

'Just that she was always going out. She was always rushing off at the end of the day to meet a friend.'

'Was it always the same friend?' Geraldine asked, concealing her sudden interest in what the girl was telling her.

'I don't know, do I? All I know is that she was always rushing off to meet her friends. She used to bring clothes to work to change into before she left.'

'What kind of clothes.'

'Oh, you know, going-out clothes. Like she was going clubbing.' She lowered her voice. 'Apparently her husband was a lot older than her, and she used to go out without him, on the pull, you know. But that's just what I heard,' she added, clearly remembering that they were talking about a woman who had recently died. 'It probably wasn't true. I mean, I don't want to gossip about the dead.'

# 31

ANOTHER VICTIM HAD BEEN reported in the news. This time a young woman had allegedly been killed outside a club in the centre of York, in the early hours of Saturday morning. The news item did not describe how she had been killed. It made no mention of the way her face had been smashed in repeatedly with a heavy weapon, after she had been suffocated. At the time, there had been no particular reason for destroying the woman's face like that, other than a passing rage against her and every other woman in the world. But that additional assault on her corpse was bound to lead the police down a false trail, suggesting as it did that the killer had been concerned to conceal the victim's identity, when in fact the dead woman was unknown to her killer, a completely random victim.

As it turned out, it was just as well that her head had caved in like that, her post mortem injuries concealing the fact that she had already suffocated. The dead do not bleed, but even that detail had been skilfully dealt with, so there was no way the police would ever work out how the victim had actually died. With a killer both bold and intelligent, the victim had been thoroughly silenced by the time the body was discovered. She had no mouth, and in any case her brain was reduced to a soggy mess of bloody torn tissue that held no memory of her killer, or anything else for that matter. She might as well never have been a person at all, considering all that was left of her. Still, it had been an unnecessarily troublesome experience, because the blood had been difficult to expunge. Nothing like that would ever be allowed to happen again. From now on, suffocation would have to be enough. That was how it would be, simple and certain, the lure of blood resisted. It was just too messy.

For a few days he seemed content, but it wasn't long before he was drawn back to his former habits, as though nothing had happened to interrupt his hidden way of life. He seemed unable to control his compulsion. However dangerous it was for him, there was no question he would continue, even though he risked exposure at every turn. The terror of discovery loomed large but there were still women for him to prey on, and in spite of everything he seemed incapable of resisting the temptation.

One day he might conquer his weakness, when he was too old and frail to continue. Sooner or later, when his turn came to fight for his last breath, he might be overwhelmed by the terror of death that would consign him to the fires of eternal damnation. But he was not yet ready to give up his addiction, and steadfastly refused to contemplate the eternal consequences of his actions. And perhaps, after all, there would be no final judgement, and this world was all that he had to enjoy, or fear. If that was the case, he would not need to feel any regret when he died, only glory in the satisfaction he had found in life. Eventually everything might yet unravel and he would be forced to confront his sins and repent. But he was not ready yet.

# 32

THE TEAM HAD BEEN looking for a connection between the two victims. If they could only find something the two women had in common, it might help them to trace the killer, but so far nothing concrete had come up. Geraldine had a feeling it could be important that they had both been employed as waitresses, albeit in different cafés, but the significance of that was not yet clear. Apart from their work, there didn't seem to be anything to link them.

'You've got to agree it's a bit of a coincidence, both of them working as waitresses in similar kinds of cafés,' Ariadne said, as she and Geraldine were discussing the case.

'It would have given them the opportunity to encounter a lot of strangers in the course of their work,' Geraldine replied thoughtfully. 'I suppose that's something we ought to be looking into.'

The missing girl, Zoe Watts, was a teenager, and still at school. The team were divided on whether her disappearance might be linked to the murders. While they were all hoping the girl had simply run away from home, as teenagers sometimes did, Eileen was keeping an open mind on the question of her connection to the murders. Along with her colleagues, Geraldine hoped Zoe would not turn out to be another victim of the murderer.

Wondering whether they had missed something, she decided to return to the cafés and question the dead women's colleagues again. Angie's unctuous manager answered all her questions willingly enough, but he had nothing to add to what he had already told her on her previous visit. The café was empty and Geraldine suspected he was keen to see the back of her as quickly as possible because he spoke very rapidly, casting frequent glances at the door in case a customer walked in.

'Is there anything else I can help you with, Sergeant?'

He did not seem to know very much about his former waitress. All the same, Geraldine continued to question him, only this time she was more interested in his customers than his employees. According to the manager, no customer had demonstrated any particular interest in the dead girl.

'She just waited at table,' he replied. 'There wasn't any more to it than that.'

The manager bristled visibly when Geraldine persisted with her line of questioning.

'This isn't that kind of establishment,' he retorted. 'My waitresses do not strike up any kind of friendship with men who come here. I would never tolerate that kind of familiar behaviour in my staff. That's not what they're paid to do. This is a respectable café. You can see that for yourself.'

He gestured around the room at tables and brown plastic chairs, dark against pale yellow walls.

The brunette waitress, Klara, was keen to help yet she too was unable to offer any useful information but resorted to babbling about her work, hinting that she had a better job in mind, once her English had improved sufficiently. Geraldine did not stay long. The visit had been a waste of time.

The second victim had only been working at her café near Lendal Bridge for about six months, and no one there seemed to know much about her. She had worked alongside two other waitresses, neither of whom appeared to have held a conversation with her.

'Sorry, but I only did the lunchtime shift and we were

always rushed off our feet,' one of them apologised. 'I hardly spoke to her, really. She seemed nice enough. It's horrible, what's happened to her.'

The manager of a shop where Leslie had been employed previously was slightly more helpful. A slightly pompous middle-aged woman, she referred to herself and the younger people working there as 'the staff'. When Geraldine asked for the contact details of anyone else who worked there, the manager raised a pencilled eyebrow.

'We are the staff,' she repeated grandly, as though she was referring to royalty.

The shop was owned by a company whose representatives rarely visited, and the manager was in effect the boss, serving in the shop with the other employees. Leslie had been employed there for nearly two years.

'We were considering letting her go,' the manager admitted, with an unconvincing show of regret.

'Why was that?'

'She was flaky,' the manager replied uneasily. 'This is just between us, isn't it? Only I do like to help the police when I can. And the poor girl is dead now, isn't she? Raped and murdered right here in York.'

She shuddered and dabbed her eyes with a paper serviette. Geraldine quickly corrected her about the nature of the assault on Leslie.

'Are you saying she wasn't raped?'

'That's exactly what I'm saying. Where did you hear that she was sexually assaulted?'

'Oh, you know how people talk,' the woman replied vaguely. 'Anyway, that's a mercy and we can all sleep soundly at night again.'

Geraldine resisted the temptation to respond to that absurd remark.

'It would help our investigation if you could tell me more

about the kind of woman Leslie was. You said she was flaky. Do you mean she was unreliable?'

The manager shook her head. 'What a terrible business,' she said. 'That poor girl.'

Geraldine repeated her question.

'Oh that,' the manager said. 'I only meant that she was often late for work, and once or twice she turned up looking like... well, looking as though she could do with a good night's sleep.' She lowered her voice. 'She struck me as the sort of girl who likes to have a good time, if you know what I mean.'

She looked meaningfully at Geraldine, who thanked her for the information and did her best to find out more. But the manager shook her head.

'I'm afraid I have absolutely no idea who she went out with. Like I said, I think she was interested in meeting men.'

'She was married,' Geraldine reminded her.

'Well, you wouldn't have thought it, the way she carried on.'

When Geraldine pressed her to explain, she described how Leslie used to change at the end of the working day before going out for the evening to pick up men.

'How do you know that's what she was doing? She could have been meeting her husband.'

The woman shook her head. 'Not dressed like that, she wasn't. He came here once to meet her, and he was definitely not the kind of man to go out clubbing, or to bars and what not. He looked like a very respectable man. He was a lot older than her. I thought he was her father. If you ask me,' she lowered her voice, 'she went out looking for other men. Well, it seems she found one.'

'Did she say anything that led you to believe she was cheating on her husband?'

'She didn't need to. I saw the way she dressed.'

Despite her belief that the dead woman had regularly gone to bars or clubs hoping to meet men, the shop manager did not know which venues Leslie had frequented or whom she might have met after work.

# 33

GERALDINE HAD THE IMPRESSION her colleague was upset about something, but Ariadne insisted she was fine. Her protestations failed to convince Geraldine. Ariadne kept laughing a little too loudly, and she grinned foolishly whenever a colleague walked past, as though desperate to convince everyone she was happy. Geraldine's suspicions were confirmed when she saw Ariadne in the toilets, sniffing and wiping her eyes. As soon as she spotted Geraldine, Ariadne turned away and blew her nose vigorously, but she knew that Geraldine had seen her crying and there was no longer any point in her maintaining the pretence that everything was fine.

'Let's go for a coffee, and you can tell me all about it,' Geraldine said.

Ariadne shook her head, insisting this was not something she could discuss at work, where she risked being overheard. So at lunch time they left the police station together and went into York for a pizza. The pub local to the police station was frequented by colleagues and Ariadne wanted to go where they could talk unobserved.

'You don't have to tell me what's troubling you, but I'm listening if you want to talk about it,' Geraldine said as she sat down.

She picked up her fork and waited.

'I've done a really stupid thing,' Ariadne blurted out.

Geraldine did not answer.

'It's Andrew,' Ariadne muttered at last, her eyes glistening with unshed tears.

'Andrew? You mean Andrew Wilder, the constable who's come to join us from Northallerton? What about him?'

Andrew had arrived in York as one of the team drafted in to help with the double murder investigation. Ariadne mumbled that she liked their new colleague. Geraldine thought about this. She had been so preoccupied with her own troubles that she had not noticed any particular intimacy developing between him and Ariadne, and was surprised to see her friend looking so upset.

'And so?' Geraldine asked. 'Is there more to this? I mean, have you let him know how you feel?'

'Yes. Kind of. That is, yes. We had a thing.'

'What do you mean?' Geraldine asked, although Ariadne's meaning was pretty clear.

'Oh for goodness sake, Geraldine. Don't be an idiot. You know what I mean.'

Hesitantly Ariadne confided that she had accepted an invitation to go for a drink with Andrew.

'I know it was wrong of me,' she concluded miserably.

'There's nothing wrong with two colleagues going for a drink,' Geraldine replied cheerfully. 'That's what we're doing right now, isn't it?'

'Yes, but there was more to it than that.' Ariadne lowered her voice although there was no one nearby who could hear her. 'I went home with him. That is, I invited him back to my flat.' She paused. 'I mean, it's a long drive back to Northallerton at the end of the working day.'

She had clearly not offered him her sofa.

'Well, he's single, and you're single,' Geraldine said. 'Where's the harm in two consenting adults spending the night together? I understand you don't want everyone to know and start gossiping, but it's not as though you've done anything wrong. I don't really understand what's bothering you. You obviously like each other, so that's good, isn't it?'

Since Ariadne had confessed to liking Andrew, Geraldine decided not to mention that he had also approached her. If he was lonely and looking for a relationship, there was no reason why Ariadne shouldn't benefit from his attention when Geraldine was not interested in him. It would be unkind to imply that Ariadne had not been his first choice of potential partner.

'The thing is, I really like him but I don't know if he feels the same way. He's never really said anything to suggest he thinks of our relationship as anything more than a fling. Is it too early to ask him how he feels? I don't want to look desperate.'

Geraldine put down her fork and spoke slowly. 'I'm hardly an expert in relationships but if you really want my advice, for what it's worth, I think you need to be patient. Give it time. Probably neither of you really knows how you feel about each other yet. Just go with it and see what happens.'

'But I'm not comfortable cheating on Nico.'

Geraldine was taken aback. For nearly a year she and Ariadne had worked closely together and become good friends, yet in all that time she had never once heard Ariadne talk about anyone called Nico.

'Nico? Who's Nico?'

'My boyfriend.'

Geraldine was even more confused. Ariadne had never mentioned that she had a boyfriend. On the contrary, she had told Geraldine that she was tired of being on her own, and wanted to meet someone. Ariadne's eyes filled with tears again, and she twisted a tissue in her fingers as she explained that she had been seeing Nico for a couple of months. He was the nephew of a friend of her mother's.

'I don't understand. If you're seeing someone else, why did

you sleep with Andrew? No, sorry, that was a stupid question.'

'What should I do? Help me, Geraldine.'

'For a start, you need to tell Nico it's over between you.'

'But what if the affair with Andrew doesn't last? I don't want to end up with no one.'

Geraldine took a gulp of her water. 'Well, which of them do you want to be with? Given that you can't keep on seeing both of them.'

Ariadne sighed. 'Andrew, obviously, I suppose, or there wouldn't be a problem. Nico's asked me to marry him, but I don't know if Andrew's serious, and it's too early to ask, isn't it? I mean, we've only been out for a drink once and then he came back to my place. That's all we've done so far. I mean, we had sex, but it's only been the once. How can I find out how he feels? I don't want to frighten him off. But I'm not comfortable about cheating on Nico.'

'It doesn't sound as though you love Nico.'

'Well, I do and I don't, if you know what I mean.'

Geraldine shook her head. 'I'm not sure I do.'

'Sometimes I think I love him. I could imagine spending the rest of my life with him quite happily. But it's different when I'm with Andrew. It's – I can't explain, but he makes me feel alive. He's exciting, you know? I don't know what to do.'

'You need to stop seeing Andrew and get over it, or else tell Nico it's over between you,' Geraldine replied firmly. 'It's not fair on any of you to carry on like this.'

'But what if I end things with Nico and then the affair with Andrew doesn't last? He's never said anything to suggest he thinks of what we did as going anywhere. I don't want to end up with no one. I'm nearly forty. It's taken me so long to find Nico. And I do like him.'

'Ariadne, you're cheating on both of them, and messing yourself up at the same time. You have to stop seeing one of them. And if you like Nico so much that you don't want to lose him, I'd say you should refuse to see Andrew again. You're probably just having last minute collywobbles about Nico because it sounds like it could be serious with him.'

'You're right,' Ariadne replied. 'I've been an idiot, haven't I? Andrew's quite attractive, isn't he? I think it just went to my head when he seemed interested in me. And I was a bit pissed. Oh well, like you said, no harm done. I won't make that mistake again, that's for sure.'

Ariadne smiled and Geraldine lowered her eyes, shocked to realise how little she really knew about her friend. Casting her mind over other people she thought she knew, she wondered what they might be keeping from her. To be fair, she was as guilty of being secretive as Ariadne, concealing her own relationship with Ian from everyone else. Thinking about her feelings for Ian, she realised she did not even understand her own reticence to be open about his moving in with her. But she was afraid to reveal it to other people, as though that might somehow ruin the relationship she was guarding so jealously.

# 34

A REPORT HAD BEEN sent by the forensic team which had been examining the bin in which Leslie's body had been transported. Extensive tests having failed to reveal any prints or DNA, Geraldine quizzed a member of the team about the disappointing results.

'Human fingermarks are left by natural oils deposited on any surface the fingers come into contact with,' the officer explained to her.

'Yes, yes, I know all that, but surely you must have found something, even a partial print, somewhere on the bin? Did you examine every inch of it?'

'Every millimetre,' the forensic scientist replied. 'The trouble is, a non-porous substance like plastic is easily cleaned using a simple solution to break down the oils. Even a damp cloth can do the job. Whoever handled this bin was careful to remove any marks that might have been left on it.'

'What about DNA? You must have found traces of DNA on the bin?'

'Only the victim's, I'm afraid,' the scientist said. 'The whole bin, inside and out, was cleaned with a strong solution of sodium hydroxide which corrodes organic materials. The bin stank of it. That would have been enough to destroy any traces of DNA, especially if the user was wearing a mask.'

Geraldine frowned. 'Someone took a great deal of trouble to cover their tracks. How easy is it to get hold of sodium hydroxide?'

'It's readily available, everywhere. It's widely used to unblock drains.'

'But wouldn't sodium hydroxide have dissolved the bin?'

'No, on the contrary, sodium hydroxide is stored in plastic containers because it damages glass, and anything else organic.'

Later that afternoon a message came through from the VIIDO team that Andrew had spotted someone wheeling a bin into the passageway beside the club on Friday at around six pm.

'Well done,' Eileen said, gazing around the room. 'It's just as well someone around here is on the ball.'

A couple of other officers mumbled discreetly, but no one minded that Eileen had singled out a newcomer for such high praise. What mattered was that they might have a sighting of whoever had deposited Leslie's body in the alley. Eileen put the footage up on the screen in the incident room and they all watched in silence as she played it through. The film was disappointing. Whoever was wheeling the bin was only clearly visible from behind, stomping along the street fairly quickly. When a camera did catch a shot from the front, the figure was moving swiftly, and the image was blurred by heavy rain. Whoever was pushing the bin had chosen a wet day when the pavement would be less crowded and any film would be indistinct.

'This killer is no fool,' Eileen muttered crossly. 'He's making it impossible for us to track him down.'

'Almost impossible,' Geraldine replied softly, and the detective chief inspector grunted.

Eileen played the short film through again. Silently they watched the killer, or perhaps an accomplice, pushing the large bin along the pavement. His hair concealed beneath the hood of an anorak under his loose hi-vis jacket, he was wearing large black shoes and thick safety gloves, looking just like any other refuse operative pushing a bin. Except that the contents of this bin were very different to the garbage it would usually contain. Snatches of film from various cameras recorded the bin and its custodian in short bursts, travelling along the pavement outside the club, until they disappeared around the corner into the alley where the film stopped. Following the film backwards, they watched the bin being unloaded from a black van with false number plates. The registration number had already been traced to a Ford Fiesta which was parked outside its owner's house at an address in Wales.

As far as they could see, only the driver of the van was involved in transporting the bin. He had jumped out, already dressed in his refuse operative's outfit, pulled the bin down a ramp from the van, and wheeled it along the street. With the bin deposited in the alley, the driver had hurried back to his vehicle and driven to where the vehicle had first appeared from a maze of side streets.

'There are a few properties with security cameras in the surrounding streets, but none of them films the road itself. They only capture the front of the houses, the driveways, and side and back entrances. They're designed to act as security for private properties,' Andrew explained. 'So we've been unable to track where the van came from. We've widened the search, but it could have been driven out of a private garage almost anywhere. It's like looking for the proverbial needle in a haystack, trying to identify where it came from.'

No one challenged Andrew's assessment of the situation.

'Can we at least tell if we're looking at a man or a woman?' Geraldine asked, staring at the image on the screen.

'The height is around five feet seven,' Andrew said, 'although the hood makes it difficult to be accurate. It looks as though there could be a hat under the hood, giving it extra height, so it could be a woman, although I think that's unlikely.' Andrew paused and glanced around, as though he was half expecting someone to contradict him. 'The hi-vis jacket looks several sizes too big for him, and it rather looks as though the shoes have thick platforms, although it's impossible to be certain about that because the trousers are too long, dragging on the ground. From their size, the shoes appear to belong to a man, but this could be a woman with unusually large feet.'

'Or a woman wearing shoes several sizes too large for her with the deliberate intention of misleading us,' Geraldine added, and Andrew frowned.

'The weight of the bin also suggests we're looking at a man,' Andrew continued, 'and getting it down from van would take some muscle power.'

'It's rolled down a steep ramp out of the van,' Eileen pointed out. 'That wouldn't necessarily take much strength, and the pavement is fairly even along there. It's not conclusive.'

Andrew nodded. 'The evidence points to a man, but it could be a woman. I'm sorry that's not very helpful,' he concluded apologetically.

If Geraldine had been unaware of what had happened between Ariadne and Andrew, she would probably have missed how her friend's eyes lingered on the constable, or else interpreted her friend's attention to the constable's words as proof of her focus on the case. As it was, Geraldine understood that Ariadne was not yet over her infatuation with the good-looking newcomer to the team, and she wondered how their relationship would play out. She hoped Ariadne would not end up feeling hurt and let down, and resolved to keep a close eye on her friend.

That afternoon, Eileen issued a press release. Along with the usual flannel about pursuing vague leads, and unspecified people helping the police with their enquiries, she mentioned that they were looking for a large hi-vis jacket whose wearer had been spotted near the scene. The comment provoked the usual flurry of calls, one of which was especially interesting. Someone called from the local council's household waste collection department to report that a hi-vis jacket belonging to one of their operatives had been stolen.

'It could have been stolen by the killer,' Ariadne said, her eyes lighting up.

'Or perhaps one of their refuse collectors disposed of his uniform himself because he was afraid it might reveal evidence that he had been handling a dead body?' Eileen added, her expression reflecting Ariadne's excitement.

# 35

GERALDINE WENT TO QUESTION the refuse collector, Harry Mellor, whose jacket had been reported stolen. The door was opened by a diminutive woman who gazed up at Geraldine with a worried expression.

'Are you from the council?' she asked.

She visibly relaxed when Geraldine introduced herself, which was a change from the usual suspicion or outright hostility she faced on announcing she was a police officer. Mrs Mellor led the way to a small living room where a man was seated watching television. As soon as Harry stood up, Geraldine suspected they had been premature in allowing their hopes to be raised. He towered over her, at least six foot in height, with long limbs and wide shoulders. Not only did his height not appear to match whoever had been pushing the wheelie bin, but his head looked larger than that of the figure captured on film, as were his hands and feet. Everything about him looked huge, unlike the person they were looking for. She could be mistaken and, even if she was right, it was possible Harry might still be able to help them. Having introduced herself, she sat down and asked him to repeat his name and tell her exactly what had happened to his jacket. Harry Mellor frowned. Beneath heavy overhanging brows his dark eyes glared at her, yet he somehow gave the impression that he was normally a good-natured man.

'I already told my manager what happened, didn't I?' he said, in an incongruously reedy voice. 'I can't believe they've reported this to the police. It was only an old jacket. They've given me another one. It's no big deal.'

Geraldine noted that he seemed keen to play down the theft, as though he was reluctant to involve the police. Casting her eyes down, she noticed that the back of his left wrist was grazed.

'You've hurt your hand,' she said, as though she was concerned for him.

'It's nothing.'

'How did you do it?'

Harry shook his head. 'I can't rightly remember. Scraped it on a wall or a gate while I was collecting bins, I guess, or I might have done it gardening.'

'Harry loves the garden,' his wife added, with a complacent smile.

'Tell me about the stolen jacket.'

'It was nicked off the back of my bike in broad daylight, would you believe? Trouble is, it's not mine.'

'Whose jacket are we talking about?'

'No, I mean, it was my jacket all right, but they provide it for me. It's the uniform that comes with the job, see. And now they expect me to pay for it out of my own pocket.'

'When did you last have it?' Geraldine asked.

'I was on my way home, on –' Harry screwed up his craggy face. 'It must've been a week ago, anyway. They made a right stink about it at work. And now they're getting you lot involved. I can't believe the fuss over an old jacket, and now I'm in trouble over it, like it was my fault some fucker nicked it.'

'In trouble?'

'Yes,' he said. 'I'm the one who's getting the blame when it wasn't my fault at all. I only stopped off to get some fags.'

'I see,' Geraldine said. 'I can't promise that we'll be able to find your jacket, and even if we do, it's unlikely to be returned to you straightaway.'

Harry shook his head. 'Who in their right mind would steal an old hi-vis jacket? And now I'm in trouble.'

'This wasn't your fault,' Geraldine assured him. 'You've done nothing wrong. So don't worry.'

Harry shook his head. 'They don't see it like that. They warn us, we're responsible for our gear.'

Geraldine did her best to calm Harry down about his manager at work giving him a hard time, but he continued to grumble. He was so emphatic in insisting that his jacket had been taken from the back of his bicycle that she began to wonder if he was telling her the truth. She probed him further about where his jacket had been taken, and he described in meticulous detail where he had left his bicycle.

'I just nipped in for a moment to buy some fags,' he explained. 'I left the bike outside, padlocked, because you can't be too careful, can you? But when I came out again, blow me if my jacket hadn't gone. That's it. That's what happened. I left the jacket rolled up in the basket on the back, in full view of anyone passing. How was I to know some fucker was going to nick it? I mean, who would want a thing like that?'

'Was anything else taken?'

'Yes it was.' Waxing indignant, Harry told her that his hat and scarf had been rolled up inside the jacket. 'I'm cut up about it because my wife knitted that hat for me for last winter.'

'It doesn't matter, dear,' his wife interrupted him. 'It won't take me long to make you another one.'

'You wouldn't think it was anything special,' Harry told Geraldine, 'just brown with a couple of wide black stripes, but she made it for me. She's making me another one, but that's hardly the point is it? It was a nice scarf too, but at least they were mine. The jacket belonged to my employers and now they're saying I shouldn't have left the jacket there, unprotected. But I was only gone for a moment, and I never expected anyone would nick it. I mean, who would think an old jacket like that would need protecting?'

He told Geraldine he had left his bicycle briefly unattended at around seven in the morning, quite possibly the day before Leslie had been wheeled into the alley. If Harry had told Geraldine the truth, and they could trace who had stolen his jacket, they might find Leslie's killer. Now they knew exactly where and when the jacket had allegedly been stolen, they could start to search through any CCTV footage within sight of the newsagent's.

'Did you often go to that newsagent's?' Geraldine asked.

Harry nodded and glanced at his wife who pursed her lips, leading Geraldine to suspect that Mrs Mellor disapproved of her husband smoking.

While Ariadne was organising collection and downloading of CCTV footage, and gathering a team to study it, Geraldine went to the newsagent's to find out whether anyone working there had noticed the theft. The newsagent told Geraldine that he and his wife both worked in the shop on Thursdays. Neither of them was sure they recognised Harry from his photograph, or even if they recalled a tall man coming in to buy a packet of a popular brand of cigarettes. Geraldine didn't reveal that Harry had told her he went to that same newsagent's every morning to buy cigarettes.

'We are a busy shop,' the man explained apologetically.

He seemed to have sensed her surprise, despite her determination to remain outwardly impassive.

'We sell a lot of cigarettes,' he went on. 'Even if this man came in here every day, I'm not sure I'd recognise him. When we hand over cigarettes and take the money, we hardly look up at customers' faces. Why would we? Our attention is on the money.'

His wife nodded her agreement. 'But what is this about, please? What has he done?'

Harry hadn't returned to the shop to tell them that his jacket had been stolen, but he was visible on the internal CCTV. Entering a few minutes before seven, he had walked straight up to the counter, waited patiently while some unidentifiable customer was served, before purchasing his cigarettes and leaving. The film merely served to confirm that Harry had gone into the newsagent's at the time he had said. It did not help them to find the thief, or even to confirm Harry's story that the jacket had been on the back of his bicycle when he had arrived outside the shop. Other officers were questioning the shopkeepers in the small parade, but no one remembered seeing anyone take anything from the back of a bicycle. No one even recalled seeing a bicycle parked there for a few minutes.

'The thief, if he existed at all, must have been opportunistic,' Eileen said. 'Harry's bicycle was only there for at most five minutes, probably less because we've seen he was only in the newsagent's for under three minutes. So someone passing saw it, grabbed it, and went on their way. It can't have been planned. We don't yet know that the stolen jacket is the same one worn by whoever was wheeling that bin into the alley.'

'It's a bit of a coincidence, a hi-vis jacket like that being stolen a week before we catch sight of the killer – or his accomplice – wearing an identical jacket,' Ian said. 'I'd put money on it being Harry's jacket the killer was wearing.'

'The killer could have spotted the jacket on the back of the bike and been following him, waiting for a chance to take it,' a young constable called Naomi suggested.

'Harry told us he went to that newsagent's regularly so perhaps someone expected him to be there and was waiting for him,' someone else said.

'We don't know the thief is the killer we're looking for,' Eileen corrected them sharply.

'And we don't know the jacket was stolen,' Ian added. 'We only have Harry's word for that. If he killed Leslie, he might have accidentally got her blood on his jacket, or was worried her DNA was on it.'

'So you're saying you think he disposed of the jacket to destroy evidence from the murder?' Eileen asked.

'I'm saying it's possible,' Ian replied.

Although Geraldine was convinced the jacket thief was the killer they were looking for, she doubted Harry was the man they had seen on CCTV wheeling the bin.

'I think Harry's too tall to be the person wheeling the bin into the alley,' she said.

There followed a brief but heated debate about the possible accuracy of an impression gained from a blurred CCTV film.

'It doesn't look like him, but it could be,' Eileen ended the discussion.

Despite all the evidence they had gathered, they were no closer to tracking down the killer.

# 36

By Friday, Geraldine was tempted to try Helena's phone, to arrange to see her. The problem was that, for all she knew, Helena was already being watched by the criminal gang who were trying to influence Geraldine. Without knowing who the criminals were, she had no way of discovering the extent of their powers. It was possible they had access to sophisticated surveillance equipment, and were monitoring Helena's phone. Unlikely as it was, she could not take that risk. She would have to visit Helena again on Saturday, without being observed, and hope her twin had not yet been moved from her home. It was possible she was still living there, and had simply been out when Geraldine had last called on her. As she was wondering what she was going to say to her sister, two unfamiliar officers strode up to her desk, a young woman with strawberry blonde hair and a square-jawed man in his mid-thirties. They were both wearing dark jackets and their expressions were completely blank.

'Detective Sergeant Geraldine Steel?' the man asked, with a curious kind of apologetic authority.

Geraldine nodded. 'Yes. Is there something I can do for you?'

'Police Integrity and Corruption Unit, North Yorkshire,' the blonde woman announced curtly, holding up her identity card.

'DS Steel, we need you to come with us,' the man said.

Geraldine cast a puzzled glance at Ariadne, who was watching in surprise.

'Is there a case I can help you with?' Geraldine asked, reaching to switch off her computer.

'Leave everything,' the woman snapped. 'Please don't touch your computer, and move away from your desk.'

'What on earth is going on?' Ariadne demanded, rising to her feet.

'This is a mistake,' Geraldine stammered.

'I'm going to tell the DCI about this,' Ariadne cried out. 'You can't do this. We're working on a murder investigation and you can't remove her from the team without the permission of our senior officer.'

'Tell Ian what's happening,' Geraldine said. 'Go!'

Startled, Ariadne hurried from the room without another word. Geraldine was led to a waiting car and driven to an interview room in an unfamiliar location, her thoughts whirling. It crossed her mind that these people who had come for her might be members of the criminal gang who were targeting her, and not police officers at all. Although their identity cards looked genuine, they could have been fake. Whoever they were, their visit must be connected to her abduction the previous week.

As well as threatening to destroy Helena's life, her attackers would have ruined Geraldine's career, but she could not imagine how they could have infiltrated the anti-corruption unit. In any case, she had not yet refused to carry out any demands made by the criminals, so they could not yet be sure of her noncompliance. It made no sense that they would want to remove her from her post while there was still a chance she might be of use to them. There was only one possible conclusion. Her escort must be part of the criminal gang, and she had gone with them without even attempting to resist. Within the space of a week, her whole life had started to fall apart, and she could not see how she would be able to straighten matters out. Her only hope was that Ian would realise what had happened, and rescue her.

The truth was she still had not come to any decision about how to react when the criminals asked her to carry out their wishes. To obey the demands of a criminal gang went against everything she believed in. Yet one injection of heroin would undo the painful months of withdrawal and rehabilitation Helena had suffered, on Geraldine's insistence and at her expense. Ian had remonstrated with Geraldine, insisting that she could not hold herself responsible for Helena's problems. But they were sisters, identical twins. Had Geraldine experienced the upbringing Helena had endured, she might easily have become an addict, and if Helena had been brought up in Geraldine's adopted family, she could have been a DCI by now. Besides, Geraldine had promised her dying mother she would take care of Helena. Whatever happened, and whatever the cost, she could not abandon her sister. She had been caught in a trap from which there was no escape.

She was not sure whether to feel relieved or terrified when her two companions drove into a police compound and led her down into a basement. When they set up an interview and started a tape, there could no longer be any doubt that they were indeed members of the anti-corruption unit. The blonde officer placed an evidence bag on the table. Geraldine could see it held a transparent bag containing white powder.

'Have you seen this before?' her interrogator asked.

'No. What is it?'

'I think you know what it is: heroin.'

Geraldine did not answer, but she was filled with sudden dread.

The woman indicated a second evidence bag. 'What can you see now?' She read out the reference number of the evidence bag for the tape.

Geraldine shook her head. Understanding the gravity of her situation, she demanded a solicitor be present, and was locked in a cell while they waited. At last the interview resumed.

'My client has not been charged,' the solicitor intoned solemnly.

He was around sixty, possibly close to retirement, rotund and rosy cheeked. In any other circumstances he might have looked more suited to the role of Father Christmas than that of a criminal lawyer. Geraldine hoped he was astute enough to grasp what was going on.

'What can you see?' the officer repeated.

'Money,' Geraldine answered. 'I can see a bag stuffed full of bank notes.'

'How much money is in there?'

'How should I know? It's not mine. I've never seen it before. But it looks like a lot.'

'How much?'

'I just told you, I have no idea.'

'Twenty thousand pounds. Do you deny it's yours?'

'Of course I deny it's mine. I told you, I've never seen it before. Where would I get hold of that kind of cash? Has there been a withdrawal of twenty thousand pounds from my bank account? And have you found my fingerprints on any of the notes? Where is your evidence to connect me to the contents of these bags?'

'How do you account for Class A drugs and a significant sum of cash being found concealed beneath your mattress in your flat?'

'What?' If Geraldine hadn't been so terrified, she would have laughed. 'That's ridiculous. You can't think I had anything to do with this.'

'They were found in your flat,' the male officer repeated quietly.

'Then they must have been planted there.'

'My client denies all knowledge of these items,' the solicitor said.

'This is an attack on my reputation, carried out by an aggrieved criminal.'

'I don't think so,' the blonde officer replied.

'In the absence of any evidence, what you think is hardly relevant,' the solicitor pointed out.

With Geraldine insisting she knew nothing about the drugs or the money, the anti-corruption officers terminated the interview and she was marched back to a cell, too shocked to remonstrate at her continued incarceration.

# 37

SEATED ON A HARD bunk in a police cell, Geraldine fought against a rising wave of panic as she gazed helplessly around the small room, taking in the familiar sight of a metal toilet, whitewashed walls, high barred window, and hard floor. She had seen the inside of such a cell many times in the past, but only once before from the viewpoint of a suspect, and that too had been as a result of her dealings with her sister. She had observed the faces of many people in custody, and they had evinced outrage, fury, terror, hopelessness, or resignation. Wondering which state of mind her own expression revealed, she did her best to maintain her outward composure while inwardly she gave in to a dark despair. After she had been sitting alone for what felt like hours, she called out to a guard and discovered that barely thirty minutes had elapsed since the door had been slammed on her. Another hour crawled by before a guard thumped on her door and shouted that she had a visitor. For a second, she hoped Ian had come to see her. She did her best to hide her disappointment when her portly solicitor entered the cell.

'You have to believe me,' she pleaded, despising herself for sounding so frantic. 'The drugs and the money that were found in my flat had nothing to do with me. I'm being set up. How else would the anti-corruption unit have known about them? Someone must have tipped them off, which means someone knew what had been stashed under my bed. They wouldn't go searching under my mattress unless they had been told what they would find there. For God's sake, I'm an experienced police officer. Do you think I'd be ignorant enough to hide Class A drugs under my bed?'

The solicitor smiled coldly at her. 'We have to make a case that a jury will believe.'

'Listen, I want to tell you something, but this has to be in confidence. I haven't yet decided what I'm going to do.'

The solicitor listened gravely to her account of what had happened.

'You're telling me you were abducted a week ago?' the solicitor asked her.

'Yes. Last Friday.'

'And you say you were blindfolded and shackled and driven somewhere in a van?'

Geraldine's hopes faltered on hearing the incredulity in his voice. If her own defence counsel refused to accept her account of what had happened, it was unlikely a jury would believe her.

'Why didn't you report the assault straightaway?' her lawyer asked.

He sounded distant, and his beady little eyes seemed to glaze over, as though he had lost all interest in her now that he reckoned he could not win the case. Mentally, he was already walking out of the room, perhaps thinking about where he was going next, or what he was going to eat for dinner that evening. It only remained for him to go through the motions of preparing the defence he was being paid to deliver.

'Yes, yes, I know I should have reported it at once, but they were threatening to kill my sister. I needed time to work out what I was going to do.'

The solicitor shook his head with an expression of distaste on his round features. 'Even if a jury believes your story, your silence isn't going to help your case. As a police officer, you should have known better than to keep this concealed from your colleagues.'

'They were threatening my sister's life,' Geraldine repeated helplessly. 'I had to think about what to do.'

'What to do? Are you suggesting you considered co-operating with these criminals?'

'No, of course not.'

'So if you weren't sure whether to report the incident via the correct channels or not, what other possible alternative could you have been considering? Surely you weren't planning to take the law into your own hands and deal with your assailants yourself?' He was growing impatient with her.

Geraldine hung her head. However she thought about it, her conduct had been inappropriate for a police officer. To anyone judging her case, it must appear that either she was now lying to cover up her involvement with drug dealers or she had concealed a crime, with the intention of taking the law into her own hands.

'Did you tell anyone else about this?' the solicitor asked.

Geraldine hesitated. She was not sure whether Ian would have broken her confidence and revealed what he knew about Helena to anyone else. No one knew he had moved into Geraldine's flat, and the last thing she wanted was to involve him in her troubles.

'I told no one,' she said, aware how easily her lie could be exposed.

'Your defence seems to be that these items were planted in your flat without your knowledge, and you are being framed by a drug dealer as a warning about what will happen to your sister if you refuse to co-operate with him?'

Geraldine nodded, aware that it sounded unlikely.

'Very well. That is the story we will tell.'

'It's not a "story",' she protested, 'it's the truth.'

The solicitor inclined his head. 'So you claim, and we will use what you have told me in putting the case for your defence. Your years of service will be taken into account.' He hesitated. 'It is unfortunate that your record is not blameless. There remains a question mark over the reason for your demotion and relocation to York.'

Geraldine did not answer.

'Can you explain why you were apprehended in a London car park for handing over a large sum of money to a known drug dealer?'

'It was part of a set-up to have him arrested,' she mumbled.

'You don't appear to have been working under cover for the drug squad at the time,' the solicitor pointed out. 'Did you ever, at any time, work for the drug squad?'

Geraldine lowered her head and did not reply.

'No, I thought not. So the question is: why did you take it on yourself to become involved with a drug dealer, without authorisation from a senior officer?'

Geraldine shook her head. It was hard to see how she could account for her actions without involving her sister. With a sigh, she explained how she had taken Helena's place, handing over a large sum of money in the hope that the dealer would leave her sister alone after that.

'I was trying to persuade my sister to go into rehab. That was the deal. I would pay off her debt to her dealer, and she would do her best to kick the habit.'

'Why couldn't she hand the money over herself?'

'That was what I agreed with her, but at the last minute she bottled it and refused to meet him. She wasn't being exactly rational, but she was clearly afraid of him. Since we're more or less identical, I agreed to see him in her place. That was the plan, anyway. Only the DS got a tip-off and I was arrested. It took some doing to extricate me from the situation.'

'I can imagine. Well, first we will need to call your sister to corroborate your story and she'll be subpoenaed to appear in court and give evidence.'

'You can't do that.'

'Geraldine, this may be your only hope if you want to avoid a custodial sentence.'

Geraldine hesitated. She was not sure her sister would agree to appear in court to defend her. Helena might refuse, and simply disappear. Worse, without Geraldine's support she might return to her former destructive habit. All of Geraldine's sacrifice would have been for nothing. Even if she escaped conviction, her career would be over. There would be no coming back from this mess.

# 38

HAVING ESTABLISHED WHERE SHE had been taken, Ian hung back from visiting Geraldine in her cell. Telling himself he wanted to have positive news before speaking to her, he knew that his resistance was partly dictated by his reluctance to see her locked in a cell. Clinging to the hope that she would soon be released, he felt awkward living in her flat while she remained incarcerated, but it seemed defeatist to move out, as though he didn't believe in her imminent release. He did his best to reassure himself that it was simply not possible that anyone would believe her capable of being involved in drug trafficking but as the hours passed and nothing changed, he began to panic. Somehow he had to find a way to prove her innocence without involving her sister, and he had to work alone. If he drew Helena into the case, Geraldine would never forgive him.

His attempt to use CCTV from Geraldine's residential block to prove that intruders had entered her empty flat drew a blank when he discovered that all the cameras in the building had stopped working for half an hour on Friday morning, soon after he had left for work. That had allowed just three hours before the anti-corruption officers had turned up to question Geraldine. Within those three hours, someone had managed to break into Geraldine's apartment, disable her burglar alarm, plant incriminating evidence, and vanish without leaving a trace of their presence. The fact that the CCTV cameras had failed at just that point in time would have been enough to alarm him, but in addition to that, the break-in had been so skilfully executed, he was seriously worried. The people who had broken into Geraldine's flat were not amateurs.

His next line of attack was to speak to his contacts on the drug squad in York. Without being able to reveal Geraldine's relationship with her sister, it was difficult for him to learn much from them. He took one of his colleagues out for a drink and attempted to pump him for information.

'It's just not possible that Geraldine would be in any way involved with drugs,' Ian insisted as he put two pints on the table and took a seat.

'Well, it's feasible. There are dealers capable of doing what you're suggesting,' his colleague said. 'Especially if she's managed to upset one of the bigger players. Some of these vermin are crafty, and they have all sorts of contacts. Breaking into a flat wouldn't be too much of a problem, even a place that's secured with decent locks and alarms and all the rest of it. No, if they're determined to gain access, they'll find a way in. Don't forget, these pariahs have criminals on their payroll used to carrying out all sorts of crimes, and the dealers often have vast amounts of ready cash. I'm talking tens of thousands, maybe more. Fortunately for us, most of them are too stupid, or too off their heads, to escape our attention for long, but as soon as we catch up with one, another one starts, and we never get near the really big players who are behind it all. They don't do their own dirty work.' He took a swig of beer and shook his head. 'There's too much money at stake for us to stamp them out completely. All we can do is try to keep a lid on it, and make their lives as difficult as possible. But the situation is volatile. You did yourself a favour sticking to straightforward murder cases. Drugs is a mug's game, for everyone involved, whichever side of the fence you're on.'

'But what about Geraldine?' Ian said, bringing the

conversation back to her. 'Who might have the skills to do that?'

His colleague frowned. 'What I don't understand is why they would target her. She's never worked in drugs, never had any of the big players arrested. She's not been a thorn in their side in any way that I'm aware of. Why would they have a score to settle with her? It's odd, mate.' He stared at Ian, screwing up his eyes. 'There was a rumour that she'd been working undercover on a drugs raid in London, only something went very wrong, and as a result she was discreetly demoted and shipped out of London. Someone high up protected her from the consequences of some shady dealing that went pear shaped.' He paused. 'Are you sure your colleague is as squeaky clean as you say she is?'

'Positive.'

'What about you? Could someone be getting at you through your girlfriend?'

'No,' Ian replied firmly. 'This has nothing to do with me. And she's not my girlfriend,' he added, a trifle too fiercely. 'She's a colleague. We go back a long way.'

'I get it, you've got a soft spot for her, but either there's something you're not telling me, or there's something she's not telling you. Because *I'm* telling *you*, this whole thing doesn't add up. In fact, there's a rotten stink about it. If I were you, mate, I wouldn't go anywhere near this, or it might all blow up in your face. You wouldn't want rumours circulating about you, would you?'

Ian shrugged miserably, doing his best to conceal his dismay. 'I've told you everything I know. I guess that's that then. But keep your ear to the ground, will you, and let me know if you hear anything.'

His colleague gave him a curious glance and agreed to do what he could. 'But don't expect too much,' he added. 'I'm telling you, this doesn't smell right.'

Ian hated himself for lying, but Geraldine had made him promise not to mention her sister, and if he broke his word and his indiscretion led to Helena's arrest or worse, he knew Geraldine would never forgive him, even if he had acted in her best interests. Somehow she seemed to have a blind spot where her twin was concerned. He suspected she felt guilty for having escaped a terrible upbringing by their birth mother, when Helena had been left behind. The twins' different opportunities in life had not been of Geraldine's making, but it hadn't taken years on the police force to convince Ian that guilt was impervious to reason and logic.

He was unable to ascertain whether or not the CCTV at Geraldine's flat had been deliberately tampered with, more evidence that the criminal gang was highly skilled. They probably bankrolled someone working in security technology. All the same, he took his findings to Eileen who raised her head wearily and nodded at him. Geraldine's arrest had clearly affected her almost as much as Ian.

'This is terrible,' she said straightaway. 'It's unbelievable. What the hell's going on, Ian? Have we really been so blind? Is it possible she was playing a double game all along?'

When Ian told her about the disruption to the CCTV filming at Geraldine's flat, Eileen sighed.

'Don't you see?' he insisted, nearly shouting in his desperation. 'That proves someone entered her flat unlawfully on Monday morning, shortly before the tip-off to the drug squad.'

Eileen shook her head. 'It proves nothing,' she said in a flat voice. 'All we know for certain is that the CCTV stopped working. Anything else is speculation. Hasn't it occurred to you that it's more likely Geraldine disabled it herself, because she was expecting a visitor and didn't want to leave any trace?'

'If she had been in communication with members of a criminal gang, do you really think she would have invited them to visit her at home? Or that she would have left drugs and a bag of cash under her mattress? Only a complete idiot would leave themselves so open to accusation, and whatever else she may be, Geraldine's no idiot. And there's no proof she handled the drugs or the money.'

'I agree, it all sounds very odd. How is she coping?'

'I'm not sure,' he replied. 'I haven't spoken to her since her detention, but I'm on my way to see her now.'

'Tell her...' Eileen hesitated. 'Tell her I'm sorry. I'll do what I can,' she added helplessly.

Before going to see Geraldine, Ian investigated her sister's circumstances. It confirmed what he had already suspected, that Geraldine was covering Helena's rent and paying her a modest allowance. Unable to do anything more to help Geraldine without speaking to her first, he went to see her. She had not yet been moved to a prison but was still being held in a police cell. Given her circumstances, she did not appear too downhearted when Ian first saw her. As he entered the cell she looked up at him and smiled sadly, but she did not break down in tears, as he had been dreading. She even smiled at him when he entered, and told him it was good to see him.

'We're going to get you out of here,' he assured her, sitting down beside her on the bunk and taking her hand in his. 'I'm going to do whatever it takes, even if I have to speak to your sister.'

'I don't want her to know anything about this,' Geraldine replied coldly, pulling her hand out of his grasp. 'This is my problem. It has nothing to do with her.'

'How can you say that? It has everything to do with her,' he protested. 'But don't worry about her. I'll have her moved to a safe house immediately, and make sure she's protected, before we do anything else.'

'No, please, Ian, don't involve Helena any more. She's been

working so hard to rebuild her life – to build a life for herself. It's not fair to put her through all this.'

'What isn't fair is that you have decided to shut her out like this. How is it going to help her if you go to prison?' he demanded, furious with Geraldine for being so stubbornly misguided.

She hesitated. 'It would keep her alive and clean,' she muttered. 'I couldn't bear to see her relapse on my account.'

But Ian had sensed her hesitation. 'She would never have kicked her habit at all if you hadn't persuaded her to go into rehab,' he pointed out. 'You paid for that, didn't you?' She didn't answer. 'And now you pay her rent, don't you?'

'How do you know that?'

'Oh please, Geraldine, give me some credit. I am a detective. It didn't take very much digging to find out what's been going on.'

'So you've been investigating my personal financial affairs behind my back?'

'Never mind all that, what I want to know is who's going to support your sister if you go to prison? Do you imagine she'll go out and get a job and support herself? And even if she does, how long is that going to last? You haven't really thought this through, have you? You've already lost your career over this sister of yours, and now are you really going to sit there and tell me you're prepared to go to prison to keep her out of this?'

Geraldine shook her head. 'I'll figure something out,' she muttered. 'It won't come to that.'

'How are you going to figure anything out? From your prison cell? Don't you think your sister's drug dealer will have you beaten up while you're inside, and possibly killed? I don't think your sister is going to be the first thing on your mind when you're being abused in prison. And if she is, all you'll be thinking is that she'll be on her own again, abandoned by the one person who promised to support her. I'm sorry to be so blunt, Geraldine, but I'm not going to sit by and let that happen. Even if you never speak to me again, I'm going to get you out of this. And we can't do that unless we stop these vile criminals, one way or another. They're not going to let this go, and nor will I.'

'No, please, Ian, don't get involved.'

He stood up and left without another word, no longer able to trust himself to speak to her without cursing her stupidity. As long as Geraldine remained locked in a cell, he was free to take whatever action he deemed appropriate. He had never fully appreciated how blind she was to her sister's shortcomings, but someone had to look after Geraldine's interests if she was too inflexible to do what was necessary to save herself.

# 39

WEEDS FLOURISHED ON EITHER side of the path and poked between uneven paving stones. Ian walked slowly up to the entrance and looked at the names scribbled beside the door. He found the one he wanted easily, but there was no answer when he rang the bell. He wasn't even sure it worked. Impatiently he tried again, but there was no answer. Afraid she had already been removed to a safe house, he rang another bell and this time a scruffy man of around thirty opened the door.

'What do you want?'

'I'm looking for a neighbour of yours.'

When Ian described Helena, the neighbour nodded. 'I know who you mean,' he said. 'She goes out a lot.' With that, he slammed the door.

Ian went for a coffee and returned after an hour to try again. This time the door opened a crack. He barely managed to conceal his shock on seeing a distorted version of Geraldine. Even though he knew they were identical twins, he was taken aback that the woman who had opened the door contrived to look the same yet very different to the woman he knew and loved. Helena's teeth were chipped and nicotine-stained; her sallow complexion scarred with tiny pock marks from childhood illness or acne, and her greasy hair was turning grey. She looked like Geraldine might in thirty years' time if she suffered from serious mental and physical illness and stopped taking care of herself; and where Geraldine's clothes always appeared to be freshly laundered, Helena's threadbare cardigan and faded jeans looked grubby and hung loosely on her gaunt frame.

'What?' she barked, squinting suspiciously at him. 'I don't want no trouble from the likes of you.'

Somehow she seemed to recognise that he was a policeman. It was a relief that she sounded nothing like Geraldine. If she had addressed him in Geraldine's voice, he might have been unable to continue, but her voice was hoarse, as though her vocal chords had been damaged from decades of smoking.

'What?' Helena repeated, scowling.

'I'm a friend of Geraldine's.'

The woman's hostile expression softened. 'What d'you want to talk about? Is she all right? Why's she sent you? Where is she?'

Responding to her evident concern, Ian pressed on. 'Can I come in?'

Helena sniffed and opened the door to admit him. Muttering under her breath, she led him down a dingy hall into a cluttered living room. The curtains were stained with mildew, and a faint stench of mould mingled with the smell of stale beer and cigarettes. A low table was covered in lager cans and empty beer bottles. An open cigarette packet lay on top of a pile of dog-eared glossy magazines. A half-smoked cigarette lay in a crusty saucer. Placing the butt in the corner of her lips, Helena lit it, screwing up her eyes as a thread of smoke wound its way up towards a single light bulb in the centre of the cracked ceiling. Gesturing impatiently to Ian to take a seat on a worn armchair, she sat down opposite him on a settee.

'I knew you was filth.'

'All you need to know is that I'm a friend of your sister.'

'What I need to know is what the fuck you're doing here and what the fuck has happened to Geraldine. Why isn't she here?'

Ian hesitated. 'She's been arrested,' he admitted at last.

'What the fuck?' Ian was startled to see the raddled version of Geraldine displaying her chipped teeth in a grin. 'Don't tell me my holier-than-thou do-gooder goody-goody saint of a sister has screwed up?'

The cigarette end wobbled precariously on her bottom lip as she cackled.

'Your dealer is putting pressure on her to protect him from the law.'

'What you mean? I ain't got no dealer,' Helena snapped, no longer smiling. 'I'm clean.'

'Your ex-dealer,' Ian corrected himself quickly.

Helena shrugged and stubbed her cigarette end out in the dirty saucer.

'Listen, if Geraldine's got herself into some fucked-up mess, she can get herself out of it. It's nothing to do with me. I got worries of my own.'

'How can you say that, after everything she's done for you?'

'But what can I do?' She raised her head and stared at him with Geraldine's eyes. 'She's a police officer for fuck's sake. Whatever it is, she can take care of it. She can take care of herself. She always has done. She'll know what to do.'

'If she could sort this out by herself, do you really think there's any way I'd be here begging for your help?'

'I don't know what you think I can do,' she replied sullenly, lowering her eyes. 'I don't even know who the fuck you are. You say you're filth but that could be a lie.'

'Listen to me. Geraldine's my friend. We're – we're close. I care about her. She's in serious trouble and you're the only person who can help her. You have to tell the truth about what happened when she was arrested. Make a statement confirming she had nothing to do with your drug dealer before that night.'

'Not bloody likely. He would shiv me.' She ran her hand up her body from her belly to her throat.

'He can't hurt you. He's locked up, remember?'

Helena gave a hollow laugh. 'You think that's going to stop him? These people, they got stooges everywhere. Even working in your nick. You want to be careful, before you start poking around in what don't concern you.'

Ian had been given exactly the same advice by his colleague in the drug squad. Somehow on Helena's lips it sounded more sinister.

'Listen,' he said, 'we'll move you to a safe house where no one can ever find you, and give you enough money to start over. I'll personally make sure you want for nothing. It'll be a new life, Helena. You'd like that, wouldn't you? A chance to –'

'I'm fine where I am.'

'Geraldine's your sister. You know she only saw your dealer to save you from him, and she risked her life doing it.'

Helena shrugged. 'There's nothing I can do,' she said, but she looked agitated. 'She's my sister. Do you think I wouldn't help her if I could? Now piss off out of my flat. I got some thinking to do.'

'This isn't just about Geraldine,' Ian persisted. 'What about you? If she goes down, you're going to lose your home, because she'll be out of a job and won't be able to carry on paying your rent. You'll be thrown out on the street and, what's more, she won't want anything to do with you ever again. Is that what you want?'

Helena sighed. 'Fine, fine, all right, all right. What the fuck do you want from me?'

'Sign a statement about what happened, and be prepared to swear to it in court.'

'I can't. They'll kill me.'

'They'll never find you. We'll get you to a safe house and give you a new identity. You can start again with a new life, where no one will ever be able to trace you.'

'They'll find me. They always do. They'll follow Geraldine and she'll lead them to me.'

'Not if you don't see Geraldine again.'

'What?'

'It's the only way to keep you safe.'

There were tears in Helena's eyes as she asked, 'Has Geraldine agreed to this?'

Ian hesitated. Geraldine didn't know he was there. She had forbidden him to involve Helena, but this was the only way to keep Geraldine out of prison, and still protect Helena. Geraldine would never be able to contact Helena again, so she would never discover what he had done.

'Yes,' he lied. 'I'm sorry.' That at least was true.

'So you're saying I won't see her again?'

'You can't risk it. You'll have a new identity, and a new life. I'll make sure of that.'

'What if I say no?'

'Then you'll be visiting Geraldine in prison for years.'

Helena glared at him. 'She won't survive in the nick, even if he doesn't have her dealt with in there. And he will.'

'You can't abandon her to that after all she's done for you.'

Helena broke down in tears. 'I'll do it, I'll do it. I'm probably signing my own death warrant, but I'll do it. Tell Geraldine if there was any other way... tell her I didn't want it to end like this... tell her I wanted us to be sisters.' She was sobbing too hard to carry on.

# 40

HIS WIFE WAS DRIVING him nuts. In the early days of their marriage, they had been happy together, but she had grown increasingly suspicious over the years, until her conjectures had begun to seem quite dangerous. Admittedly, he had not always behaved exactly as he ought, but he was hardly the only man ever to have strayed. Even when other men's transgressions were discovered, their wives often turned a blind eye, rather than upset their whole marriage over a few indiscretions. As if what happened outside the marriage really mattered, in the context of spending year after year together. Yet in his case, his wife seemed determined to control every aspect of his life. The more he tried to break free, the more she wanted to pin him down. Was it any wonder he strayed from time to time? In the end, he had to have some relief.

Thinking about it, his life had never really been any different. He had never felt free. Few men would have reacted in so controlled a way to the cross he had been forced to bear. After his father left, his mother had treated him with sustained and deliberate brutality. The physical abuse had been hard to take, but the emotional cruelty had been far worse. It was a miracle he had managed to remain married for as long as he had, without raising his hand against his wife, given the violence he had been subjected to as a child. But he could not be expected to behave impeccably all the time. He had to break out sometimes. He was only human. No sane person in possession of all the facts would blame him for doing what he did. It wasn't as though he did it very often. Hardly ever, if the truth were told. And if a few women were hurt in the process, that was hardly his fault. They had all known the risk they took in becoming involved with a stranger. If it ended badly for them, well, they should have been more careful in the first place. His conscience was clear.

In the meantime, despite his wife's nagging, she had not succeeded in exposing his transgressions, and she never would. No one would, because he was careful to cover his tracks. It was becoming increasingly difficult with his wife constantly on his case, but even she couldn't watch him all the time. The more risky it became, the less he seemed able to control his urges. So be it. As long as he was careful, everything would be fine.

# 41

LAURA WOKE UP LATE on Saturday. For a moment she lay in bed, in a pleasant half-dream state, luxuriating in the knowledge that she didn't have to get up for school. Catching sight of Zoe sitting on the floor beside the bed, she remembered the situation she was in, and sighed.

'You have to leave,' Laura muttered.

'You said a few more days,' Zoe replied in an urgent whisper. 'I can hardly walk out of here at the weekend, can I? Not while your parents are at home.'

Laura stomped off to the bathroom without answering. She regretted ever having agreed to allow Zoe to stay. To begin with it had seemed like a fun idea, but she had never expected Zoe to hang around, stinking, for nearly two weeks. Angry with herself for allowing the situation to drag on for so long, Laura went downstairs and discovered her mother in the kitchen, busy baking flans and biscuits. A huge birthday cake stood on the worktop, still in its box.

'Don't interrupt me, I'm in the middle of things,' her mother said, flustered and red from her exertion in the kitchen. 'You'll have to get your own breakfast.'

'I always do.'

'Don't give me any of your cheek, and don't make a mess.'

'What are you doing?'

Her mother frowned, without taking her eyes off the biscuits she was shovelling onto a plate.

'Damn,' she muttered as one of the biscuits broke. 'What does it look as if I'm doing? Pass me the cling film, will you? It's in the middle drawer, at the back. If you want to help you can find a plate big enough for the cake. It's still in the box.'

Laura found the cling film.

'I can see you're baking,' she said. 'I'm not blind. What I meant was, why are you doing all that? What's going on?'

'Laura,' her mother replied reprovingly, as she covered the plate of biscuits with cling film. 'Don't tell me you've forgotten.'

'Forgotten what?'

'It's grandma's birthday. Everyone's coming over for tea.'

'Everyone? Everyone's coming here?'

'Yes, Aunty Pauline and Uncle Ben, with Tansy and Jed, and…'

Laura scarcely listened as her mother reeled off the names of all the family, including several cousins around Laura's age. Usually she was pleased to see them, because they had fun hanging out together, but now the prospect of them all descending on the household en masse filled her with dread, because her cousins sometimes went upstairs to her bedroom to play on her computer.

'I hope your bedroom's tidy,' her mother said sharply, registering Laura's expression.

'No, no, it's not,' Laura replied in a panic. 'It's a tip.'

'Well, you'd better go and see to it, and when you've finished you can come back down and help me get the living room ready. We need to move the kitchen chairs into the dining room, and then I thought you might want to put up some decorations. I've brought the Christmas tinsel in from the garage, and there's a packet of birthday balloons that need blowing up.'

Laura did not hear the rest of her mother's list of things

to do, because she was already running upstairs.

'You have to hide,' she panted as soon as she reached her room. 'They're coming!' She closed the door softly behind her.

Zoe jumped to her feet. 'What shall I do?'

'They'll be here this afternoon!'

'This afternoon?' Zoe glanced at the time on her phone. 'Who's coming? It's the weekend. Is it my parents? Where are they now? Don't tell me they've actually noticed I've gone.'

'What are you talking about?'

'My parents. I'm not surprised it's taken them this long to notice I left home. They don't care about me. Believe me, they're not like your parents. So, where are they? Are they here?'

'Your parents? No, no, why would they be coming here? They never come here. No, it's my family, all my aunts and uncles and cousins. They're coming over because it's my grandmother's birthday. You have to get out! You have to leave!'

Zoe sat down on the bed. 'Where am I supposed to go?'

'I don't know. Anywhere. But you can't stay here.'

'Why not? Won't you all be downstairs having tea? I'll be really quiet, and we'll keep the door shut, and no one will know I'm here. I can be quiet, you know I can. Your parents haven't heard me, have they? I suppose there'll be a birthday cake,' she added wistfully.

Laura drew in a deep shuddering breath and explained that her cousins sometimes went in her room to use her computer, and she did not want them to find Zoe hiding there.

'My parents would go apeshit,' she wailed softly so as not to risk being overheard by her mother. 'If they find out you're here, they'll never forgive me. They'll never trust me again. Never.'

'I might have a little more sympathy for your situation if mine wasn't so much worse,' Zoe muttered crossly. 'Where am I supposed to go?'

'Go home.'

'I can't. And what's more, I'm not leaving, so you'll just have to make sure no one comes in here.'

Laura shook her head and hid her face in her hands, mumbling, 'I don't know what to do, I don't know what to do.' After a few moments she raised her head. 'I'm sorry,' she said, 'but you have to leave. Now.'

'Where's your mother? What if she sees me?'

'I'll say – I'll say you just popped round.'

'Just popped round? Doesn't she know I've run away from home? How could I just pop round, when I've been missing for ages? What are you talking about? Listen, you have to stop your cousins from coming in here.'

'I can't.'

'Well if you can't stop your cousins from coming up here, then you have to hide me somewhere.'

Hurriedly they hatched a desperate plan. First of all, they cleared a pile of clothes out of Laura's wardrobe. They lay them in a pile on the bed, and covered them with the duvet. Unless anyone lifted up the bed cover, or realised that the duvet looked unusually high, they were hard to spot.

'I'll leave the door ajar so you can hear if anyone's coming up the stairs,' she told Zoe. 'If I'm with them I'll talk really loudly to make sure you hear us, but it might just be one person coming up to go to the toilet without my realising, so you need to listen out really carefully, all the time. Don't lose focus for a minute.'

Zoe nodded. 'And as soon as I hear anyone coming upstairs, I'll creep into the wardrobe and wait in there.'

Just then they heard Laura's mother calling for her to come and help. Ignoring Zoe's whispered demand to be brought some birthday cake as soon as she could get away, Laura hurried downstairs to help her mother, leaving her bedroom door ajar.

# 42

A BULKY CUSTODY SERGEANT opened the door of Geraldine's cell and nodded at her, his wide face creased in a smile.

'Go on, sling your hook,' he said amiably.

Geraldine stood up and stretched.

'What's going on?'

'It seems they've decided you're not a dangerous criminal after all,' he grinned. 'Bunch of idiots those ACU officers,' he muttered. 'You're free to go,' he added loudly.

'How come?' Geraldine asked in surprise. 'What's happened?'

He entered the cell and pulled the door to behind him, answering in a low voice. 'Don't ask me. I'm just the messenger. But if I were you, I'd make yourself scarce while you can, before they change their minds. There's no predicting what they might do from one day to the next. Throwing their weight around, if you ask me. Nothing else to do but pick on innocent officers just to make a point. It's a job creation scheme for police officers who don't want to deal with real criminals. Go on, get home and clean yourself up. You look terrible.'

Geraldine was taken aback at being so unceremoniously released. As she was driven home, her initial wave of relief was overwhelmed by apprehension. There was something about her release that didn't feel right. Barely an hour later, she was back at the police station, having showered and changed her clothes. Bewildered and not a little scared, she went to report to Eileen. The two anti-corruption officers who had arrested Geraldine were waiting for her in the detective chief inspector's office. The female officer explained that new evidence had come to light which cast serious doubt over her guilt and possible conviction.

'What new evidence?' Geraldine demanded.

'That's confidential.'

'So now I'm a matter of national security?' Geraldine asked, investing her voice with as much sarcasm as she could.

The anti-corruption officer gazed at her impassively. 'No you're not,' she replied. 'You know this has nothing to do with you. The information is confidential.'

'Nothing to do with me?' Geraldine blurted out, momentarily too incensed to control her temper.

Eileen interrupted briskly. 'Never mind about that. Thank you for returning my sergeant to her duties. I expect a full report about this farce to be on my desk first thing tomorrow. I suppose an apology to my sergeant is too much to hope for? And now, if you don't mind, we have real police work to get on with here. You can show yourselves out. And don't come back,' she muttered after the anti-corruption officers had left, giving no assurance that an explanation of Geraldine's arrest would be forthcoming.

'Bunch of incompetents,' Eileen said. 'What a balls-up. They had no reason to come after you. No reason at all. I'm going to lodge an official complaint. Why didn't they unearth their so-called new evidence before putting you through all this? Locking you in a cell overnight. It's outrageous. And they took you away from our investigation. Now, Geraldine, we need to get back to work. We have a briefing due to start.'

Still confused by what had happened, Geraldine followed Eileen to the incident room. She looked around at her colleagues with a curious sense that she had been away for a long time, and was almost surprised that nothing seemed to have changed. She did notice that no one seemed to want to meet her eye, but it wasn't unusual for everyone to be focused on Eileen when she addressed them. There was still nothing definite linking the two murders, and nothing had been found that connected the victims during their lifetimes. Geraldine wasn't sure whether it would be worse to look for one multiple murderer, or two different killers who had each claimed one victim. Either way, they didn't seem to be making much headway with the investigation. Eileen kept repeating that it was 'early days', but it was obvious she was becoming frustrated. Despite a major search, there was no sign of the hi-vis jacket that had allegedly been stolen outside the newsagent's.

Back at her desk, Geraldine had the same sense of unreality. She had only been in custody for twenty-four hours and off work for one day, but once again she had the feeling that she had been away for weeks. After giving Geraldine a few inquisitive glances, Ariadne invited Geraldine to join her in the canteen for a coffee, 'To discuss the case,' she added quickly, as Geraldine began to protest that she had too much work.

'So, I just wanted to warn you that there's been a bit of gossip while you've been away,' Ariadne said, when they were seated with drinks. 'I mean, not everyone has been talking about you, but a few of the constables have been saying you ran off with Andrew.'

'Andrew?'

'Yes, he's been recalled to Northallerton to help with an investigation he's been working on for over a year. The point is, he left at the same time as you disappeared, so the gossip is that your brush with the anti-corruption unit was a fabrication, and the two of you ran off together.'

Geraldine laughed. 'That's ridiculous.'

'Well, I know that. I'm just telling you what I heard.'

Geraldine launched into her rehearsed speech, hinting that her brush with the anti-corruption unit had been a mistake.

'You know how gung-ho they're said to be. Well, it seems their reputation is well deserved.'

Her colleagues would all be thinking there was no smoke without fire, and she must have done something to merit investigation, so she was not unhappy about the story linking her absence to Andrew's departure. When the truth came out, Ariadne would remember that Geraldine had covered it up. But it was quite possible no one would ever find out where she had been taken, and why, because the officers of the anti-corruption unit never spoke about their work to anyone. All Ariadne had seen was Geraldine being marched away, but that could easily have been in the course of an investigation into someone else. The fact that she had returned to work so soon after leaving in the company of the anti-corruption officers surely confirmed that she was of no real interest to them. So she smiled at her colleague, as cheerily as she could, and reassured her that everything was fine.

Ariadne nodded and spent the next ten minutes bringing Geraldine up to speed on the murder investigation.

'I've been liaising between all the teams checking CCTV film from the vicinity of both crime scenes, but we're no further forward.'

Geraldine nodded, silently preoccupied with her own troubles. Only one thing seemed clear; somehow Helena held the key to the recent confused turn of events. She called her repeatedly, but Helena's phone failed to connect. Trying not to panic, Geraldine turned her attention back to her work but it was difficult to focus on the murder investigation.

# 43

ALL WAS QUIET FOR a while, and then Zoe heard the door bell and voices mumbling downstairs in the hall. The bell rang again and there were more muffled voices. After that, she heard only the occasional burst of laughter, or shrill voices raised in excitement, competing to be heard. Zoe couldn't understand why Laura had been so agitated when all she had to do was enjoy a birthday tea party. Zoe was the one who was stuck upstairs, unable even to use the toilet without risking discovery. She was the one who should be feeling put out, not Laura. But it was typical of her friend to panic. Her mother had just invited a few people over for tea, that was all. There was no reason why anyone should discover Zoe hiding in Laura's room. It had been a lot of fuss over nothing, emptying out Laura's wardrobe and hiding clothes under the duvet. Irritated, she threw herself down on the bed and closed her eyes. She hoped Laura wouldn't forget to bring her some cake when all the guests had gone home. It would be typical of her to finish it all off herself and forget to bring any up to Zoe.

When she heard footsteps they sounded as if they were just outside the door, although she had not heard anyone coming up the stairs. She leapt off the bed, dashed to the wardrobe and flung herself inside, pulling the door closed behind her with a thud. She had to keep her head lowered and her arms pressed to her sides in the dark interior of the wardrobe. As she stood there, scarcely daring to breathe, the door of the wardrobe swung slowly open and a shrill voice addressed her.

'Hello. I heard you, but when I came in, there was no one here.'

Zoe twisted her head around and saw a fair-haired boy of about six. He had a freckled face and a snub nose, and he was staring inquisitively at her.

'What are you doing in there? Are you hiding? It's not a very good hiding place,' he added with a shrewd air. 'I found you straightaway, because I'm good at finding people. Some people would have taken a long time to find you, but I found you really quickly. Why don't you want any cake?'

Zoe didn't answer.

'You're not very good at hiding. I saw the wardrobe door closing as I came in,' he went on. 'It was easy to find you. Who are you and why are you hiding in the cupboard?'

'You found me very quickly,' Zoe replied. 'You mustn't tell anyone I'm here or you'll ruin the game.'

The boy reached into his pocket and brought out a squashed sandwich. 'I'm Richard. Who are you? Would you like a sandwich? My mum won't let me have any cake until I've eaten a sandwich, but I put it in my pocket.' He laughed.

Zoe took the sandwich and gobbled it down gratefully.

'Are you going to come out of the cupboard?'

'No,' she replied crossly, 'I told you, I'm hiding. So you'd better not tell anyone you've seen me.'

'OK. I won't.'

The boy turned and scampered away. Zoe wondered whether it was safe to come out of the wardrobe, or if she might be wiser to stay where she was in case anyone else entered the room. It was stuffy in there, and cramped, and she decided it was stupid to spend the whole afternoon in there, when all of Laura's family were downstairs having tea. She had just lain down on the bed again when she heard footsteps on the stairs, accompanied by childish voices raised in excitement and several other voices all talking at once. She jumped off the bed and barely had time to fling open the door of the wardrobe before Laura's mother burst into the room, closely followed by Laura and a rabble of children and adults.

'Good lord!' a woman exclaimed. 'Is this a friend of Laura's? Why isn't she downstairs?'

But Laura's mother had recognised Zoe instantly and was staring at her in astonishment.

'I'm calling the police,' she said, recovering from her shock.

'The police?' the other woman said. 'But she's a child. Don't you know her, Laura?'

'Yes,' Laura muttered. 'I know her.'

'Then it's hardly a matter for the police –'

'Oh, do be quiet, Betty,' Laura's mother interrupted the woman crossly. 'You can't come into my house and behave as though you're in charge. I know what I'm doing. Now take all the children back downstairs, and I'll deal with this. Go on, go.'

Having shooed everyone but Laura out of the room, she turned to her daughter.

'Now, Laura, I'd like you to explain. But first I'm calling your parents, Zoe. You must realise they've been going out of their minds with worry, and the police have been searching everywhere for you. There is no excuse for wasting so much of their time. Where have you been?'

Zoe lowered her eyes and tried to look contrite. 'Here,' she mumbled. 'I've been here.'

Laura's mother glared at Zoe. 'You've caused a lot of people a lot of trouble with your nonsense.'

Zoe drew herself up to her full height. 'It's not nonsense,' she replied haughtily. 'I've run away from home. And if you'd just let me get past you, I'll leave your house and you'll never see me again.'

'As for you,' Laura's mother went on, ignoring Zoe's protest and turning her attention back to Laura, 'I expected better from you. I'm not responsible for Zoe's childish running around, but I will be dealing with you very severely. Let's hope we're not all in trouble with the police for harbouring a runaway.'

'The police can't arrest Laura,' Zoe began, 'she's too young –'

'Be quiet,' Laura's mother snapped. 'You've caused enough trouble already. Now, sit down on the bed, both of you, and don't say a word.' She tapped the keys on her phone. 'Police please. I'd like to report that we've found the missing girl, Zoe Watts. Yes, that's Zoe Watts, reported missing ten days ago. She's here, in my house and it seems she's been here all along.'

Zoe glared helplessly at her friend while Laura's mother gave the police her name and address. 'That snotty nosed kid, Richard, betrayed us,' she muttered.

Laura shut her eyes and began to cry.

'I don't know what you're crying for,' Zoe hissed. 'I'm the one who's been caught. The police are probably going to lock me up now, because I'm not going home.'

# 44

ZOE AND LAURA WENT downstairs. Once Laura's mother recovered from her vexation, she wasn't angry with Zoe at all. Smiling, she sat her down and gave her a thick slice of cake, and insisted she eat it.

'You look half starved,' she said. 'How on earth did you manage to survive, hidden up there all this time?'

'I took food up to her,' Laura answered for Zoe, whose mouth was crammed with cake. 'I've been looking after her. Zoe's my friend, and her parents are horrible to her.' She burst into tears.

Laura's parents were very kind to Zoe, assuring her that she wasn't in trouble.

'There's no need to feel frightened,' Laura's mother said gently.

Zoe was about to point out that she wasn't afraid of anything, but Laura silenced her with a warning frown and a slight shake of her head.

'You did what you felt you needed to do, both of you,' Laura's father said. 'No one can criticise you for that.'

'But next time you have a difficult situation to deal with, speak to us, Laura. You shouldn't have tried to deal with this on your own,' her mother added seriously. 'And the same goes for you, Zoe.'

It wasn't clear if she was telling Zoe she ought to speak to them or to her own parents, but before they could continue the awkward conversation there was a knock at the door. Two police officers had arrived to collect Zoe. One of the two policewomen spoke quietly to Laura's parents, while the other one sat down next to Zoe and talked to her.

'Hello Zoe. My name is Susan and I'm here to make sure you have everything you need. We know you've had a spot of trouble at home, and we're here to help you get this sorted out, and make sure you're happy with what happens next.'

'Thank God you're here,' Zoe heard Laura's mother say. 'I had no idea she was here. She's been hiding upstairs for nearly two weeks! I called you the moment we discovered her hiding up in Laura's room. Please, she can't stay here. I don't know what to do with her. And her poor parents must be going out of their minds with worry. If I'd known, I'd have got in touch with them immediately.'

'I'm not going home,' Zoe cried out, springing to her feet. 'If you take me back there, I'll run away again. I don't want to go back.'

The policewomen were surprisingly nice about it, and she heard them reassuring Laura's mother that they would only need a statement from her about what had happened, and there would be no further action taken.

'I had no idea,' Laura's mother kept repeating, pale and agitated. 'This was all my daughter's doing, and she's barely thirteen. She didn't know what she was doing.'

'I didn't want her staying here for so long,' Laura muttered. 'I kept telling her to go home but she wouldn't.'

At last they left the house, and Zoe sat in the back of the police car, twisting her knitted hat in her lap and staring miserably out of the window. It should have been exciting driving away in a police car, but she was too worried about the future to enjoy the ride.

'What will happen to me now?' she asked.

'We're taking you to the police station so that we can ask you a few questions,' the policewoman who was sitting in the back of the car with her explained.

'Are you going to arrest me?'

'Of course not. You haven't committed any crime. We just want to find out what you want to happen, and whether you can be reconciled with your parents. Then you can go home.'

'What if I don't want to go home to my parents' house?'

The policewoman smiled gently at her. 'That's what we want to discuss with you. Don't worry. No one's going to force you to do anything you don't want to do. We just need to work out what's the best way forward for you.'

It all sounded very reasonable, and when they arrived at the police station, Zoe was offered tea or orange juice and chocolate biscuits which the policewoman told her were reserved for special visitors.

'What's so special about me?' Zoe asked.

She wondered why everyone was being so nice to her.

The policewoman smiled. 'You haven't broken the law, which makes you our guest.'

'Does that mean I can go whenever I want?'

The woman didn't answer her question, telling her instead that they just wanted to talk to her. After that, Zoe was questioned by another woman, this one a social worker, but the nice policewoman stayed with her, at her request. It was tiring and after a while it grew boring. They kept on asking her why she had run away from home.

'I hate my parents,' was all she would say.

At last the woman left the room and returned with Zoe's parents. Her mother burst into tears and flung her arms around Zoe who promptly began to cry too, and her father put his arms around them both, with tears in his eyes. Zoe sobbed, unable to recall exactly what had prompted her to leave home, but then she remembered how her parents argued all the time, and she drew back from them and wiped her eyes.

'I'll come home,' she said, 'but only if you promise to stop shouting at each other all the time.'

Out of the corner of her eye, she saw the policewoman and the social worker exchange a glance, and wondered if she should have been more discreet about the arguments at home. Turning to her parents, she saw that far from being angry with her, they looked frightened. An unexpected sense of strength coursed through her, because in some way she understood that she could exert power over her parents. From now on, they would have to behave nicely or she would run away again, only next time she would go straight to the police and tell them everything. With a sigh, she agreed to go home with them. Having been keen to bring this about, the social worker seemed to change her tune. Now she looked concerned.

'Are you sure that's what you want, Zoe?' she asked. 'You can stay here for a while and think about it. There's no pressure to decide straightaway.' She leaned forward and lowered her voice. 'Would you like your parents to leave the room so we can talk?'

But Zoe was tired, and she was fed up with the interrogation. She wanted to go home, have supper, and watch television, not sit endlessly answering stupid questions.

'I want to go home,' she said. 'I'm sure. That's what I want.'

As her parents turned to leave, the nice policewoman held out the knitted hat Zoe had been wearing. 'Here,' she said, 'this is yours.'

Zoe shook her head. 'I don't want it,' she replied. 'You can keep it.' And she hurried out of the room after her parents.

# 45

THERE WAS A GENERAL mood of relief at the team meeting once it was announced that Zoe had been found and reunited with her parents. At least that potential tragedy had ended well, and they all hoped that Zoe would settle down from now on. It wasn't altogether clear why she had left home in the first place, but given her readiness to return, the consensus was that she had probably run off in a teenage strop and been too bloody-minded to swallow her pride and go back.

'She probably had some tests at school,' one of the older constables suggested.

'Is that what you used to do then? Run away from school when you had a test? Afraid of being put in the dunce's corner?' one of his colleagues teased him.

The officers who had been occupied searching for Zoe were now free to join the team working on the double murder investigation, although a small increase in man power wasn't likely to move them forward when what they really wanted was a new lead. Returning to their desks, Geraldine and Ariadne discussed Harry's reaction to losing his jacket.

'Isn't it a bit odd that he didn't go back into the shop and ask if they had seen anything, or even whether it had any CCTV camera covering the street outside?' Ariadne asked. 'He seems to have just gone off without any attempt to find out if anyone had noticed someone near his bike.'

'I don't know if he noticed it had gone until he arrived at work and went to put it on,' Geraldine replied.

221

'So it could have fallen off anywhere,' Ariadne replied. 'It wasn't necessarily stolen. Someone could have found it.'

'It's possible,' Geraldine agreed. 'The VIIDO team has checked, and it's not clear if the jacket was on the back of the bike before Harry reached the shop, and not there when he left. But if it did fall off, it would have been somewhere close to the newsagent's, and there's no sign of it. A team went out looking and asking around and couldn't find any sign of it anywhere else.'

The unreality continued for Geraldine, when it turned out that there had been little development in the case in the twenty-four hours since her arrest. Somehow, sitting in a cell for what had felt like weeks, she had expected at least the hi-vis jacket to have been found while she was away, if not the murderer himself. With a sigh she settled down to read all the reports that had been logged over the past twenty-four hours, but nothing helpful had been uncovered. When she went home at the end of the day, all she wanted was to be alone to think about what had happened to her, but Ian was there, sitting in the living room, waiting for her.

'Geraldine, are you angry with me?' he asked, seeing the expression on her face when she caught sight of him. 'I was hoping, now you're out, that we could go back to how we were before everything went wrong.'

'You haven't told me how you got me out.'

Her ferocity seemed to take him aback. 'What?'

'Don't play the innocent with me, Ian. I was behind bars facing a serious drugs charge and then, all at once, I was released without a word of explanation. It was you, wasn't it? Wasn't it?'

She was nearly shouting with a rage she had been suppressing for days.

Ian hesitated. 'Shall we go and sit down and discuss this sensibly?'

'How can there possibly be a sensible explanation for what you did?' she snapped.

Ian glared back. 'What makes you assume your release had anything to do with me? Think about it, they held you for twenty-four hours without any evidence to convict you and at the end of it they let you go because they still couldn't prove you were guilty.'

'They found all the "evidence" they needed in my flat.'

'But they had no proof you put it there. They must have believed your story about the criminal gang who were angry because they failed to blackmail you. Geraldine, you've done nothing wrong and they were misled into accusing you, but they were only doing their job. Now, let's put this behind us and get back to our life together.'

Geraldine wanted to fall into Ian's arms and agree with everything he said, but the suspicion nagged at her that he had done some kind of deal to free her. He could have forced Helena to give a statement to the anti-corruption unit, proving Geraldine had only been in contact with the drug dealer in London to save Helena herself from having to see him. If that was the case, he might have put Helena's life in danger.

'I'll listen to you once I've had a chance to speak to Helena,' she said. 'Until then, I'd like you to go back to your own flat. It'll just be for tonight. I'll go and see her tomorrow, and arrange to move her somewhere she won't be found.'

Ian gave her a look of such desperation she was afraid her suspicion was right. He had betrayed her and gone to see Helena.

'I don't understand what's wrong,' he said. 'Don't you trust me?'

'I just want to see that my sister's all right.'

'Why wouldn't she be?'

'Just for tonight, Ian. Please, go. I really want to be alone.'

# 46

GERALDINE CAUGHT THE FIRST train to London the next morning, arriving at King's Cross at ten. From there it was under an hour on the tube to Helena's flat in Hackney. Filled with dread, she walked to the block where Helena was living and rang the bell. There was no answer. She rang again and this time she heard footsteps approaching. The door opened and Geraldine's relief evaporated. A stranger was staring at her, a tall skinny woman with greying hair and a sallow complexion.

'What do you want?' the woman asked, puffing on a cigarette as she spoke.

'Where's Helena?'

'Who the fuck's Helena?'

'Helena Blake. She lives here.'

Geraldine turned to the card scrawled beside the bell and was dismayed to see that Helena's name had been removed.

'Nah.' The woman dragged on her cigarette. 'This is my place. I haven't put my name up yet, but I'm not Helena.'

'I know you're not Helena,' Geraldine snapped, fear making her irate. 'How long have you lived here?'

'I just moved in today. About an hour ago as it happens. So whoever you're looking for, you just missed her.' She lowered her voice. 'The place is a shit house. Still,' she went on more cheerfully, 'beggars can't be choosers. I've lived in worse, though I'm sure I can't remember when.'

'Do you know where the previous resident has gone?'

'Back to the gutter she crawled out of, I expect. You have to see the state of this place to believe it.'

'Did she leave any forwarding address?' Geraldine asked desperately, although she knew there wouldn't be one.

If Helena had moved out without telling Geraldine, it could only be for one of two reasons. Either she needed to disappear without trace because her former associates had been threatening to kill her, or else she had been relocated in secret by the police.

'Did she leave any message for her sister? For Geraldine?'

She knew any such hope was vain. If Helena had needed to vanish in a hurry, she wouldn't have left any messages.

'Nah. I never set eyes on her.'

The door closed abruptly. After searching for her birth mother for years, Geraldine was not sure she had the energy to start all over again. In any case, when she had been looking for her mother, she had known the name of the woman she had wanted to trace and had found her address fairly easily. Only her own reluctance to meet the mother who had abandoned her at birth had kept her from going to see her straightaway. This was different. She had not discovered the existence of her twin sister until she had finally contacted her birth mother. Since their first meeting, the sisters' relationship, rocky at first, had slowly developed as Helena came to trust Geraldine. Now they knew one another and Geraldine was distraught at the prospect of losing contact with the twin she had found as an adult. But she did not know the name Helena was now using. Without that, it was going to be difficult to know where to begin looking for her. She tried repeatedly to reach Helena on her phone, and was informed that the line was unavailable every time. Her twin seemed to have vanished without trace.

Geraldine had not yet confessed to her adoptive sister, Celia, that she had discovered a twin sister who had been separated from her at birth. When Geraldine had first heard about Helena, Celia had been pregnant, and Geraldine had decided not to upset her by introducing her to Helena. The longer Geraldine had kept silent, the more difficult it had been to disclose the secret she had been keeping. Now, it seemed she might never need to tell Celia about Helena at all. Helena had vanished from Geraldine's life, as though she had never existed.

Thinking over the situation on her way back to King's Cross, Geraldine concluded that it was unlikely that Helena would have been able to organise that without help. She had barely been able to cope with simple everyday survival when Geraldine was supporting her. Alone, she would be completely at sea in the world, and disappearing so completely required both money and expertise. Either her drug dealer associates had taken Helena somewhere very private and disposed of her, or else someone had assisted her in ensuring she could not be traced. In return for immunity and a new identity, Helena might have been persuaded to give a statement that Geraldine had played no part in the drug deal that had ended in her arrest in London.

Geraldine had a shrewd idea who might have arranged that. If Ian was behind Helena's disappearance, he would have succeeded in rescuing Geraldine from prison, but only at a great cost to her personally.

Furious with Ian for interfering, she was impatient to confront him about Helena's disappearance as soon as she could do so face to face. Disappointed as well as infuriated, she took the train back to York. Ian had no right to relocate her sister on his own initiative without first consulting her. She would find out from him where Helena had gone, and somehow find a way to make contact with her without compromising her safety. There was always a way. But as the train sped north, she wondered with a sickening feeling whether she would ever see her twin sister again. They had only just begun to communicate without Helena's anger and Geraldine's guilt undermining their attempts to understand each other. The thought that this could be the end of their embryonic relationship was devastating.

It made no difference that there was no logical reason for Geraldine to feel any guilt. It was hardly her fault that she had been given up for adoption at birth, to be raised in a prosperous and caring family, leaving Helena struggling to survive with their dysfunctional mother. Now, just as they were beginning to establish friendly relations, Helena had been snatched away. Geraldine closed her eyes and tried to rest, but it was impossible. Helena's troubled features haunted her mind and she wondered whether they had really lost each other again, this time for good.

She did not call Ian. The conversation they needed to have was too important to conduct on the phone. She wanted to see his expression when she accused him of arranging Helena's disappearance. If he lied about it, Geraldine would know. Even her feelings for Ian came second to her need to see her sister. She and Helena were identical twins. By an accident of birth they were closer than either of them could ever be with anyone else, and they had only relatively recently met for the first time. If Ian had indeed had a hand in coming between them, Geraldine was afraid she would never be able to forgive him for his unwanted intervention. He must be aware of the strength of her feelings for Helena, but he had simply ignored her wishes and gone ahead with his plans to extract her from her cell. She wondered angrily if he expected her to be grateful to him. If he *was* involved in Helena's disappearance, as she suspected, he would probably lie about it. If that was the case, how could she ever trust him again?

Her anger against him had barely begun to form yet, but she did her best to keep it under control until she had confirmed what had happened. There was still a possibility that Helena had left of her own accord, and Ian knew nothing about it. Deep down she knew that wasn't the case and that it was possible to hate someone she loved. However keen she was to exonerate Ian, she knew he was responsible for Helena's disappearance.

In the meantime, there was a murderer to pursue, perhaps even two if Angie and Leslie had been attacked by different killers. Geraldine's problems would have to wait. However complicated and unsatisfactory her personal life might be, from now on she had to ignore anything that continually threatened to distract her from her job. Helena had disappeared in a miasma of uncertainty. The two bodies Geraldine had viewed at the mortuary were both horribly real. Their killers had to be found, at whatever personal cost to the members of the investigating team. Geraldine had no choice. She had to walk away from searching for her sister.

# 47

ON MONDAY MORNING, GERALDINE did her best to put Helena and Ian out of her mind and focus on the case. A team had been set up to question Harry's colleagues at work, while other officers approached his neighbours to find out whether they had seen anything suspicious. So far every avenue had drawn a blank and they were casting around, waiting for new leads. There was nothing urgent for Geraldine to do. She knew murder investigations could take time, and there was no point in trying to rush things, but it was difficult for her to forget about her own troubles while there was nothing pressing to occupy her mind. The detective chief inspector was keen to find out more about Harry.

'What was your impression of him, Geraldine?'

Geraldine hesitated. 'I can't imagine he killed two women,' she said.

'Based on what?' Eileen asked.

'I can't give you anything specific. You asked me for my impression of him,' Geraldine reminded her. 'That's my impression.'

'Let's look into him, search his house,' Eileen said. 'If he did do it, there could well be some trace of the victims there.'

In the absence of any evidence pointing to Harry being guilty, under normal circumstances a request for a search warrant would have been refused. Given that this was a double murder investigation, Eileen obtained an emergency warrant and a search team was sent to Harry's house to hunt for proof of his guilt. Keen to take her mind off her personal problems, Geraldine went along to observe and assist. It was beginning to drizzle as she arrived, and she hurried along the street to the house, pulling her collar up against the chill wind. She was interested to see how Harry reacted to this intrusion into his home. He and his wife were standing outside the house, remonstrating with a uniformed officer.

'But you can't lock us out of our own house,' Harry's wife was protesting.

Harry stood at her side, scowling, his hands thrust in the pockets of his trousers. Several neighbours were watching from their own doorways.

'We're living in a police state, mate,' one of them called out as Geraldine arrived. 'This is just the beginning.'

'What's going on?' Mrs Mellor asked, catching sight of Geraldine and darting forward to grab her by the arm. 'This isn't on. My Harry hasn't done anything. All he did was get his jacket stolen. He didn't mean to leave it unattended. It was only for a moment. It's not fair to persecute us like this, in front of all our neighbours.'

Geraldine asked the Mellors quietly if they would prefer to go in the house.

'As long as you leave us alone to get on with our search,' she said, 'you don't have to wait out here.'

She led them to the front door and spoke to the constable standing there.

'Mike, this isn't a crime scene.'

'Not yet,' the constable replied stolidly.

'There's no reason why these people should be kept waiting outside in the rain,' Geraldine continued. 'They've undertaken not to interfere with the search, and I'll keep an eye on them.'

The constable nodded and stood aside to allow Geraldine to lead Harry and his wife back into their house. They all sat in the front room, and Geraldine explained that the search would not take long.

'It will be over soon,' she assured them. 'And then you can return to normal. I'm sorry for the disruption, but we're investigating a serious crime and we have to leave no stone unturned. You are not the only people whose property is currently being searched,' she added untruthfully.

If she could gain the Mellors' trust, there was a chance they might relax with her and become more talkative, and she suspected Harry knew more about his missing jacket than he had yet admitted. His wife was still flushed with indignation, while Harry sat, fidgeting wretchedly with the buttons on his shirt, staring at the floor. He looked ungainly, slouched on the sofa beside his dainty wife.

'Harry, is there something you haven't told us?' she asked gently. 'If there is, then now's the time to come clean. The longer you leave it the worse it will be.'

'What are you talking about?' Harry's wife replied for him quickly. 'My Harry isn't a liar. Why is he being treated like a criminal? You've all made up your minds he's guilty before he's even been tried. And what's he supposed to have done, anyway? Surely all these police can't really be here about one old jacket? It wasn't even new. Haven't you got more serious crimes to worry about? You're just persecuting him because he's an easy target. He won't be bullied into confessing to something he didn't do.' She turned to her husband and patted his hand. 'Don't worry, whatever story they come up with, they won't have any evidence.'

'Harry's not on trial,' Geraldine replied gently. 'We're investigating a double murder and we think Harry might be able to help us.'

Harry and his wife both looked shocked, but the latter continued with her tirade, more vigorously than ever. 'Well I know my husband, and he had nothing to do with any

231

murders, or any other crime for that matter. He can't help you, so you can leave him alone.'

Geraldine turned to the wretched man sitting at his wife's side. 'Harry,' she said gently. 'What are you not telling us about your missing jacket?'

Harry hung his head, and his large hands hung loosely between his legs. He heaved a deep sigh.

'It wasn't on my bike,' he mumbled.

'What are you saying?' his wife interrupted him. 'Harry, don't say another word. Whatever you say, they'll twist it, and if you admit you lied once, they'll distrust everything you say and you won't be able to defend yourself.'

'We only want the truth,' Geraldine said. 'Harry, if you're innocent of any serious crime, as I'm sure you are, then you have nothing to be afraid of. Just tell me what happened to your jacket. It could be really important for us to know when and where it was taken. We believe whoever took your jacket could be involved in a very serious crime.'

'Harry, don't say another word,' Mrs Mellor interposed.

He glanced miserably at his wife and shook his head. 'I have to tell them what happened. God help me, I have to tell the truth. I can't bear this, Peggy. It's driving me crazy. You heard the woman. They're investigating a murder. How can I keep quiet?'

Mrs Mellor turned to Geraldine in desperation. 'My Harry's not a liar,' she said. 'He hasn't done anything wrong. If he didn't tell it exactly right, it's only because he was frightened.'

'I understand. Now, Harry, suppose we go from the beginning. What really happened to your jacket?'

'It was like this,' he replied. 'That jacket wasn't on my bike. I never had it there when I went out that morning but I said it was on my bike because I wanted them to think it had been stolen.'

'Who is "them"?' Geraldine asked. 'It would help if you

could be as clear as possible with what you're telling me. Who did you want to believe it was stolen?'

'My manager at work. I thought if I told them it had been stolen they wouldn't think it was my fault.'

'So what did happen to it?' Geraldine asked.

It was like pulling teeth, extracting any information from Harry.

He sighed. 'I lost it.'

'Where did you last have it?'

Harry shrugged.

'Please, Harry, it's very important you tell me where you last had it.'

She wondered whether to explain that once the police knew where Harry had left his jacket, they might be able to find an image of whoever had taken it, and actually see an image of the killer. She could scarcely conceal her excitement, even though she knew it was probably misplaced. The chances of the killer being caught on film, seizing the jacket and gazing straight at the camera to give a clear and identifiable image of his face, were so remote as to be virtually impossible.

Her hopes were further dashed when Harry said he didn't know.

'How can you not know?' she asked, doing her best to control her impatience.

'It was on the back of my bike, like I told you, and it fell off somewhere, I don't know where. It must have happened as I was cycling along. I mean, it was there when I left home, and I'm pretty sure it was still there when I stopped at the newsagent's. I mean, I would have noticed if it wasn't there when I got back on my bike. But when I got to work, it had gone. It must have fallen off. Trouble is, I didn't dare tell the boss I'd lost it, so I said it had been stolen. What else was I supposed to do? Not that it helped me much,' he added morosely.

Assuming Harry's convoluted account was accurate, the jacket had fallen off the back of his bike somewhere between the newsagent's and the refuse collection depot where he worked, a distance of about three miles.

# 48

As soon as Geraldine arrived back at the police station, and before she had a chance to speak to Eileen about Harry's revised story, the waitress from Angie's café rang her. Even talking face to face Klara was difficult to understand, and it was almost impossible to hold a conversation with her over the phone. All Geraldine could make out was that she was saying something about her murdered colleague.

'Are you talking about Angie?' Geraldine asked.

'Angie, Angie, yes I talk Angie,' Klara replied, sounding almost hysterical as she repeated her garbled message.

'Where are you?' Geraldine asked. 'Can you come and see me at the police station, or shall I come to you?'

As she put the question, she hoped that Klara would agree to come to the police station because she was not sure she would be able to understand her if Klara gave an address. So she was initially relieved when Klara said she would come and speak to her at the police station.

Having concluded the conversation, Geraldine went to find Eileen so they could discuss Harry's revised statement. After listening to Geraldine's update, Eileen immediately authorised her to set up a check on any surveillance cameras they could track down in the streets between the newsagent's where Harry had last seen his jacket, and his place of work. The detective chief inspector gave no obvious outward sign that she shared Geraldine's cautious excitement, but her eyes brightened. From having no new leads at all, suddenly there

235

seemed to be two more possible lines of enquiry. Eileen gave Geraldine an approving nod before she turned her attention back to her screen, and Geraldine went to arrange the surveillance check.

'We seem to spend an awful lot of time arranging teams of visual identification image detection officers to watch hours and hours of CCTV footage,' Ariadne grumbled when Geraldine brought her up to speed. 'I wouldn't mind, but they always turn out to be a waste of time.'

'I don't know how they do it,' Geraldine replied. 'It would drive me nuts if I had to spend all day just staring at a film captured on a security camera. Give me real people to question any day.'

'I think I'd struggle to stay awake if I had to do what they do. It can be hours before anything happens. Most of the time it's like watching paint dry.'

'Well, it's just as well some people are happy to do it,' Geraldine said.

After that she busied herself recording Harry's statement and writing up her decision log while she waited for Klara. After an hour, she began to suspect that Klara was not going to turn up. She rang her mobile, but there was no answer. Kicking herself for not driving straight to wherever Klara had called from, she phoned her again, but still Klara did not pick up.

'Is something wrong?' Ariadne asked.

'I think I've just lost a potential witness,' Geraldine said. 'Klara, the waitress who worked with Angie, called me and wanted to talk. I asked her to come here because I really struggle to understand her over the phone. But she's not turned up.'

As she was speaking, the message came that a woman had arrived asking to speak to Geraldine. She leapt to her feet and heard Ariadne wish her luck as she hurried from the room.

Geraldine was too old and experienced a detective to allow herself to hold out much hope that this meeting might actually lead to an arrest, but she almost ran along the corridor in her eagerness to hear what Klara had to say.

'I sorry, I sorry,' Klara began, and burst into tears. 'I not know what happens,' she said when she had controlled her sobbing enough to speak. 'I not know is murder. I think she fall in river and drown. I think is accident. I see in paper is murder. My husband show me. "This is girl you work with," he says to me. Yes, Angie, it is murder.' Covering her face with a large white handkerchief, she broke down in tears again. 'Is horrible. I know her. Who kill her? I must know, please. And he must be with punishment.'

Gently Geraldine explained that the police were working hard to find out who had committed this terrible atrocity.

'But you know who kill her? You know?' Klara insisted.

'I'm afraid not. We will find out, but we don't know yet. Now, if there's anything you can tell us, anything at all, that might help us to find the killer, please tell me.'

'Yes, yes, I know, I know,' Klara replied, an earnest expression on her childlike face. 'I know.'

Geraldine waited. Klara did not say anything else, but sat, sniffling quietly into her handkerchief.

'What do you want to tell me?' Geraldine prompted her after a moment. 'Why did you come here?'

Klara nodded her head. 'Bad man,' she said at last, making a visible effort to pull herself together. 'Bad man kill her.'

Geraldine stifled a sigh. If that was all Klara had to say, it was hardly going to advance the investigation.

'Yes,' she said, as calmly as she could, 'I think we can all agree that the man who killed Angie was a bad man. A very, very bad man.'

'He come to café many days,' Klara went on. 'Every day he ask where is she. He come to café and he look for Angie.'

Geraldine snapped to attention, her weariness gone in an instant.

'A man was looking for Angie?' she asked, when Klara didn't continue.

Klara nodded. 'Many times.'

'Who was? Who was looking for Angie?' she asked, no longer making any attempt to hide her impatience.

'Bad man,' Klara repeated. 'He come in café. He come to kill her.'

'What makes you think this customer killed Angie?'

'I not think. I know. I tell my husband. He say "Go to police, Klara, you must go to police". So I here.'

'And this man, the one you say killed Angie, who was he?'

'I tell you, he come in café. He come many times to see Angie and she tell me he give her creeps. She tell me she not want serve this man at table. He bad man. Yes, she afraid him. She see him, she run in back.'

'Did you ever see this man who was frightening her?'

'Yes, I tell you, he come many time in café. He say he like Angie very much. So she afraid. She say he want give her money. When he in café she go in kitchen. She run. She not come out.' She smiled sadly at the memory. 'She not come out when he there. He not see her. This important to her. So I help. I give man tea. Angie not go to him, never. I help her. My poor friend, Angie.'

Klara's description of the man in the café was not very helpful, but by working with her, an e-fit officer managed to produce an image that satisfied her.

'Yes,' she said, nodding at the face staring back at her from the screen, 'He him. He him.'

Armed with the e-fit image, Geraldine returned to the café to quiz the manager there about Klara's 'bad man'. It wasn't much to go on, but it was something. The manager gazed at the picture of a bald middle-aged man with a sharp nose, piercing dark eyes, and fleshy jowls.

'Do you recognise this man?'

The manager hesitated. 'Possibly. It's difficult to be certain from a sketch like this.'

'If it is the man you think it might be, what can you tell me about him?'

'Only that he's been in here a few times,' the manager replied uncertainly. 'I can't be sure though, and I can't tell you anything about him, other than that he's an occasional customer here. I can't say when he was last here.' He looked up at Geraldine with a stricken expression. 'I'm sorry I can't be of more help to you. Is this about Angie?'

'We're not sure,' Geraldine replied. 'But we'd like to talk to him.' She handed the man her card. 'If he comes in here again, please will you call me urgently? Never mind what else you might be doing, please call me the minute you see him.'

He nodded, and she left, hoping she would hear from him before long. A middle-aged man stalking Angie and offering her money had to be a likely suspect. Eileen smiled grimly when Geraldine told her everything the manager of the café had said.

'If he didn't exactly corroborate what Klara told me, at least he didn't contradict it. And Klara seemed convinced that this customer was stalking Angie and that she was frightened of him.'

'Well done,' Eileen said, her square face set in a determined expression. 'Let's hope we get somewhere with this new lead.'

Geraldine had been working with Eileen for long enough to know that she was feeling positive about the outcome of the investigation. She hoped the detective chief inspector's optimism was justified, and Klara's 'bad man' would not turn out to be another dead end.

# 49

THE PRIORITY NOW WAS to hunt for the suspect Klara had brought to their attention. They had only her vague description, and her word that the e-fit image of her 'bad man' was accurate. In charge of organising the search, Ian came to Geraldine to ask whether Klara had mentioned anything else that might possibly help them in their search. Geraldine had to restrain herself from snapping at him that if there had been anything else, she would have reported it already.

'Yes, Ian,' she replied instead, with exaggerated meekness. 'Thank you for that helpful suggestion. As if we don't all know what to do.'

Immediately she regretted her muttered outburst. Ian looked puzzled, and she looked away, waiting for him to remind her that he was her senior officer and she should address him with respect. But he turned on his heel without a word and stalked away. At the desk opposite Geraldine's, Ariadne kept her head down and her eyes on her screen. Either she had not heard Geraldine's crotchety retort or she was wisely ignoring it, as Ian had. Dejected, Geraldine tried to focus on her work. Every aspect of her personal life was a disaster, from losing contact with her sister to her own rejection of Ian. And the investigation did not seem to be faring much better. All they had were vague statements from two witnesses, one unreliable, the other barely intelligible, and an e-fit image that might or might not resemble someone who might not bear any relation to the case, even if they managed to find him.

A few hours had passed in desultory reading and comparing statements when Geraldine's phone shrilled, startling her from a miserable reverie.

'Hello? Hello? Who is this?'

'He's here, he's here!' an unfamiliar voice hissed.

'I'm sorry. Who is this?'

'It's me. I'm calling from the café. You asked me to call you –'

The voice was abruptly cut off mid-sentence, but Geraldine had heard enough. She called Ian and together they raced to the car. They drove all the way in silence, reaching the café ahead of the patrol car that was following them. Geraldine looked at Ian from time to time as they drove, but he sat staring fixedly at the road ahead and did not once glance at her. If he shared her sense of strangeness at working as partners again, after their break-up, he gave no sign of it. She was relieved, yet slightly piqued, to see that he had his feelings for her so tightly under control. No one observing them would have the slightest suspicion that they had recently been romantically involved.

They drew up outside the café and she hurried inside after him. The manager was hovering anxiously near the counter while a waitress Geraldine hadn't seen before came towards them. Ignoring her, Geraldine went straight over to the manager who nodded towards a table in the corner.

'Is there another exit?'

'What?'

'Is there another way out?' she asked urgently.

'Yes, round the back. That's him.'

She turned and saw a stout man in his forties. His balding head was sprinkled with tufts of fluffy ginger hair, and from across the room she could see that his pale face was dotted with freckles. Geraldine and Ian walked over to his table and sat down, boxing the man in. Small blue eyes glared at them in surprise.

'Here, what's the meaning of this?' he asked. 'I don't remember saying you could join me. In fact, I don't recall you having the manners to ask if you could sit at my table.'

Geraldine held up her identity card. 'We're police officers.'

'I don't care who you are. There are other tables free. Go and sit somewhere else.'

'And we'd like to ask you a few questions,' Geraldine went on quietly, ignoring the man's protest.

'Of all the impertinence –'

'We're investigating a murder,' Ian said.

'And we'd like to ask you a few questions,' Geraldine repeated doggedly.

'I have nothing to say to you.'

'We have a few questions we'd like you to answer,' Ian repeated. 'Let's start with your name.'

Sullenly the man told them his name was Jeremy Flannery, and he lived in York. Geraldine made a note of his address.

'Can I go now?' he asked. 'I haven't got anything to tell you.'

'We'd like you to accompany us to the police station, sir,' Ian said, in a tone of command that made it clear this was not a request that could be declined.

Nevertheless, the man did his best to refuse, although there was not much he could do but bluster and grumble, since he couldn't get past them.

'Oh, very well,' he conceded. 'What is it you want to know? Make it quick, will you? I haven't got all day.'

Ian politely explained that they could not say how long the questioning would take.

'We believe you may be able to give us some information that could assist us in a murder enquiry,' he explained. 'So you understand this is important. Now, if you'd like to come with us, please.'

The man opened his mouth to protest and half stood up.

'You're not going anywhere,' Ian said.

'There are two uniformed constables waiting just outside, and two more at the back door,' Geraldine said. 'Even if you push past us, you won't get out of here.'

The man sat down again.

'Come on then,' Ian said, standing up. 'Let's go.'

As they walked out to the street, the man looked around.

'Let's not take any chances, shall we?' Ian replied, pulling the man's hands swiftly behind his back and whipping handcuffs on.

'What's this? What's going on?' Jeremy demanded.

'We just want to ask you a few questions,' Ian repeated stolidly.

Once they were at the police station, they set to work but Jeremy's face told them more than his words. He flatly denied having known anything about a waitress working at the café.

'I went there for the all-day breakfast,' he said. 'It's cheap, and bloody good. There's no other place can beat it.'

A few beads of sweat appeared on his pale forehead and he wiped them away impatiently with the back of his sleeve.

'Is it too hot for you in here?' Geraldine asked.

The room was not even warm.

'Not at all.' He scowled. 'I'm just nervous. Who wouldn't be, hauled off the street and dragged here in handcuffs, like a common criminal?' He rubbed his wrists and grimaced, as though the handcuffs had injured him. 'And now this, being questioned like you think I'm guilty of some crime. A man would have to be made of stone not to feel nervous. What is it I'm supposed to have done?'

Geraldine gave an encouraging smile. 'You're not being accused of anything, Mr Flannery.'

'Not yet,' she thought.

'So what am I doing here, and why did you bring me here in handcuffs?' He was beginning to sound irate. 'I'm not going to take this, you know. This harassment is just not on. I'm going to lodge a complaint. You had no right to drag me here against my will.'

'When we first spoke to you in the café, you were unwilling to co-operate, and we do need to talk to you,' Geraldine said. 'We're investigating a very serious crime.'

'We could charge you with obstruction,' Ian said impatiently. 'So let's stop hedging and get some answers.'

Jeremy insisted he had never met anyone called Angie. 'I just went there for breakfast. They do a really great breakfast. Since when was enjoying your breakfast a crime?' He rolled his eyes.

# 50

WHILE THEY WERE TALKING, there was a tap at the door and Naomi came in. Tasked with looking into Jeremy Flannery's history, she had been busy researching his records while Geraldine and Ian were questioning him. She indicated that she had found some interesting information, and they stepped out of the room to hear what she had to tell them.

'I've got something on him,' she said.

Although her face remained impassive, her voice betrayed her excitement.

'What? What have you found?' Geraldine asked, catching her colleague's enthusiasm.

For answer, Naomi handed Ian a report. He scanned through it, frowning, before passing it to Geraldine.

'It's just a summary,' Naomi said.

'It's very interesting,' Ian muttered, and waited for Geraldine to read it.

Two women had independently reported Jeremy Flannery to the police, citing harassment. Seven years ago, a young woman called Jane Stanhope had complained about him to the police, after he made a series of unwanted phone calls. Jane lived alone, and claimed that Jeremy had repeatedly followed her home. Having seen him loitering outside her apartment over a period of several weeks, she had been afraid to go out on her own, especially after dark. After speaking to her family, who did not live locally, Jane had changed her mobile number. Somehow Jeremy had discovered her new number and resumed calling her. After that, she had become seriously frightened, and reported him to the police, who asked her to make a note of dates and times whenever she saw him following her home from work, or hanging about in the street outside her apartment. Although Jeremy had denied the charge, insisting he had never verbally threatened or physically assaulted her, nevertheless she had been seriously frightened by his unwelcome attention. Before she had applied for an injunction against him, the matter was resolved between the two parties, and the charge dropped. After that he stopped bothering her. Five years later another woman lodged a complaint against him: Angie Robinson.

Ian and Geraldine took this new information straight to Eileen who listened carefully, smiling grimly all the while.

'Good work,' she said, when Ian had finished telling her what Naomi had found. 'It looks as though we've got our man. He's been stalking her. Take a DNA sample, and let's see if we can place him at the murder scenes. I'll sort out a search warrant for his home, and in the meantime find out as much about him as you can. If you can get him to confess straight away, so much the better. Push him as hard as you can and I dare say he'll cave in and it'll be all over bar the shouting.'

Her smile softened the customarily stern features of her square face, making her look quite kindly.

'Do you think he killed them both?' Geraldine asked.

Eileen grunted. 'Impossible to say,' she answered after a pause. 'Leslie could have attracted his attention. We know he has a history of stalking women. What do you think?'

Geraldine frowned. 'It all seems a bit off. Surely if he was intending to kill her he wouldn't have been so blatant about his stalking?'

'True, but we don't know he intended to kill her, do we? It might have been a moment of frustration,' Eileen said.

'Two moments,' Geraldine replied thoughtfully.

Geraldine suggested they leave Jeremy to sweat in a cell for the rest of the afternoon, while they went to question Robert and Greg about Jeremy.

'We should have a closer look at Naomi's findings before we speak to Jeremy again. And let's see if we can find out any connection between Jeremy and Leslie, or between Angie and Leslie.'

'We need to gather everything we can against him or he might slip through our fingers,' Eileen agreed.

'Assuming he's guilty,' Geraldine said.

'His DNA is going to link him to both victims,' Ian said. 'He could easily have encountered both of them while they were working as waitresses. It all adds up. Everything points to Jeremy.'

'We don't know it's his DNA at the scenes, and we don't yet know whether he met Leslie,' Geraldine pointed out.

She was reluctant to challenge Ian, especially in front of the detective chief inspector, but she was concerned that Eileen might be encouraged to leap to conclusions in her eagerness to tie the case up. Geraldine had noticed that impatience in Eileen before. It was a weakness in a detective.

'Let's not waste time casting about blindly,' Ian said. 'We've got him here, let's force a confession from him.'

'We can't force him to confess if he's innocent,' Geraldine protested.

'No, but we can do our best. A man who stalks a woman until she's terrified of him has to be a likely suspect.'

'Maybe, but what if he didn't kill either of the two victims? You seem to have already made up your mind he's guilty.'

'And you seem set on believing he's innocent, before we've even had a chance to look for a link between him and the two victims.'

Geraldine glared at Ian, no longer caring that she and Ian were engaged in a spat in Eileen's office.

'He's a nasty little man,' Eileen interrupted their exchange, 'but we can't seek a conviction for a double murder on the grounds that he stalked one of the victims. We'll have to wait for the result of the DNA tests. In the meantime, speak to the widowers of the victims and gather whatever else you can from them. And send a team of constables to question Jeremy's neighbours and work colleagues. Within twenty-four hours we need to have more witness statements confirming that he was potentially violent, and DNA evidence that places him at both scenes. We won't leave him any wriggle room. We want a cut and dried case to present to the CPS.'

Leslie's husband listened carefully to Geraldine's question before shaking his head.

'Jeremy?' he repeated, with an anxious frown. 'Jeremy, you say?'

Geraldine nodded but refrained from passing on any more information about their suspect.

'So did you ever hear Leslie talking about someone called Jeremy?' Ian asked.

Robert shook his head. 'No, never. I'm sorry.'

Greg took a while to open the door. He looked sleepy, and had clearly been drinking.

He glared belligerently at Geraldine. 'Well?' he asked. 'Have you got him yet? Listen,' he leaned forward and Geraldine took a step back, afraid he was going to fall on her. 'Have you got him? You have to let me know the minute you've got him so I can smash his fucking face in. I'll pulverise the sick bastard. Listen, you have to let me at him.'

'We haven't made an arrest yet,' Geraldine replied, 'but we're following several leads and we do have someone helping us with our enquiries.'

'Let me at him,' Greg repeated, his words slurring into one another. 'Jusht let me at him.'

'As I said, we don't yet know who was responsible for this

terrible tragedy, but we are looking into it and hope to make an arrest soon. I want to ask you for your help.'

'Yesh, yesh, anything,' he replied, his eyes growing glazed and his voice increasingly slurred. 'Jusht let me at him when you get him. Jusht a few moments, that'sh all I want. Jusht a few moments alone with him and then he'll be all yoursh. What'sh left of him.'

It would have been an easier conversation if he had been sober. Geraldine was wondering whether to return at another time when Ian took over.

'Did your wife ever say anything to you about being followed?'

'Followed? What do you mean?'

'I mean,' Ian tried again, 'we have reason to believe it's possible your wife's killer was not a random stranger, but someone who had been stalking her.'

Greg's green eyes widened in surprise, and he seemed to sober up a little. 'Stalking her? He was stalking her? Why the hell didn't she tell me? I would have sorted him out.'

'Did you ever hear your wife mention the name Jeremy?' Ian persisted.

'Jeremy? Is that his name? Where is he?' He raised a clenched fist. 'I'll show him what happens to scum like him.'

Geraldine glanced at Ian. She could tell that, like her, he was wondering whether Greg had 'sorted out' his wife. He had just shown a potentially violent side of his character they had not previously known about. From having no suspects, they now seemed to have three: Jeremy, Greg, and possibly Harry.

# 51

IT WAS STRANGE THAT Angie had gone to the police about her stalker without even mentioning him to her husband. Her discretion said little about her dealings with Jeremy, but quite a lot about her relationship with Greg. Geraldine would have liked to discuss this slightly surprising aspect of the case with Ian, but he merely grunted when she asked him what he thought about it.

'It says something about their marriage, don't you think?'

She tried to explain her impression of the dead woman's relationship with her husband.

'You can have no inkling of what goes on in a marriage,' Ian replied brusquely.

He did not add that she was not even capable of sustaining a relationship for longer than a few months, but she was sure that was what he was thinking. After that, they drove back to the police station in uncomfortable silence. Once they arrived back at the office, Ian was keen to try and persuade Jeremy to confess. It would certainly be a shortcut. By now the duty solicitor had arrived, a twitchy mousy-haired girl who looked too young to have qualified. Geraldine remembered her from a previous case where she had been very quiet, but on this occasion she was more forthcoming, even slightly flirtatious in the way she glanced at her client. It was unpleasant to think that sweaty Jeremy had probably worked hard to charm her with compliments. The solicitor looked as though she was unused to receiving much attention from men.

Geraldine began by reeling off a list of dates. Jeremy listened in apparent perplexity.

'Do those dates mean anything to you?'

'No. Why? Should they?'

Jeremy glanced enquiringly at the solicitor who merely raised her eyebrows.

'My client has no recollection of these dates, and no idea why you are bringing them to his attention,' she stated.

'These are the dates on which you contacted or followed Jane Stanhope.'

'Who's she when she's at home?' Jeremy asked, giving a credible impression of baffled innocence.

'Jane Stanhope,' Ian repeated roughly. 'The woman you're pretending not to remember. But then, why would you remember her? You only stalked her for three years.'

Jeremy shook his head and stared at Ian. 'I don't know what you're talking about.' He turned to the lawyer. 'They're making this up to scare me. I never stalked anyone.'

'Do you deny having pursued a woman named Jane Stanhope?' Ian asked. 'You might want to think carefully before you answer.'

There were records of his phone calls and emails, and Jane had handed in signed cards he had sent her, on her birthday and on Valentine's Day, and at Christmas. Jeremy hesitated before claiming that Jane was his former girlfriend.

'Not according to her,' Ian retorted. 'You only left her alone when you were faced with the threat of an injunction against you for stalking her.'

'That's a lie,' Jeremy muttered, flushing with anger. 'I'm telling you, that woman couldn't get enough of me.'

He glanced at the lawyer who blushed, giving Geraldine a horrible suspicion that he might have been busy lining up the object of his next infatuation.

'And then there was Angie Robinson,' Ian went on.

Jeremy shook his head again, and a few beads of sweat trickled down his forehead. At his side the lawyer looked faintly uneasy.

'Angie Robinson?' Jeremy repeated, frowning. 'Who the hell is that?'

He was sweating more profusely now, fidgeting with the buttons on his shirt and avoiding meeting Geraldine's gaze. There was no doubt that he was nervous.

'Angie Robinson, as you well know, is the woman who complained to us about you stalking her.'

'Oh yes, I remember her all right,' Jeremy said, 'I just didn't know her full name. That woman was a hundred per cent crazy. We met a few times, but she became obsessed with me. I'm telling you, she wouldn't leave me alone. In the end I had enough of it and I told her straight, it was over between us. She went berserk and that's when she went to the police and accused me of running after her, when it was entirely the other way round.'

'She was married,' Geraldine pointed out. 'Happily married by all accounts.'

Jeremy shrugged. 'All the more reason for her to leave me alone,' he muttered.

'So you don't deny you knew Angie Robinson?' Geraldine said quietly.

It wasn't a question.

'I told you, she wouldn't leave me alone,' Jeremy muttered sullenly.

'You have a history of stalking women, don't you, Jeremy?' Ian asked.

'No.'

'Jane Stanhope was going to take out an injunction against you for stalking her,' Ian went on. 'Or was she also following you? Did the police get that the wrong way round too?'

'It was a mistake,' Jeremy blustered. 'She was my girlfriend. She was crazy.'

'Another mistake? Jane was threatening to take out an injunction against you to stop your harassment, and then Angie complained you were stalking her.'

'No, no, I told you she was lying.'

'You admit you knew her,' Ian said. 'She reported you to the police for stalking her, and now she's dead.'

'Dead?' Jeremy's jaw dropped and he looked genuinely shocked. 'What do you mean?'

'Inspector, is this going anywhere?' the lawyer asked. 'My client hasn't been charged with anything and he would like to go home.'

Ian glanced at Geraldine then turned back to the suspect.

'Jeremy Flannery, I'm arresting you on suspicion of the murder of Angie Robinson.'

Jeremy sat dumbfounded while Ian read him his rights. Then he turned to the lawyer.

'They can't do this. Do something. Get me out of here.'

Ian sighed. 'This will be a lot easier for everyone concerned if you stop denying what you did, and tell us exactly what happened between you and Angie.'

'No, no, I didn't do anything to her. I never touched her. Listen, I'll tell you everything. It's true, I liked Angie. I did. I really liked her. I would never have hurt her. I couldn't have. I liked her too much. She was – she was special.'

'She was married,' Geraldine replied curtly.

'So?' Jeremy blustered. 'What's that to me? I suppose her husband killed her, because he was jealous.'

'Of you?' Geraldine made no attempt to conceal the scorn in her voice.

'Yes, why not?' Jeremy face flushed. 'What's so funny about that? You think because she was married she would have preferred her husband to someone else?'

'Someone like you?' Geraldine smiled.

'Can you account for your movements on these dates?' Ian asked, citing the dates of the two murders.

Geraldine was not surprised when Jeremy said he had no idea where he was on the nights when Angie or Leslie were presumed killed. It did not take much research to discover that he had been away visiting family in Scotland three weeks earlier, when Angie had been killed. Leslie had been wheeled into the alley eleven days before the interview, and they were keen to place him at that scene at least.

'The Saturday before last?' Jeremy repeated, his face breaking into a worried smile. 'Yes, I know exactly where I was that night. It was my grandmother's birthday, and we all went to Edinburgh to see her. Ask anyone. If ninety-five isn't something worth celebrating, I don't know what is. I hadn't seen some of my cousins for years. We don't keep in touch, and I can't say I care. I wouldn't have gone, but I never fell out with my grandmother and I thought it might be the last time I would see her alive.'

If Jeremy's alibi checked out, he couldn't have been the figure who had wheeled Leslie's body into the alley. Either he had an accomplice or else he was innocent of any involvement in the murder of Leslie and the disposal of her body. They took a break while Jeremy's alibi was being investigated.

'He's bluffing,' Ian said. 'He has to be. It's too much of a coincidence his being in Scotland when both murders were committed.'

While the police in Edinburgh were looking into Jeremy's alibi, tracking down his grandmother and the other members of his family, the results of the tests arrived, establishing that no DNA found on either victim was a match with Jeremy Flannery's. They had no evidence to link him to the bodies, only supposition. A handful of witnesses were willing to swear he had been in Edinburgh on the night Leslie was killed. CCTV footage of him boarding the train confirmed his story.

'Could it be – Could he have –' Ian stammered.

'Ian, what part of "It wasn't Jeremy Flannery" don't you understand?' Eileen snapped.

Clearly as disappointed as everyone else that they had failed to nail the suspect, she told Ian to release Jeremy. Geraldine went to the VIIDO office and watched the footage of the bin being wheeled into the alley once again.

'You know the definition of insanity, Sarge?' a middle-aged VIIDO officer asked her, his round face creased in a cheerful grin.

'Working in this place?' she replied, returning his smile.

'That too,' he agreed. 'But I meant doing the same thing again and again hoping to get a different result. We've studied this repeatedly, and you must have watched it right through at least ten times, and it hasn't shown us the killer's identity yet.'

'Just play it for me once more,' she said.

The portly constable complied and together they stared at the grainy grey image. It gave very little away. The height and stature of the figure was obscured by his loose jacket and the way he bent over to push the bin. It wasn't even clear whether the figure was a man or a woman. Geraldine watched it again, this time focusing not on the person pushing the bin, but on other pedestrians. Even at six o'clock on a Friday the pavement was fairly busy outside the club, although it was not yet open, although nowhere near as crowded as later in the evening. The bin with its macabre cargo trundled past a number of people, none of whom appeared to take any notice of it. All the same, it was possible someone might remember seeing it, and recall the appearance of the person pushing it along the pavement. Geraldine put her idea to Eileen, who organised a plea on the local news bulletin that evening. She addressed anyone who had been walking past the Livewire

Bar at around six o'clock two Fridays ago, and recalled seeing a garbage bin being wheeled along the pavement, urging them to come forward. They all knew it was a long shot, but it was worth a try.

# 52

EVERYTHING HAD BEEN WORKED out to ensure the operation worked seamlessly. The plan was actually foolproof, so it came as a shock to learn that the police knew about the bin. After so much care and meticulous attention to detail, it was galling to learn from the media that the police had found out how the body had been moved into the alley beside the Livewire Bar. No, it was worse than galling, it was maddening. The police had no business snooping around the streets like that. It seemed that no one was safe from their prying. But the fact that they had discovered the bin was neither here nor there. It didn't matter that they had traced it on CCTV all the way back to the van. It must have taken them hours and hours, and no doubt they thought they were very clever to have found the van at all. But so what? It made no difference, because they had no idea who had been driving the van and pushing the bin, and they were never going to find out.

In the end, in spite of all that time and effort, nothing the police had done had made any difference to their investigation. Even spotting the van on film wasn't going to help them, because there was no way they were going to trace it. There was no longer anything that could link the van to the woman's corpse. Only a thorough search for DNA in the back of the van could possibly throw up proof that the body had been transported in it, and that was never going to happen because the van was safely locked away in a garage with its genuine registration number showing once again. The false registration plates were probably already in landfill by now, after being wrapped in black rubbish bags and thrown away days ago. That was the kind of attention to detail that guaranteed the police would never stumble on the truth. Without any leads, they were reduced to crashing around blindly. Used to dealing with idiots, drunks, crackheads and petty criminals too dumb to do anything even vaguely intelligent, they were helpless against someone with real brains.

It was faintly worrying, yet at the same time entertaining, to see how the media reported the story. They had begun calling the killer 'The Shadow', because no one had the faintest idea who was behind the deaths.

'Never before have the police hunted for so elusive a killer, a killer who leaves no clues,' one of the local papers said. That was a very nice compliment. 'This killer really seems to be as impossible to pin down as a shadow,' the reporter went on. Another journalist claimed that 'a man' was helping the police with their enquiries, but that was just sheer desperation on the part of the police. It meant nothing. The police had to talk to the media, even though they had nothing to say. Nothing at all.

For now, it was time to lie low and resist the temptation to kill again, at least for a while. That was the hardest part, having to be patient and do nothing. But it would be foolhardy to claim another victim just yet, and The Shadow was no fool. Two women had been killed, and the police were completely clueless about who was responsible. They were running a massive investigation, and most killers would have been caught by now. But not The Shadow. The national papers were already running articles, although the story had not yet reached their front pages. One more victim and The Shadow would be headline news. Meanwhile, The Shadow was the perfect name for a killer who was never going to be caught. Two women had been killed so far, and there would be more. Soon everyone in the country would be talking about The Shadow. It was an exhilarating and terrifying thought. Not that The Shadow was interested in notoriety. No, these murders were driven by a different motive. And that was why The Shadow would never be caught.

# 53

GRADUALLY THE PAIN OF losing her sister grew less raw and Geraldine was able to focus on her work without a constant ache at the back of her mind, draining her energy. It was still an effort to stop herself thinking about Helena, but she forced herself to concentrate on the case, pushing every other consideration from her mind. She even began sleeping better, and her nightmares grew less frequent. Although it hurt her to think that she might one day remember her unfortunate sister without becoming emotional, she knew that was better than continuing to torment herself about what could have been. Helena had gone, and had probably forgotten about her by now. If she hadn't moved on with her life, she soon would. Geraldine tried to think of her sister developing relationships with friends who knew nothing about her sordid past, and finding peace at last. The idea made Geraldine want to weep.

Further testing had discovered an unattributed trace of DNA on the lid of the bin that had been used to transport Leslie's body. For days a team had been working to collect DNA samples from all the refuse operators working in York, and the forensic lab had been busy testing the samples and comparing them with the trace left on the bin. It had taken nearly two weeks, but they had all now been eliminated, along with the people who worked in the shops near the alley. No one who gave a sample admitted to having been in the alley, or to having touched the bin or opened the lid to peer inside.

'It could be from a rough sleeper,' Ariadne suggested.

'Whoever it was, someone touched that bin and we need to know who it was,' Eileen said.

So a team of constables was sent to the shelters and the breakfast club, and to walk around the streets in the evening, collecting samples from all the homeless people they could find. At the same time, Eileen prepared to make another television appeal, this one slightly unusual. They all knew they were going to receive a lot of calls from members of the public after the broadcast, and more officers were drafted in to answer the phones.

If you were near the Livewire Bar around two weeks ago, we need you to come forward as you may have vital information that can help us in the course of an investigation into a serious crime.'

The following morning, Geraldine received a letter addressed to Detective Geraldine Steel, Police Station, York. The envelope was handwritten in an untidy childish scrawl, and the wording was peculiar. Faintly curious, she slit open the envelope and drew out a slightly grubby sheet of paper. As she read the opening words of the letter, she felt a strange sensation, as though she had slipped into a dream. She blinked, but she wasn't mistaken. The letter was still there, clutched in her trembling hand. Barely able to see for the tears that suddenly filled her eyes, she stumbled to the toilets and sat down in a cubicle to read the whole letter.

'You will never find me but don't you be sad about that. I already caused you enough grief. You always tried to take care of me but now I'm on my own and believe me it's better that way. I never was any good for you. All I ever did was mess things up for you and you know that's the truth. Now I've been given a second chance at life, and that's thanks to you. I got clean and I'm going to try and stay that way. One day at a time. But I'm sorry it had to end like this between us because I think we would have been good sisters. You showed me how to try but now I won't have a chance to show you I can be a good sister too, same as you was to me. When your friend came to see me he said you sent him but I knew straight away he was lying. He told me you had agreed never to see me again, but I never believed him. I knew you wouldn't let me go without you saying goodbye to me. But if it was your doing that we never had that chance I want you to know I forgive you. And whatever happens from now, I want you to know that I love you. And I never loved anyone before. And that's because I never knew how. You were the only person ever to be nice to me because of who I am and we will always be sisters. Now I'm going to stop because thinking about you and how we can't see each other again is making me so sad I can't bear it and I never want to feel so desperate again that I do something stupid and you know what I mean. I'm going to stay clean for you so you will always know you done that for me. I want to do something for you and that's all I can do and that's a promise. You won't ever see me again but I won't ever stop thinking about you. That's another promise. And I never promised nothing to anyone before except our mother and that doesn't count because she was a crackhead same as me.'

The letter was unsigned. Helena hadn't even written her name. All she had given Geraldine was a promise for an unknowable future. Geraldine would never learn whether her sister had kept her word. Clearly she intended to, but there was no guarantee that she would succeed in staying off drugs, day after solitary day, year after weary year, without Geraldine to support her. A promise wasn't enough. Perched uncomfortably on the lid of a toilet seat, in a locked cubicle, Geraldine wept silently.

'There you are,' Ariadne said when Geraldine returned to her desk, hoping it wouldn't be obvious that she had been crying. 'Eileen's been asking for you.'

Geraldine went straight to the detective chief inspector's office. Eileen gave her a curious glance.

'Geraldine, at last. Where have you been? Never mind. No time for that.'

Eileen told her that they had a match for the DNA found on the bin.

'It's a young man who worked Saturdays in the shoe shop near the Livewire,' she said. 'He's only recently been tested, but according to the constable who took his swab, he didn't seem reluctant to give a sample of his DNA. He wanted to know how long we would hold on to it and why we wanted it, all the usual questions, but once he knew we were taking swabs from all his colleagues he couldn't refuse to co-operate. There was nothing suspicious about his behaviour, according to the constable who saw him. I want you to talk to him straight away, see if he can shed any light on all this.'

With a nod, Geraldine hurried away to talk to the man whose DNA had been discovered on the bin and discover whether they had found an oblivious passerby, a witness, or a killer.

# 54

PHIL JAMIESON WAS A student at York St John's University living in digs outside the city in a house near the village of Heslington. Geraldine drove out there that evening, hoping to catch him at home, and a young man of about twenty answered the door. He blinked sleepily at her, although it was only around eight o'clock in the evening.

'Are you Phil Jamieson?'

'What? No.'

'I'd like to speak to Phil please.'

'OK. I'll get him.'

The young man shut the door and Geraldine waited on the doorstep. One of the uniformed constables with her scuttled round to the back of the property, while the other one hovered by the side entrance. After a few moments the front door opened again and a different youth looked out.

'I'm Phil,' he said, gazing at her through a shaggy straw-coloured fringe. 'What's happened? What's up? Who are you?'

His smile faded when Geraldine introduced herself.

'I haven't committed any crimes, nothing that need involve the police, and if this is about that window, I already told the landlord my parents are going to pay –' he began, but she interrupted him.

'We haven't come here to accuse you of any wrongdoing. We think you might be able to help us with some information that could be relevant to a case we're working on.'

'OK, go on then, what do you want to know?'

Geraldine gave what she hoped was a reassuring smile. 'We'd like you to come along to the police station and answer a few questions there, if you don't mind accompanying me.'

Perhaps it was her use of the plural pronoun, but Phil glanced around and caught sight of the uniformed constable standing by the side of the house. He frowned and turned back to Geraldine.

'Do I have to come with you?'

'It would be better for you if you did,' she replied.

'OK then,' he answered, cheerfully enough. 'Let me get my shoes.'

Geraldine signalled to the constable who ran over and followed the student into the house. A moment later they both reappeared, and he walked quietly to the car with them.

'Can you at least tell me what this is about?' he asked once they set off.

'We're investigating a double murder,' Geraldine said solemnly. 'And anyone who might possibly have seen anything that can help us is being called in for questioning.'

There was no need to mention that Phil's DNA on the bin made him a potential suspect. It would only frighten him if he was innocent, and alert him to their suspicions if he was guilty. Somehow Geraldine did not think he had killed two women with his bare hands, but she was experienced enough to know that people with the most violent tempers often appeared placid and easygoing. The young man declined to have a solicitor present, on the basis that he had not been accused of committing a crime, and once Geraldine had him seated in an interview room, Ian joined them. He did not waste any time in telling Phil that traces of his DNA had been found on the lid of a bin. Phil frowned, apparently baffled.

'A rubbish bin?' he repeated with a nervous laugh. 'Is it illegal to touch a rubbish bin?'

Ian showed him a picture of the large brown bin. 'Do you recognise this bin?'

'Recognise this bin?' Phil repeated, frowning. 'I don't know what you mean. It's a bin. It looks like any other bin.'

'Do you remember seeing it on the street near where you work, the Saturday before last?' Geraldine asked patiently.

Phil looked puzzled.

'Someone might have been pushing it along the pavement,' she added cautiously.

Phil's expression cleared as she spoke.

'Oh wait, yes, I do remember seeing a bin just like this one. That is, I don't know if it was the same one, but it could have been. I remember it because you're right, someone was wheeling it along the pavement, and nearly barged right into me as I was coming out of the shop. He nearly knocked me over. Bashed right into me and I've still got the bruise to prove it.'

He rubbed his thigh as though to emphasise his point.

'About what time was that?'

'I don't know. I was leaving work so I guess about five thirty or thereabouts.'

'And did you see who was pushing it?' Geraldine asked.

She held her breath and was dimly aware of the tension in Ian's face as they sat, side by side, waiting for an answer. This could be the break they had been waiting for.

Phil shrugged. 'Not really.'

'Can you remember anything about him? Anything at all?'

He shook his head. 'I'm sorry, no.'

It was almost unbearable to have found a witness who had actually seen the killer, or his accomplice, and even had a fleeting encounter with him, yet could not help them to trace him.

'I'm sorry,' Phil repeated, sensing their disappointment. 'It was a busy day. I mean there are always a lot of people around on a Friday at that time, and I was more interested in trying not to get mowed down.' He paused. 'He was wearing a hood, I think.' He screwed up his eyes with the effort of trying to remember. 'He was wearing a hood,' he repeated lamely. 'His jacket was – it could have been dark. Although no, I think it might have been one of those bright yellow ones, like the refuse collectors wear. I'm just not sure.'

'Can you remember if he was taller than you?'

'Not really, because he was kind of hunched over the bin he was pushing, like it was really heavy or something, and he... no, I just can't remember. I'm sorry.'

There was nothing more they could do but thank the witness for his help. He had merely confirmed what they already knew, that the bin had indeed been wheeled past the club at around five thirty, and pushed into the alley. It was frustrating to feel they had come so close to finding a witness who could describe and possibly even identify the killer, yet they still had nothing that could lead to an arrest.

# 55

WALKING THROUGH THE POLICE station the following morning, Eileen spotted a knitted hat lying on a window sill.

'Whose is this dirty old thing?' she asked officiously, picking it up by the edge between one finger and a thumb, and holding it up so everyone in the room could see it. 'I won't tolerate an untidy office. That's how things get misplaced. If it's evidence, let's bag it and record it properly.'

A constable called Naomi jumped up and explained that it was of no significance, but had been left at the police station by a member of the public who didn't want it any longer.

'I'm not surprised no one wants it,' Eileen remarked as she dropped it in the bin. 'It smells disgusting.'

With a loud sniff, she strode away. Geraldine watched her thoughtfully.

'Are you all right, Geraldine?' Ariadne asked suddenly.

Geraldine nodded without answering.

'You look as though you've seen a ghost.'

Geraldine shook her head. 'There's something,' she muttered. 'There's something there.'

'I'm not sure I understand what you mean.'

In the back of her mind, the sight of an old knitted hat had sparked an idea Geraldine thought might be important, but she was struggling to bring it to mind. She closed her eyes, waiting for the memory to surface.

'There's something about that hat,' she said. 'I don't know what it is.'

On a sudden impulse she leapt to her feet and retrieved the hat from the bin where the detective chief inspector had dropped it. Eileen was right. The hat smelt unpleasantly of rain and sweat. Geraldine slipped it into an evidence bag and made a note on the plastic before putting it away in her drawer.

'Collecting presents to give for Christmas?' Ariadne laughed.

Geraldine took the evidence bag out of the drawer and stared at the hat. It was brown, with wide black stripes. Closing her eyes, she recalled the only person who had recently mentioned a knitted hat, very similar to the one she was now holding. It was hardly an unusual pattern, but it was a strange coincidence that a hat matching the description of Harry's missing hat should turn up at the police station just a week after he had reported his stolen, and two weeks after the theft. She went over to the constable who had answered Eileen's question about it.

'You said a member of the public left this here,' she said. 'Who was it?'

Naomi looked surprised to see the hat in a bag.

'What do you want with that?'

Geraldine shook her head. 'I'm not sure. Where does it come from? This could be important,' she added, aware that she was probably overreacting, reading too much into the appearance of an old hat.

But there was a chance this could provide them with a lead.

'Who brought it in?' she asked again.

Naomi frowned. 'I'm not sure, actually. I mean, Susan put it on the window sill, and she said someone had left it here. She thought she'd hang on to it for a week or so in case they changed their mind and came back for it.'

Susan seemed surprised when Geraldine approached her with the hat.

'What do you want that for?' she asked, making the same

joke as Ariadne had about collecting presents to give for Christmas. 'I hope I don't get your secret Santa.'

But she remembered exactly who had left the hat at the police station.

'Zoe?' Geraldine repeated, startled in her turn.

'Yes, Zoe Watts, the girl who was missing.'

Before she spoke to Zoe, Geraldine decided to go and see Harry again to establish whether the hat left at the police station could possibly be the one that had fallen off his bicycle. She was probably setting off on a wild goose chase, because there seemed little chance that Harry's hat could have ended up in Zoe's possession. But a slim chance was still a chance. And if Harry recognised it, and forensic testing confirmed it as Harry's, then Zoe Watts might know something about the missing hi-vis jacket?

'It's probably nothing,' Geraldine said to Eileen as she outlined her idea.

Eileen nodded. 'You're right, it sounds unlikely, but it won't do any harm to check it out. Maybe Harry will have remembered something else, while you're there.'

Geraldine drove to Harry's house. He greeted her cheerfully and thanked her for the crime number which, he said, had kept his line manager off his back.

'They couldn't be too hard on him,' his wife said smiling amiably. 'Not after he was the victim of a crime.' She smiled at her husband. 'Poor lamb.'

Harry was as unlike a lamb as anyone Geraldine had ever met. Suppressing a smile she took the hat out of her pocket. Through the plastic of the evidence bag, the pattern of wide black stripes on brown was clearly visible.

'My hat!' Harry burst out, delighted. 'You've got my hat. Look Peggy, it's my hat.'

'Are you sure it's yours, and not just a similar one?'

'It's mine, it's mine,' he crowed.

More circumspect than her husband, Mrs Mellor came over to examine it. She scrutinised it closely through the plastic.

'Oh yes,' she said at last, 'there's where I dropped a few stitches.' She tutted. 'It's never the same when you redo it, however careful you are. The tension's always slightly different. This one's going to be better,' she added, nodding complacently at the knitting on her chair.

Harry held out his hand. 'You don't need to make another one now, Peg.'

Geraldine moved the hat away. 'I'm afraid I can't let you have this just yet.'

'But it's my hat. I'm not lying to you. Peg, tell her, you know it's mine, don't you?'

'Yes, dear. It doesn't matter where it's been,' she added, turning to Geraldine. 'It's machine washable.'

Geraldine did not explain that where the hat had been might actually matter very much.

'I'm sorry but we need to hold on to it for a while longer. It could provide us with vital evidence.'

'Ah, you're going to find out who else has been wearing my hat and get the fucker who took my jacket,' Harry grinned. 'I told you the police would get him,' he added, to his wife.

Once again, Geraldine did not tell them that she was working on a far more serious crime than the theft of Harry's hi-vis jacket.

'Good,' Harry said. 'You hold on to my hat for as long as you need. And thank you for letting me know you got it back for me. That's made my day that has.'

'And don't you worry,' his wife repeated, smiling. 'It's machine washable wool. I never use anything else these days.'

Geraldine wondered if they would be quite so complacent if they knew the hat might have been worn by a murderer.

# 56

GERALDINE DROVE TO ZOE'S school, accompanied by Susan, the constable trained in working with teenagers who had previously collected Zoe from her friend's house. They spoke to the headmaster and to Zoe's form teacher, who told them Zoe had added nothing to the statement she had given at the police station. They were still unclear why she had run away from home, but she was being monitored by social workers.

'And we're keeping a close eye on her,' the headmaster said earnestly, peering at Geraldine over his glasses.

'Yes, I don't doubt it,' Geraldine smiled.

The headmaster arranged for Geraldine to question Zoe in his own office. He insisted on being present, along with Zoe's form teacher and her mother, in addition to the two police officers.

'Hello Zoe,' Susan said, and was rewarded with a tentative smile.

'I just have one question for you,' Geraldine said, holding out the hat, still in its evidence bag. 'Can you confirm that this is the hat you left at the police station? Do you recognise it?'

Zoe frowned. 'Yes, that's it. But I don't want it back. It stinks and it doesn't fit me anyway.'

'Where did you find it? Please think very carefully. It's important we know the answer to that question.'

Zoe looked surprised. 'It was in the hall,' she said.

'The hall?'

'Yes, it was raining when I ran away – when I left home,'

she corrected herself, 'so I just grabbed it as I was leaving the house. It's not mine.'

'Just to be absolutely clear, you found it in the hall of your house?'

'Yes,' Zoe replied, muttering that she had already said that.

'I suppose you've seen your father wearing it?'

'No, I haven't. I never saw him wearing it. I don't suppose he's missed it.' She wrinkled her nose. 'It stinks.'

'Thank you.'

Zoe's mother showed no surprise at the line of questioning, but she denied having seen the hat before. There was not much more they could ask Zoe, so they left. As soon as they returned to the police station, Geraldine sent the hat away for forensic testing. They already had a DNA sample from Zoe, from when she had gone missing, and were extremely interested to find out who else had worn the hat. The results of the tests were disappointing, showing that the hat had been worn by Harry, and Zoe, but no one else. There was also a woman's DNA, which they assumed must belong to Harry's wife, since she had knitted it.

'Damn,' Eileen said.

'Whoever took the jacket presumably hadn't intended to take the hat as well,' Geraldine said. 'Harry told us it was folded up inside the jacket. But how did it get into the Watts' hall? If Zoe's telling us the truth, someone left that hat there, and whoever it was could also have taken Harry's jacket.'

'It's looking that way,' Eileen agreed. 'The Watts seem to be more closely involved in this case than we thought. Let's bring the father in and question him. We haven't really spoken to him, apart from when his daughter was missing. This hat has introduced a whole new line of questioning. Bring him in, and let's put some pressure on him.'

'Shall we search the house?'

'Let's bring him in first and see what he has to say. In fact, bring both Zoe's parents in, and let's get to the bottom of this hat business. It looks as though Zoe was lying about where she found the hat and, in any case, if the killer never wore it, the lead is unlikely to go anywhere.'

Geraldine agreed. 'I'm not sure Zoe's a very reliable source of information.'

'Still, we need to question them, find out if they know anything about Harry's jacket. And while we're about it, I'll get a search warrant. The jacket could be at the house.' She smiled grimly at Geraldine. 'It's possible we may be getting somewhere.'

Geraldine had the same feeling, but she did not say anything. In the course of this investigation, they had both had that impression before and been proved wrong. Even though she was not in the slightest bit superstitious, the investigation had been so confusing, she did not want to do anything that might jinx it. In the car on the way to the hotel where John worked, Ian spoke severely. In the periphery of her field of vision, Geraldine was aware that he had turned his head towards her, but she resisted the urge to look at him.

'We need to talk about this untenable situation,' he said. 'It's been going on for long enough and I need to know where I stand. We can't go on like this. I can't go on like this.'

'What do you mean?'

'Geraldine, please don't make out you don't know what I'm talking about. Less than a week ago we were living together perfectly happily. At least, I was perfectly happy... '

He broke off as though waiting for a response. Geraldine kept her eyes firmly fixed on the road ahead and refused to respond to his unspoken question.

'Geraldine, please, tell me what's going on.'

'Nothing's going on.'

'You know what I mean.'

'Ian,' she sighed, 'this is not the time or the place for a

heavy discussion. In a few minutes we'll be interviewing the Watts, and we need to focus all our attention on them.'

'Yes, of course work is our immediate priority, but at least agree with me that we do need to talk. You can't just walk away from our relationship as though it never happened. That's not fair to either of us.'

'Yes, we'll talk, but not now. We're here.'

Geraldine did her best to hide her emotions, but it was hard. She had an uncomfortable feeling she was being cruel in shutting Ian out, but her anger with him was still raw and she was afraid she might be provoked into saying something she later regretted.

'I need time to think,' she muttered as she pulled up and opened her car door.

'I get that, but how much time do you need?' he replied irritably.

She strode towards the house without another word. The truth was, she could not answer his question. What made her situation so painful was that she loved Ian, but he had robbed her of the chance to build a relationship with the only living blood relative she knew of. That was a grief she would carry for the rest of her life, and she honestly didn't know if she would ever be able to forgive him for his meddling, however well intended it had been.

# 57

ZOE HAD RETURNED TO school without any fuss, and seemed to have settled back to her studies. The school had been very understanding about it all, and the teachers seemed to have gone out of their way to reassure Bella and John that they would keep a close eye on her from now on. After the meeting with the two police officers, the headmaster spoke to Bella to explain that teenagers often rebelled, and although running away for a few days could have put Zoe in danger, she had actually been very sensible in going to stay with a friend. No harm had come to her, and the only injurious aspect of her disappearance was the distress she had caused her parents. Bella watched him as he spoke. He was a large man with a big head, who spoke with the confidence of a man used to dealing with the vagaries of teenagers. Somehow, he made Bella feel as though she was a schoolgirl again.

The headmaster reassured her that the school would be keeping a very close eye on Zoe from now on, and he said he was happy that she had returned to school as though nothing had happened. His only caveat was that Zoe agree to talk to the school counsellor about her experience.

'The important thing is that Zoe has returned home, unharmed, and seems to want to return to her studies. The police are no longer interested in her escapade, and hopefully she's got this rebellion out of her system, and won't be causing you any more worry,' he concluded.

The interview was decidedly one sided, with little time

for Bella to comment, beyond agreeing with the headmaster and thanking him for his help at this difficult time. All in all, Bella had to agree that things could have turned out a lot worse. As she drove home, she dared to hope that life might improve from now on. John would realise how important his family was to him, and stop his wickedness, which couldn't end well. If he carried on transgressing, not only would more women suffer, but he must know that his sins couldn't continue undetected forever. Sooner or later he would be caught out. He had to be stopped before he ended up in serious trouble.

Bella made herself a mug of tea and sat down in the kitchen, relieved that Zoe was home and seemingly happy at school. Soon, the whole episode would be nothing more than a horrible memory, and they could all concentrate on returning to normal. Zoe's flight might even turn out to be a blessing in disguise, because there was a chance John might abandon his compulsion and focus on his family, now that he understood how his behaviour was affecting them all, his daughter as well as his wife. Bella prayed that he would be transformed by the experience which had threatened to tear their family apart.

Finishing her tea, she set to work, and was folding laundry when she heard the bell ring. Peering out through the window in the hall, she saw two police cars parked outside the house, and her spirits sank.

'Is it about Zoe?' she asked as she opened the door. 'Has something happened to her?'

'Zoe's fine, but we need to take a look around.'

'What do you mean?'

Bella stumbled backwards and tried to close the front door, but the policewoman had already stepped over the threshold and had one polished leather shoe in the hall.

'No, you can't come in,' Bella stammered. 'There's no need

for this. Zoe's back now. She's fine. I've been to the school and everything's all right. We don't need you any more. You can go away and leave us alone. We've had enough trouble. We just want to be left alone so we can get back to normal.'

'We have a warrant to search the house,' the policewoman said quietly, waving an official looking document in the air.

'What do you mean? Search it for what?'

'We have a warrant to search your house,' the policewoman repeated quietly.

'What for?' Bella repeated, her unease increasing to alarm. 'What are you looking for? What's going on?'

'While the search team are taking a look around,' the policewoman went on, 'I'd like you to come with me.'

Bella could hardly speak for terror. 'What for? Where to?'

'I'd like you to accompany me to the police station.'

'The police station? Why?' Bella began to cry. 'Leave us alone, please, please, leave us alone.'

The policewoman watched her calmly. 'There are a few more questions we'd like you to answer,' she said at last, ignoring Bella's hysterical weeping. 'This is just routine. There is no need to upset yourself.'

'Very well,' Bella replied, controlling her sobbing with an effort. 'I'll just go and get my things.'

'No, there's no need for you to bring anything. Please just come with me.' She picked up Bella's bag which was lying in the hall. 'Are your keys in here?'

'I need to call my husband.'

'There's no need for that. He'll be joining us at the police station.'

'No! You can't do this to us, not after all we've been through. I can't leave the house right now. I need to finish doing the laundry.'

'I'm sorry to disrupt your routine, but you do need to come with us. The sooner we get started, the sooner this will all be over. Now, come this way, please. Hopefully we won't keep you long.'

'Please,' Bella begged, 'at least let me call my husband and tell him to call a lawyer. I need to speak to my husband.'

'You can make a call once you get to the police station. Now please come with me.'

Bella had no choice but to allow the police officer to escort her to the vehicle that was waiting outside. With tears streaming down her face, she sat in the back of the police car, sobbing.

'Why are you doing this to us?' she whispered. 'Haven't we suffered enough?'

'We just want to ask you a few questions,' the policewoman repeated stoically. 'There's no need to upset yourself. And there's absolutely nothing to worry about, assuming you have nothing to hide,' she added quietly.

# 58

JOHN WAS EMPLOYED BY a large chain of hotels, and had worked his way up to become a local manager in an establishment located near Monk Bar. Ian and Geraldine drove in and left the car in the 'Pick Up Only' area outside the main entrance. The revolving door spun automatically, giving on to a spacious foyer. There was no one at the reception desk.

'How are people supposed to check in?' Ian grumbled, gazing around the deserted foyer. 'There isn't even a bell to ring for service.'

'It's probably all done online now,' Geraldine replied.

'Come on, let's try the bar. There's bound to be someone there. At least, you'd think there would be.'

A young man behind the bar was making a coffee for a guest, and they waited for him to finish before asking for the manager. Instead of John, a pretty young blonde turned up.

'Can I help you?'

'We're looking for John Watts,' Ian replied, holding up his identity card.

The woman's eyes widened slightly, but she maintained her composure. 'I'm afraid he's on the phone,' she replied.

'Please take us to his office and we'll wait outside,' Ian said.

'You can wait here —'

'No, thank you,' Ian replied. 'We'll wait outside his office. When you take us there, you can put your head round the door and let him know we're waiting. If he takes too long, we'll have to cut his call short. This won't take long,' he added. 'We just need to ask him a few questions.'

The woman nodded. 'Is this about his daughter?'

'It's connected, yes,' Ian said vaguely.

The woman took them through a staff door and along a short corridor. Leaving them in the corridor, she knocked on a door and entered the room, closing the door behind her. Ian nodded at Geraldine before pushing the door open and marching in. John was seated at a desk, phone in hand, while the blonde woman was leaning over him, talking quietly. They both looked up as Ian and Geraldine entered the room with a uniformed policeman. The woman appeared surprised, but John did not seem to be disturbed by the intrusion. He put his hand over the receiver he was holding.

'I won't keep you a moment,' he said calmly.

He began talking rapidly into the phone, something about a complaint and a voucher for a free dinner. At last he finished his conversation and put the phone down.

'Thank you, Becky,' he said, dismissing the blonde woman with a smile,

He was an attractive man, confident in the power of his charm and good looks.

'Yes, sir,' the girl replied, blushing.

'Becky, I've told you before,' he said, with assumed impatience, 'my name's John, not sir.'

He smiled at her again, and her cheeks flushed a deeper red.

'Now, Inspector,' John said, addressing Ian but still directing his dazzling smile at his assistant, 'how can I be of assistance? Can I offer you some refreshment? Tea? Coffee? Something stronger? Just say the word and I'll have it brought in here in a jiffy. My wife and I are very grateful to you for returning our daughter to us,' he added.

'Nothing, thank you,' Ian replied.

'And for your colleagues?'

Ian glared coldly at him. 'Nothing for any of us. Now,' he went on briskly, 'we'd like to ask you a few questions.'

Just then John's mobile rang. Glancing at it, he frowned. 'Excuse me, but my wife's calling me. Would you mind if I take the call? She gets very twitchy if I don't pick up.'

Without waiting for a response, he answered his phone. Ian and Geraldine exchanged a glance. They knew why Bella was calling him and watched as John's face darkened in alarm. They would have preferred to question John before he was aware that a team had arrived to search his house, but he could hardly be refused permission to speak to his wife, given that he had not been accused of committing a crime. Not yet.

'All right, all right,' John said at last, when he had been listening for a few minutes, 'just calm down, will you? There's no need to become hysterical. I've got a couple of police officers here now –' He paused, listening again. 'No, no, they haven't come here to arrest me. Don't be ridiculous. For goodness sake, what would they be doing that for? No, they just want to speak to me about Zoe. So let me get off the phone and I'll tell them what's going on and I'm sure we can sort it all out. It's obviously a misunderstanding, searching the house.' Listening again, he began to look agitated. 'Well, I suppose they want to see if Zoe left any clues about who might have put her up to her stunt of running away like that. They probably want to check her computer and her phone in case she was being groomed by a paedophile.' He paused. 'No, no, of course she wasn't. I'm well aware that she was staying with Laura the whole time. But the police must have to check these things. Now let me go and I'll sort this out, I promise.'

He hung up and turned to Ian, his face flushed with anger. 'Would you mind telling me what the hell is going on?' he demanded. 'My wife says you have a team searching my house. If that is true, I'm going to lodge a formal complaint about this harassment.'

There was no point in pretending they were only there to talk about Zoe.

'We'd like you to accompany us to the police station and answer a few questions,' Ian said.

John frowned. 'You can ask your questions here. I can't take any more time off work than is strictly necessary.'

'I'm afraid we'd like you to come with us to the police station, and we'd like you to come now,' Ian replied impassively.

'And if I refuse?'

'It isn't a request.'

'This is outrageous.'

There was nothing John could do but demand a lawyer.

'Of course,' Ian said, 'or we can arrange a duty brief to be present when we talk to you.'

'What the hell is this about? Are you arresting me? If so, I'd like to know why.'

'That rather depends on your answers,' Ian replied. 'This shouldn't take long, but we do need to ask you a few questions.'

Still protesting, John allowed them to escort him to the car.

# 59

THEY QUESTIONED JOHN FIRST, without letting him see his wife. He expressed outrage at the treatment he was receiving, even though Ian reiterated that they only wanted him to answer a few questions. Meanwhile, the lawyer sat at John's side and made no comment. A thin, young man, with black-rimmed glasses, he barely moved in his chair but appeared to be listening intently.

'I don't know what this is all about,' John protested. 'My daughter is home, and as far as we're concerned, the incident is over. Even the school is satisfied that nothing happened.'

But he blanched when Geraldine showed him a photograph of Leslie.

'For the tape, the interviewee is being shown a picture of Leslie Gordon.'

'Who is that?' John asked, his demeanour suddenly subdued.

'How do you know this woman?' Geraldine demanded.

John let out a sigh. 'I wouldn't say I knew her, exactly. We – we met, just the once. She came on to me in a pub one evening. It was quite late and we both had too much to drink. But she threw herself at me. It wasn't the other way round. If she tries to tell you I approached her, it's a lie. Anyway, it was just the once, a stupid pointless fling.'

'What happened?' Geraldine asked gently.

'I took her to the hotel, to an empty room, and well, it happened. But I swear I never saw her again after that one time.' He paused and turned to Ian. 'It's difficult to resist when a woman like that throws herself at you, and you have the keys to any number of empty bedrooms at your disposal.' He shrugged. 'I'm only flesh and blood, and my wife –' He sighed. 'I'm not proud of what I did, but it happened, and it's not as if we committed a crime. It was just sex. Just a bit of fun. And her name isn't Leslie,' he added. 'It's – something beginning with F.' He frowned with the effort to remember. 'Felicity? Phoebe? I'm embarrassed to admit that I can't actually remember her name.'

He frowned when Geraldine put a photograph of Angie on the table, and mentioned her name for the tape.

'Angie Robinson,' John looked puzzled. 'I've heard that name before.'

The name certainly should have been familiar to him. It had been mentioned repeatedly in the media for weeks. The lawyer's mouth dropped open, and his shrewd eyes narrowed behind the thick lenses of his glasses, but he said nothing.

'I may have met her,' John said, frowning. 'The name rings a bell.'

'You do not have to answer any more questions,' the lawyer interrupted, suddenly shifting in his chair.

'And did you take her back to the hotel as well?' Geraldine asked. 'There's no point in denying the truth. We are checking CCTV cameras at the moment.'

If that was not true, it soon would be.

John's frown darkened. 'It was just sex, that's all.'

'And then you were afraid they would tell their husbands,' Geraldine suggested.

'No. Neither of them was married. They were in the pub, looking for a good time.'

'You were afraid they would tell your wife,' Geraldine pressed on.

'No, no, it wasn't like that. I told them I was single. They didn't know my real name, and I don't think they gave me their real names either. They understood it was just sex. No strings. No expectation of seeing each other again. It meant nothing. Nothing.'

'And now both of these women are dead,' Ian said flatly.

'What? What do you mean? Have I caught some disease? Oh my God.' John dropped his head in his hands.

'They were murdered,' Geraldine said.

John's head jerked up. 'What did you say?'

At that point the lawyer insisted on taking a break so that he could confer with his client in private.

Geraldine and Ian discussed the interview with Eileen.

'He doesn't seem to have known they were dead,' Geraldine said. 'He seemed genuinely startled to hear they had been murdered.'

'Are you saying you think he's insane, and has no memory of the women he picked up?' Eileen asked. 'Or is he merely trying to give that impression?'

'We have his confession that he met them both, took them back to his hotel, and had sex with them. Isn't that enough?' Ian asked.

'It doesn't mean he killed them,' Geraldine replied.

Eileen scowled. 'Everything points to him, but so far all we have is circumstantial evidence. He must be our man, but he's been clever enough not to deny having met these women. He suspects we might be able to prove he had sex with his victims, but he also knows we can't prove he killed them. So he's told us the truth about everything except that he killed them. We need to set up a thorough search of the hotel. We have to find evidence that he killed these women.'

'The search of the house may come up with something,' Ian said. 'In the meantime, should we continue to press him for a confession?'

'Do your best,' Eileen replied, 'but this man is no fool.'

John continued to claim that he was innocent. 'No, no,' he insisted, 'I met them both, and had sex with them, but I never killed anyone. It wasn't me. It wasn't me.'

'We know it was you,' Ian replied quietly. 'You have nothing to gain from persisting in denying your guilt. Why not be sensible, John, and co-operate with us? It will help you in the long run. You know you're not going to get away with this.'

However earnestly they worked on John to convince him that it would help his case to confess, he remained adamant in his protestation of innocence.

'My client has given you a full and unforced account of his meetings with these two women,' the lawyer said, his eyes masked by the light reflected off the lenses of his glasses. 'Sexual relations between consenting adults is not a crime.'

'But murder is,' Ian muttered.

'Charge my client or release him,' the lawyer said. 'In the absence of any evidence that he has killed anyone, I suggest you stop this interview right now and let him go.'

Ian nodded briskly and proceeded to arrest John on suspicion of murdering Angela Robinson and Leslie Gordon. John glared helplessly at his lawyer, who merely shrugged.

'If you are innocent, they will not find any evidence of guilt,' he said calmly. 'You have nothing to worry about.' He turned to Ian. 'Someone killed those two women, but it wasn't my client. You are wasting time harassing him, instead of focusing on finding the killer.'

'Can I go home now?' John asked in a voice that shook.

'Soon,' his lawyer replied. 'Very soon.'

# 60

WHILE THE SEARCH OF John's residential and work premises intensified, Geraldine and Ian turned their attention to John's wife who had been locked in a cell for hours, waiting to be questioned.

'With any luck she'll have come to her senses,' Ian said.

'Come to her senses?' Geraldine repeated. 'You mean she'll tell you what you want to hear.'

Ian did not answer.

'I want to see my husband,' Bella shrieked when she was led into the interview room. 'I want to see my husband.'

In the space of a few hours, her appearance had altered almost beyond recognition. Her eyes were swollen and bloodshot from crying, and her skin blotchy.

'Please take a seat. We would like to ask you a few questions,' Geraldine said.

'No, no, no more questions, please.'

Sobbing that she just wanted to go home, Bella listened as Ian told her about John's infidelities.

'Why are you telling me this?' she whispered, her fingers fidgeting with her sleeves.

'You must have known about your husband's affairs?' Ian asked.

Geraldine watched, uncomfortable with the way the interview was proceeding, although she understood that corroboration of John's guilt could prove crucial in a prosecution.

Bella shook her head. 'No, no, it's not true,' she said. 'He loves me. He loves me. You are lying, trying to turn us against one another, but you won't succeed. I know he's innocent. I know it.'

She soon became hysterical again, and Eileen decided the best course of action was to send her home and summon a doctor to sedate her. After the stress of dealing with her daughter's disappearance, she was clearly too fragile to discuss the possibility of her husband's guilt. It was a pity, but there was no point in even attempting to question her.

'We only broached the subject of his infidelity,' Ian grumbled. 'We hadn't even got as far as the murders, and she completely freaked out.'

Arrangements were made for Zoe to stay with an aunt in Leeds, while a constable stayed with Bella, in case she broke down and began to talk about her husband. With Bella in a state of emotional turmoil, and John still adamant that he was innocent of murder, they all hoped that evidence would be found to convict him. But the search of his house and work space produced nothing to indicate he had been involved in murder. However forcefully Eileen insisted they needed to find proof, no evidence was forthcoming.

'It's odd that we can't find anything to verify his guilt,' Geraldine said.

CCTV footage was found showing John arriving at the hotel with young women on several occasions. Two of his partners were almost certainly Angie and Leslie, but they did not accompany him on the nights of their deaths. So far all the VIIDO evidence had done was confirm everything John had already told them, that he was a serial adulterer who had abused his position as a hotel manager, deceiving his employers as well as his wife. All of the young women John took to the hotel walked out of the premises again within a few hours of their arrival. Along with the rest, Angie and

Leslie left after a few hours. In each case, John emerged around half an hour after them, presumably returning home to his wife having cleared away all trace of his visit being anything other than professional. The set-up was too easy. John had bedrooms and showers at his disposal, together with an excuse for staying out late.

'But none of it means he's a killer,' Geraldine said. 'A philanderer and an adulterer, a sexual predator, and a thoroughly nasty man, who took advantage of any number of vulnerable women, but his victims all walked out of the hotel.'

There was nothing to suggest John had killed anyone. Nevertheless, two of his conquests had been murdered, and most of the officers working on the case were confident they had caught the killer.

'All we need is one scrap of incontrovertible proof,' Ariadne said.

'I still think it's worrying that we haven't found anything,' Geraldine replied.

Armed with what they had discovered about his womanising, Ian and Geraldine talked to John again the next morning.

'You are saying you have proof that my client visited the hotel with several women, two of whom have been killed,' the lawyer repeated softly. 'I think his wife might be concerned to learn about this, but it is hardly a matter for the courts.'

'So far as we know,' Ian pointed out.

The lawyer shrugged. 'All you have is speculation,' he pointed out.

'And two corpses,' Ian said.

'Which have nothing to do with my client.'

'Both of them went to his hotel with him. He knew them both. That alone is enough to cast suspicion on him.'

John shook his head, muttering about 'consenting adults'. 'But I never killed anyone,' he added angrily.

'Why?' Ian asked. 'Why those two in particular? What did they threaten to do? Were they going to expose you? To tell your wife?'

John glanced helplessly at the lawyer.

'Take a deep breath,' the lawyer said. 'They are casting around in desperation. They clearly have no evidence against you or they would have produced it by now.'

Geraldine produced the knitted hat.

'Where did you find this?' she asked.

John frowned at it, looking puzzled. 'It's not mine,' he said. 'What would I want with that?'

'Your daughter found it in your house,' Geraldine told him.

'Well, I don't know how it got there.'

'It's a hat,' she said.

'Yes, I can see that. But I've never seen that filthy thing before in my life.'

'It was in your house. Zoe says she found it in the hall.'

'My client has just told you he has never seen it before. Apart from the fact that you have given no indication as to what bearing it might have on this case, do you have any forensic evidence to prove my client ever wore it?'

He sniffed dismissively, before requesting a break.

'You just had a break,' Ian replied.

'I need to speak to my client,' the lawyer replied quietly.

Geraldine and Ian went to discuss their lack of progress with Eileen.

'We can't prove he wore it,' Geraldine said. 'There are no stray hairs, no DNA on it to indicate he even touched it.'

Eileen sighed.

'It's machine washable,' Ian pointed out. He turned to Geraldine. 'What's wrong with you? Why are you being so negative about this? We've arrested him, haven't we?'

'But we need evidence if we're to get a conviction,' Eileen replied.

Geraldine and Ian went to the canteen to grab a quick coffee while they were waiting to press on with the interview.

'What if we're wrong?' Geraldine asked.

'What do you mean? How can we be wrong?'

'Oh please. That's a ridiculous thing to say. All we have against the suspect is circumstantial evidence and speculation. You know as well as I do that just because we can prove he met them, doesn't mean he killed them.'

'How else would he have the refuse collector's hat?' Ian asked her.

Geraldine scowled. 'Bella said her husband was innocent.'

'She would say that, wouldn't she?'

'She said she knew he was innocent. Bella said she knew it wasn't John who killed those girls.'

'Yes, we have the word of his hysterical wife on that. So what?'

'So either she has no idea who her husband really is, or she's lying to protect him,' Geraldine said.

'He could easily have done it without his wife knowing about it,' Ian said, with a touch of bitterness in his voice. 'Marriage is no guarantee of anything.'

Remembering how Ian's own wife had deceived him, Geraldine felt a fleeting sympathy for him.

'She certainly convinced me when she said he didn't do it. I think she genuinely believes he's innocent. But it's possible she's just putting on an act. I'm going to have another word with her.'

Ian offered to accompany her, but she shook her head. A female constable was already at the house with Bella, and in any case an emotional woman might be more inclined to talk to another woman.

'Do you really think she knows more than she's letting on?' Ian asked, gazing curiously at Geraldine. 'If we could get her to corroborate our suspicions, that would be it.'

She shook her head. 'It's a long shot. But if it was John who killed them, which is the most likely theory, Bella might say something that drops him in it, even without meaning to. It has to be worth a try, and I think she's more likely to talk at home than here across a table in a formal interview. Who knows what we might discover if she actually talks to us? Of course, it's still possible that John had nothing to do with the murders, but either way, this might help us get to the truth.'

# 61

BEFORE GOING TO SPEAK to Bella, Geraldine talked to the next-door neighbours.

'Yes, we heard them rowing,' one of them replied promptly. 'I've already told your colleague about it.'

The woman lived in the house attached to John and Bella's, and she seemed like a reasonably sensible witness.

'Were you able to overhear what they argued about?'

'Oh yes. That is, we could only catch the odd word, but the gist of it seemed to be that she was accusing him of running after other women, and he was denying it. I never saw him with another woman, but of course he probably wouldn't have brought her home with him if he was seeing someone else. I can't tell you if he was having an affair, but I am pretty sure his wife thought he was. Does that help?'

'It does. Did she sound angry with him when you overheard them arguing?'

'I really don't know how she was feeling. It's difficult to tell, just from overhearing the odd argument, especially from the other side of a wall, but from the little I could hear, I'd say she was upset rather than angry. He kept yelling at her to stop crying, because there was nothing to cry about.'

Thanking the neighbour, Geraldine went to ring Bella's bell, aware that there was a slim chance this encounter might prove a turning point in the investigation. With luck, Bella would go to pieces and admit that she knew her husband was the killer the police were searching for, and could prove it, even by accident. Alternatively, she might say something to incriminate herself. The likelihood was that she would do neither of those things, and Geraldine would leave the house feeing just as frustrated as when she had arrived. Doing her best to remain positive, she rang the bell again, determined to convince Bella to talk to her.

'What do you want?' Bella snapped, peering out and glaring when she saw who was on the doorstep. 'I haven't got anything else to say to you, so you might as well give up and stop pestering me. And send my husband home.'

She stood leaning against the door jamb for support. Her eyes were still bloodshot, and her lips moved as though she was talking to herself, but she no longer looked as anxious as when she had been at the police station. Geraldine had been right to suspect Bella would be more relaxed in her own home than she had been in an interview room. She smiled as gently as she could, hoping to persuade Bella to let down her guard.

'Hello, Bella. Can I come inside for a few minutes?'

'What for?'

'So that we can talk more comfortably.'

'Huh! You've not come to search the house again, then?' Bella asked with a surly scowl. 'When is John coming home?'

'Can I come in and talk to you?' Geraldine repeated her question. 'I need to ask you a few more questions, and we can do that here or back at the police station. It's up to you. But the sooner we get to the bottom of all this, the sooner John will be released, assuming he's innocent.'

Grudgingly, Bella stood to one side to allow Geraldine to enter, and led her into the living room. There was no sign of Susan in there. As she sat down, Geraldine enquired where her colleague was.

'That other trollop? I sent her packing,' Bella replied.

For the first time, Geraldine felt a flicker of unease. Susan had not reported leaving the house, which was slightly irregular conduct in a police officer, but perhaps she was waiting until she reached the police station to tell Eileen that Bella had thrown her out. In the meantime, Geraldine was alone in the house with Bella, and there were no witnesses to confirm what she said.

'The constable and I must have crossed on the way,' Geraldine murmured.

Bella did not respond.

'You told me you were sure your husband didn't kill those two women, Angela Robinson and Leslie Gordon,' Geraldine began. 'What I want to know is how you can be so sure?'

'Because he's my husband,' Bella replied with a strange kind of fervour. 'John would never kill anyone. I know he wouldn't. I told you that already. I'm not going to change my mind, however many times you ask me.'

'But how can you *know*?'

'I told you, I just know. That's why you have to let him go. He has to have a chance to redeem himself.'

Geraldine kept her voice even and calm, as she enquired what Bella meant by that. She had the impression she was about to discover what might trigger Bella to talk openly to her, but she would have to proceed carefully, or Bella might clam up and refuse to say any more.

'I don't understand,' she said cautiously.

'My husband is a sinful man,' Bella replied. 'He must be given a chance to redeem himself.'

'A sinful man?' Geraldine repeated. And just like that, she had an unnerving suspicion that Bella knew exactly what her husband had done. 'But is your husband truly worthy of redemption, Bella?' she asked softly, goading Bella to explain.

Sitting opposite Bella, Geraldine calculated the best way to extricate herself from the situation should the need arise. Bella's moods were volatile, and that made her behaviour unpredictable. At any moment she might become hysterical, or lash out, and Geraldine was, effectively, trapped. She judged the distance to the door with her eyes. It wasn't far, but Bella was seated right in front of her, blocking her way. Somehow she would have to persuade Bella to move, or else barge her out of the way, if she needed to get out of there. Meanwhile, Bella was answering her question.

'Everyone is worthy of redemption,' Bella said. 'The Lord is merciful. But you have to leave us alone, all of you. Don't you understand? It is women like you who are the cause of our problems. You are the reason for his downfall. This is all your fault, not his. My husband is a sinner only because he is weak. He has been tested many times, and he has failed, but with my help he will be saved. No one is beyond redemption. No one. My husband is ready to repent. I know he is.'

'Bella, you can't keep protecting him like this. You can't protect him from the law.'

'You're not listening to me. I told you, he is ready to repent. He deserves his chance at salvation.'

'What about the two women he killed?' Geraldine asked. 'Where is their opportunity for repentance and redemption?'

'Women? What women?'

'Don't pretend you don't know what I mean. Shall I spell it out for you? I'm talking about Angie Robinson and Leslie Gordon, the two women your husband murdered.'

'Oh that,' Bella said dismissively. 'They weren't women at all. They were servants of Satan, sent here to lead my husband astray. You have to understand, we could have been happy together. We were happy, so happy, until Satan sent his fiends to tempt my poor husband. And he fell, many times. But the demons were sent back to hell, where I pray they will be tormented for all eternity for tempting him to sin.' She stared at Geraldine, her eyes narrowing in accusation. 'You were there when John was arrested, weren't you? Are you one of them?' She stirred in her seat.

For an instant, Geraldine thought Bella was going to strike her, but she remained seated in her chair and continued speaking in a curiously cold voice although her eyes burned with rage.

'You have failed, all of you. I know he is not guilty of murder. And he will repent.'

Geraldine shifted to the edge of her chair and sat, poised to make a desperate dash for the door.

'My husband is guilty of sin, but I can save him. Do you understand what I am telling you? He is a soul on the edge of damnation. And you want to prevent me from saving his soul, don't you?' Her voice rose in a shriek. 'You have come here to stop me, but you are the one who will be silenced. He must have his chance at redemption. I shall save his soul and we will spend eternity together. He belongs to me. Me! He is my husband!'

Bella's eyes seemed to bulge in their sockets as she pitched forwards, her lips parted in an unearthly scream. At the same instant, Geraldine sprang to her feet and hurled herself sideways. Her attempt to avoid an attack came too late, as Bella lunged at her, brandishing a kitchen knife. A sharp pain sliced into Geraldine's side, and she fell to her knees with a cry of pain.

# 62

BELLA SPRANG BACK AS though she had been stung.

'Look at it!' she cried out, waving the knife in front of Geraldine. 'Just look at it!'

Geraldine drew back in alarm, afraid that Bella intended to slash her again. Partly shielded by the back of an armchair, she grabbed a cushion and clutched it firmly against her side in an attempt to stem the bleeding. Gasping with pain at the pressure against her injured side, she struggled against the panic that threatened to overwhelm her. Above all else, it was imperative to control her terror so that she could think clearly. Once Ian discovered Susan had left Bella's house, he would call Geraldine, and when she did not answer her phone, he would come looking for her. But that would only happen if he discovered that Susan had left Bella's house before Geraldine arrived, and it was quite likely he would not notice. Not only that, but since Geraldine had asked him to move out of her flat, there was no reason why he would realise that she was missing overnight. Probably no one would be aware of her absence until she failed to turn up at her desk the following morning, by which time she might have been attacked again, if she hadn't already bled to death from her existing injury.

Staring into Bella's crazed eyes, Geraldine shivered.

'Look!' Bella repeated, her face twisted in an expression of dismay. 'Look at it! Blood! There's blood everywhere!' She stared at the knife in fury, muttering under her breath. 'No more blood. No more blood.' She looked up and glared at Geraldine. 'How am I supposed to hide the evidence this time?'

'This time?' Geraldine whispered.

For all Bella's fussing and carping, there was very little blood soaking into the cushion. It seemed to be dribbling from her injury, rather than gushing, suggesting Geraldine had received a nasty scratch, rather than a deep stab wound. Admittedly her injured side was agonising, but she told herself it must be a superficial wound, and tried to block out the pain as well as she could. She could not afford to allow anything to distract her from her priority, which was to make her escape. In this moment, nothing else mattered.

Bella's eyes swivelled round to fix on Geraldine again. 'You made me do that,' she hissed, 'and now look what's happened. There's blood everywhere. What a mess. How am I ever going to clean this up? Look! There's blood on the chair. Can't you see it? Blood everywhere.'

Stupefied, Geraldine looked at where Bella was pointing, and saw a bright red smear on the fabric. All at once, she felt nauseous, sickened by the realisation that she was being compelled to gaze at her own blood, as if this was a crime scene from which she was completely detached. Forcing herself to remain outwardly calm, she watched Bella closely. Her attacker was still gripping the handle of the knife tightly, her knuckles white with the effort. There was no way Geraldine would be able to disarm her, without risking further injury. But she was not so dazed that she failed to register Bella's dismay at the sight of blood on the chair.

Tentatively she suggested that Bella might want to put the knife down. 'If you don't want to get any more bloodstains on your furniture,' she said, 'it might be best to take that knife very carefully back to the kitchen and rinse it under the tap. Otherwise you might touch the walls or another chair with the blade, and you can see for yourself that it's covered in blood.'

As Bella glanced down at the knife in her hand and hesitated, Geraldine made her move. Whipping the cushion round so that she was holding it in front of her like a shield, she darted out from behind the chair. With one swift blow, she knocked the knife out of Bella's hand. Dropping the cushion, she seized Bella's wrists. It was the work of a moment to subdue her adversary now, the action automatic, after so many years of training. Twisting one of Bella's arms up behind her back until she yelped in pain, Geraldine pushed her roughly down on to the floor. At the same time, she became aware that her wound was beginning to bleed more profusely with all the movement, and she started to feel faint.

'Get up!' she shouted urgently, jerking Bella to her feet. 'Walk!'

Holding both Bella's wrists in one hand, as soon as she could reach her bag, Geraldine tipped out its contents on the sofa and found her handcuffs. With Bella's hands secured, Geraldine was finally able to collapse on the bloodstained chair, shaking, with her phone in her hand. There were seven missed calls, six of them from Ian. Before she could call him, there was a deafening crash, and a loud voice bellowed that the police were entering the premises.

'Put down your weapons!' the voice yelled. 'We have an armed response team surrounding the property, and we are coming in! Stand away from the door and put down your weapons! Arms where we can see them.'

'Oh for goodness sake,' Geraldine murmured irritably.

She could have done without this additional drama. Too weak to raise her voice to remonstrate at such a pointless waste of police time and resources, she clambered unsteadily to her feet, and staggered out of the living room into the hall.

'Geraldine!' Ian cried out, rushing forward.

'Keep back!' a masked figure called out.

'It's all right, it's over,' Geraldine told the armed officer.

'There's no threat. She's not armed. She's in there,' she nodded at the living room door, 'and she's handcuffed.'

'You're injured,' Ian said, his eyes alert with alarm.

'Yes, she had a knife, but she's no threat to anyone now. It's all over.'

'Stand down!' a deep voice called out.

Behind her, Geraldine heard movement, and then uniformed officers were running past her, jostling and shouting. Overhead there was the sudden roar of a helicopter circling.

'What is all this fuss?' she asked Ian, who barely managed to catch her as her legs gave way.

'You're getting blood on your clothes,' she murmured, aware of his breath on her face as he leaned over to brush her forehead gently with his lips.

'No need for any of this,' she murmured as she passed out.

# 63

EILEEN DID NOT BOTHER to remonstrate when Geraldine turned up at the briefing the next morning, although she did raise her eyebrows and ask if Geraldine was sure she was all right.

'I'm fine,' Geraldine replied. 'I'd like to be present when we interview Bella. I don't think she'll try to cover up what she's done if I'm there. She knows I know.'

Eileen frowned. 'Do we have to talk in riddles?'

'What I mean to say is, Bella made a confession, of sorts, while she was attacking me.'

'We can get her for assaulting a police officer, if nothing else,' Ian said, with barely concealed anger.

'We should be able to get her for at least two murders as well,' Geraldine said.

'At least two?' Eileen repeated.

'Yes. She as good as admitted she killed Angie and Leslie, although she didn't say so in exactly those words.'

'What did she say?' Eileen demanded.

'She told me they weren't women at all, but demons sent by Satan to lead her husband astray.'

Eileen laughed bitterly. 'So she's preparing a plea of temporary insanity?'

'We can't let her get away with that,' Ian said. 'These murders were very carefully planned. She knew exactly what she was doing.'

'I'm not sure her insanity is temporary,' Geraldine replied. 'I think she genuinely believes Satan tempted her husband to sin, and it's her sacred duty to save his soul from eternal damnation.'

'Oh please,' Ian said. 'Spare us the mumbo-jumbo. Those two women were killed.'

'I'm not sure they were her only victims,' Geraldine said. 'She seemed very exercised about my blood on her furniture.'

'Well, it is a bit of a giveaway,' Eileen said. 'Apart from your testimony, she can hardly deny having attacked you with a knife that has your blood on the blade and her prints on the handle.'

'Yes, but her reaction was odd. She seemed very angry about the blood. Fortunately it was just a scratch. I didn't bleed very much and most of it soaked into a cushion, and there was a fairly small bloodstain on the arm of a chair. But she told me there was blood everywhere, and it was my fault, and then she wanted to know how she was supposed to get rid of it. She kept repeating, "No more blood", and asked me how she was going to hide the evidence this time. I definitely had the impression this wasn't the first time she had stabbed someone.'

It did not take long for a match to be found for Bella's DNA. Two years earlier, a young woman had been fatally stabbed in her own bed, in Leeds. DNA of an unidentified female had been discovered at the scene, which proved a match with Bella's, along with a single partial fingerprint that was a possible match. Armed with this new evidence, Geraldine and Ian prepared to interview Bella, who was formally charged with committing three murders and assaulting a police officer. Bella listened to the charges in silence while her lawyer looked anxious. Geraldine wondered whether he had managed to get any sense out of his client.

'Well?' Ian asked. 'Do we have to go through the charade of hearing you deny the charges, or are you going to save everyone time by giving us a full confession?'

Bella stared blankly at him and muttered that she wanted to see her husband. 'He's my husband. I have a right to see him.'

'I'm afraid you waived any rights when you decided to embark on a killing spree,' Ian replied.

'You make it sound so wicked,' Bella replied, 'but it's your accusations that are pernicious.'

Geraldine snorted. 'Committing murder hardly gives you the moral high ground.'

Bella sat forward suddenly in her chair. At her side, her lawyer stirred.

'You do not have to say anything,' he muttered urgently.

Ignoring the interruption, Bella looked straight at Geraldine. 'Surely that depends on who you kill. You understand, don't you? Of course you do. You deal with the wicked all the time. You know, better than anyone, that there are fiends among us who do not deserve to live. They come among us but they are not human. Sometimes they have to be destroyed, to protect the innocent. But the blasphemous libertarians who guard our morality refuse to allow that. Look at any other period in history. Witches were burnt, and demons exorcised. What do we do to protect ourselves from the forces of darkness now?'

'So you are claiming to be carrying out some kind of moral purge by murdering innocent women who happened to catch your husband's eye?' Ian asked. 'It seems pretty obvious that the only people in need of protection are innocent women who end up in bed with your husband.'

'It is my duty to save my husband from the demons who are sent to corrupt his immortal soul.'

'Oh, I've heard enough of this nonsense,' Ian snapped. 'Your husband is a serial adulterer who abused his position as a hotel manager to seduce young women. Adultery isn't a crime, but if it were he would be locked up for life for what he did. As his wife, you faced two choices: put up with his infidelity, or leave him. It's a choice many women have to make. There's nothing special about you or your husband. Some men are unable to keep their dicks in their trousers, and he's one of them. We all get that, except you. Out of some misguided sense of entitlement, you couldn't face the fact that your husband was unfaithful. Refusing to blame him for his behaviour, instead you channelled your rage against the women he seduced. You lashed out and ended up killing at least three. For all we know, there could have been more. You can try and hide behind this pretence of insanity, but the fact is you are a violent, possessive woman, and you chose to murder your rivals out of sheer jealousy. This has nothing to do with morality, or God, or the devil. And you are going to be locked up for the rest of your life. Prison is too good for you.'

Bella shook her head, her eyes blazing with fury. 'The Lord will save me,' she cried out. 'He will save my soul and you will burn for all eternity.'

'Very well,' Ian said. 'Perhaps you're too good at this to end up in prison, and you'll spend the rest of your life in a padded cell. I don't really care what happens to you, as long as you're incarcerated somewhere. In a previous era, you would have been burned at the stake, of course,' he added softly.

'The Lord will smite you down with a flaming sword,' Bella screeched.

'Oh, give it a rest, will you?' Ian replied.

Bella's lawyer spoke for the first time. 'My client is not of sound mind. You are obliged to speak to her with respect.'

'Tell that to the families of her innocent victims,' Ian said, 'you know, the women she murdered.'

'Those women are not innocent,' Bella raged. 'They were sent by the devil. I was carrying out the Lord's work when I ended their lives.'

'We'll take that as a confession then, shall we?' Ian said.

'Thank goodness for that. I don't know about anyone else, but I've heard enough of this nonsense. Interview terminated at fifteen twenty.'

# 64

IT WAS ALL OVER now, bar the procedure. Following a trial, Bella would be locked up for the rest of her life, probably in a psychiatric unit. The lives of her husband and her daughter had been destroyed, along with the lives of her victims and the people who had loved them. Yet it was a result of a kind, and the mood at the team's celebratory drink was one of bitter triumph.

At her flat that evening, Geraldine handed Ian a large glass of wine.

'Tell me what happened with Helena,' she said.

She was pleased that her voice sounded steady, although her hand shook as she poured a glass of wine for herself.

Ian sighed. 'Can we spend one evening together without arguing about your sister?'

'Tell me,' she repeated, glaring at him.

'Oh, very well. You're obviously spoiling for a fight.'

'I just want to know what happened.'

'For goodness sake, did you think I would ignore what was happening to you?' he replied. 'Geraldine, look at me. Did you really think I was going to abandon you to those idiots in the anti-corruption unit, without making any attempt to rescue you?'

'So you went ahead and acted on your own, knowing you were going directly against my wishes.'

'It's not out of order to bend the rules to protect someone you care about.'

'Isn't that what Bella was doing?'

'Don't be ridiculous. How can you compare my actions with those of a murderer? On the contrary, what I did probably saved you from being killed in prison. You can't honestly say what I did was wrong. Or did you want to spend the rest of your life behind bars? Geraldine you're being unreasonable. You must know I couldn't abandon you to a life in prison.'

'You couldn't abandon me, but you were happy for me to abandon my sister,' she replied bitterly. 'This was never about me or what I might want. It was about you. You had no right to interfere.'

She was aware that she was being harsh, but she was too upset to even attempt to control her fury.

Ian stared at her. 'What else was I supposed to do?'

'You could have spoken to me. '

'I knew what your answer would be.'

'So you admit you knew I wouldn't condone what you did.'

'Condone it? You didn't know what you were doing. I rescued you from yourself, Geraldine.'

'And I'm supposed to be grateful?' she demanded coldly, hating herself for her bitter resentment, yet unable to stop herself. 'You think I should be grateful to you for betraying my trust?'

'Geraldine,' Ian said, very quietly. 'Stop it. You know how I feel about you. You know that I love you.'

'That isn't love, Ian. You can't use love as an excuse to do whatever you want.'

Ian rose to his feet and gazed at her in dismay. 'Geraldine, I really don't know why you're being so unreasonable. Listen, first of all I never broke my word to you.'

Geraldine stared at the floor and clutched her wine glass. When she spoke, her voice sounded oddly forced.

'When I tried to speak to Helena, I found that her phone had been disconnected. So I went to see her, and do you know what I discovered? Yes, of course you do, because you arranged it. Someone else had moved into Helena's flat. Now if I try to find my sister, there'll be no record of her anywhere. It's as though she never existed. She disappeared without trace, and it happened overnight. Someone arranged for her to vanish. She could be dead, or living somewhere else with a new identity.' She raised her head and looked at him, no longer making any effort to control her tears. 'I'll never know.'

Ian heaved a sigh and sat down. In a faltering voice, he explained how he had been unable to leave her locked in a cell.

'I couldn't bear to think of you in there. I couldn't sit back and do nothing, just as you couldn't abandon Helena to her addiction. You risked your career to save her from her drug dealer. Is the risk I took to protect you any different from what you did to save her?'

'Only now neither of us can find out where Helena is, because if I ever try to contact her again, it would risk revealing her location. And there are men out there who will seize any chance they can to put pressure on me to do whatever they want. Everything that has happened in this case has been about people trying to protect one another, and it has all gone horribly wrong.' She paused, shaking her head. 'You do realise that, thanks to your intervention, I'll never see my sister again. Never. I dare say you couldn't tell me where she's gone even if you wanted to, because any trail will have been expunged by now. She's probably no longer in the country. She could be anywhere. She might be dead.'

'What alternative did I have?' he demanded, growing angry. 'Was I supposed to leave you in a cell to await trial, and see you sent down on a false drugs charge? Do you have any idea what serving a prison sentence does to a police officer? The screws have it in for you for being corrupt, and the other prisoners hate you for being a cop. What are the chances you'd have left there alive? Tell me, what would have happened to your sister then? And now look at you. You're not in prison. You're free and you're back home and in your job again. Whatever happened, you would have been forced to abandon your sister. Are you seriously saying you would have preferred to spend years behind bars, beaten up repeatedly, for no purpose at all?'

'You should have discussed what you were planning to do to ruin my life before you did anything, instead of going ahead and telling me afterwards,' she said.

She knew she was being cruel, but in her suffering she felt an irresistible urge to lash out, and had a fleeting insight into how Bella must have felt when she discovered her husband's infidelity.

'She's my *sister*, Ian, my identical twin,' she went on. 'I don't have any other blood relatives, and even if I did, no one can be closer than identical twins. I'll never be that close to anyone else ever again.'

She could not explain the sense of isolation she felt, severed from the twin sister she had known for such a brief period.

'I can't believe you're behaving like this,' Ian replied. 'Anyone else would be thanking me.'

'You had no right to act without asking me first. I didn't even say goodbye to her.'

'There was no time. You were going to be charged and her enemies would have been on to her as soon as they found out you'd been arrested.'

'So? What you did was still unforgivable.'

'Are you serious? And what the hell do you mean by saying to me, of all people, that you can never be as close to another person as you were to an addict you barely knew?' His voice rose in frustration. 'You were strangers for Christ's sake. What does that say about our relationship?'

Geraldine stood up, feeling her legs shaking. 'I'd like you to leave,' she said, without looking at him. 'Leave and don't come back.'

'I understand you need some time alone, but please don't be hasty. Take some time to think about what you're saying. You're still in shock after everything that's happened. Take time to process it all. Speak to a counsellor and clear your head.'

'My head is perfectly clear. I don't want you living here any more.'

'Here we go again,' Ian muttered. 'Face it, Geraldine, you never really wanted me living here, did you? Be honest with me.'

He rose to his feet in one swift movement and walked out. Geraldine did not call him back, and a few seconds later she heard her front door slam. With a broken cry, she sank back on the settee, too exhausted to follow him. She was not sure she wanted to continue living in her flat without Ian, constantly reminded of the time they had spent together, and tormented by seeing him at work every day. It was difficult to see how she could carry on at all, having lost everyone she cared about. Perhaps Ian was right, and she was incapable of sharing her life with anyone. She had hesitated for so long about allowing him to move into her apartment in the first place, and not long after that she had asked him to leave. Through her own desperate need for privacy, she had trapped herself in a lonely existence.

Self-pity overwhelmed her, and she reached for another bottle of wine. The more she drank, the worse the future looked. Everything had gone horribly wrong, but somehow she had to wrest back control of her life. It was time to make a drastic change. She had worked hard in her career, but she no longer had the will to continue the struggle. Something had to give. Drunk and sobbing, she sat down to write a letter of resignation. Taking early retirement, she would move back to Kent where at least she would have family nearby. That would be preferable to the loneliness that stretched out in front of her if she stayed where she was.

The following morning she overslept, and drove to work feeling hungover and looking frowzy.

'Looks like someone had a bad night,' Ariadne chuckled.

Geraldine did not look up but sat at her desk with a strong coffee, mentally preparing herself to hand in her letter of resignation and walk away from the career she loved, and the man she loved. She was still fiddling with her coffee cup when Eileen summoned her. With the envelope in her hand, she walked heavily down the corridor.

'I have some news for you,' Eileen said briskly, as soon as Geraldine entered her office.

Clutching her letter, Geraldine waited.

'Your exemplary conduct as a detective sergeant since your arrival here in York has not gone unnoticed,' Eileen went on.

Hesitantly, Geraldine muttered her thanks.

'I am very pleased to tell you that you are being restored to your former position,' Eileen announced, breaking into a grin. 'Congratulations, Detective Inspector.'

For a few seconds, Geraldine was too startled to respond.

'This is good news,' Eileen prompted her. 'I always knew you were too effective to remain a sergeant for long.'

Returning Eileen's smile, Geraldine mumbled her thanks and stumbled out of the room, her letter still in her hand. It was hard to take in that her stint as a detective sergeant was actually over, and she had been restored to her former position. Suddenly giddy, she leant against the wall feeling her heart racing. Her career was not over yet, and with that realisation, everything seemed to pivot and settle back where it should have been all along. Seized by a wild hope that happiness was still possible, she made her way to Ian's office. In saving her from prison, he had rescued her career, and probably her sanity as well. She understood as well as he did how terribly she would have suffered in prison. The torment would not only have been physical.

Ian looked up warily, and watched her in silence as she closed the door.

'Ian,' she began, and hesitated, unable to find the right words. 'I've been an idiot,' she muttered at last. 'A complete idiot.'

He waited, motionless, as she struggled to continue.

'I've made a complete hash of things, haven't I?' she blurted out. 'What I mean to say is, I don't think I can bear to live without you. I just can't bear it any longer. Please, please, come home.'

'Come home?' he replied. 'I've only just got here.'

But he was smiling. Through her tears, Geraldine smiled back.

'It's your turn to cook,' he said as she turned to leave.

Hurrying to the toilets to check her make-up, it occurred to her that she did not know what Ian's favourite dinner was, let alone how to make it. They had been friends for years, but they still had much to learn about each other. Within the space of a few minutes, the future had suddenly become full of promise. Thinking about what lay ahead, she realised she had forgotten to tell Ian that she was an inspector. It didn't matter. He would find out soon enough. Contrary to her expectations, it seemed she cared more about her personal relationship than about her career. Not only did she have much to learn about Ian, she had much to learn about herself as well. Dabbing her glistening eyes with a tissue, she grinned at her reflection.

'You're looking pleased with yourself,' Ariadne commented as Geraldine returned to her desk.

'Things are looking up,' Geraldine replied.

'Excellent. You've been looking really despondent lately.

Whatever it was that was bugging you, I'm glad to hear you're sorting it out.'

Geraldine nodded. 'Yes,' she replied. 'I'm sorting it out.'

One day she would trace her sister, but for now she was content that her career and her love life were back on an even keel.

'Two out of three isn't bad,' she added aloud.

Ariadne raised her eyebrows. 'If you say so,' she replied. 'I've absolutely no idea what you're talking about, and I guess you're not going to tell me, but it's good to see you looking happy again. Fancy a drink after work?'

Geraldine shook her head. 'Sorry, prior engagement,' she said, and broke into a grin.

# Acknowledgments

I would like to thank Dr Leonard Russell for his medical advice.

My thanks also go to Ion Mills, Claire Watts, Clare Quinlivan, Jayne Lewis, Lisa Gooding and all the tireless team at No Exit Press for their support, and belief in Geraldine Steel. I would love to spend every working day in the company of such inspiring and generous-spirited people, and it is a privilege to continue working with them after so many years.

Geraldine and I have been together for a long time now. For over ten years, not a day has passed when I haven't written about her or thought about her and her colleague, Ian Peterson. Another woman has been with us from the very beginning, so I would like to thank my editor, Keshini Naidoo, without whom Geraldine and I would never have come this far.

I don't think any of us realised what we were letting ourselves in for when we produced the first book in the series, all those years ago.

Someone else has been with me every step of the way, and I would like to conclude by thanking Michael, who has cheered Geraldine on from the start and remains her staunch supporter.

# A LETTER FROM LEIGH

Dear Reader,

I hope you enjoyed reading this book in my Geraldine Steel series. Readers are the key to the writing process, so I'm thrilled that you've joined me on my writing journey.

You might not want to meet some of my characters on a dark night – I know I wouldn't! – but hopefully you want to read about Geraldine's other investigations. Her work is always her priority because she cares deeply about justice, but she also has her own life. Many readers care about what happens to her. I hope you join them, and become a fan of Geraldine Steel, and her colleague Ian Peterson.

If you follow me on Facebook or Twitter, you'll know that I love to hear from readers. I always respond to comments from fans, and hope you will follow me on **@LeighRussell** and **fb.me/leigh.russell.50** or drop me an email via my website **leighrussell.co.uk**.

That way you can be sure to get news of the latest offers on my books. You might also like to sign up for my newsletter on **leighrussell.co.uk/news** to make sure you're one of the first to know when a new book is coming out. We'll be running competitions, and I'll also notify you of any events where I'll be appearing.

Finally, if you enjoyed this story, I'd be really grateful if you would post a brief review on Amazon or Goodreads. A few sentences to say you enjoyed the book would be wonderful. And of course it would be brilliant if you would consider recommending my books to anyone who is a fan of crime fiction.

I hope to meet you at a literary festival or a book signing soon!

Thank you again for choosing to read my book.

With very best wishes,

*Leigh Russell*

# BECOME A
# **NO EXIT PRESS**
# **MEMBER**

BECOME A NO EXIT PRESS MEMBER and you will be joining a club of like-minded literary crime fiction lovers – and supporting an independent publisher and their authors!

## AS A MEMBER YOU WILL RECEIVE

- Six books of your choice from No Exit's future publications at a discount off the retail price
- Free UK carriage
- A free eBook copy of each title
- Early pre-publication dispatch of the new books
- First access to No Exit Press Limited Editions
- Exclusive special offers only for our members
- A discount code that can be used on all backlist titles
- The choice of a free book when you first sign up

**Gift Membership available too – the perfect present!**

FOR MORE INFORMATION AND TO SIGN UP VISIT
**noexit.co.uk/members**